THE Abulon DANCE

by Caro Soles

Baskerville Books
Toronto, Canada

The Abulon Dance
© 2001 Caro Soles

The Abulon Dance
ISBN: 0-9686776-2-2

Canadian Cataloguing in Publication Data

Soles, Caro
  The abulon dance

(The Merculians ; bk. 1)
ISBN 0-9686776-2-2

I. Title. II. Series: Soles, Caro. Merculians ; bk. 1.

PS8587.O41819A72 2001   C813'.6   C00-932801-7
PR9199.3.S64A62 2001

Cover design by Kevin Davies
www.kevindavies.com

Published by:
Baskerville Books
Box 19, 3561 Sheppard Avenue East
Toronto, Ontario, Canada M1T 3K8

www.baskervillebooks.com

Caro Soles can be reached at soles@sff.net
web site: www.dm.net/~caro-soles

Printed in Canada

Dedicated to the memory of

Warren Harding

who always enjoyed a good performance.

ACKNOWLEDGEMENTS

Those who are helpful and encouraging to writers, those who enjoy what we create, or at least claim to, are appreciated far more than they may ever realize. Know that sometimes a single word of praise is all that keeps us from despair.

Now is my chance to thank some of those who were helpful along the way with The Abulon Dance. *Thank you to Iréna Zvagulis, who was there at the birth of the Merculians and kept dropping in to find out what happened next; to Nancy Kilpatrick and Helen Lightbown who were unfailing in their editorial insights; to Karl Schroeder and the members of my old writing group who helped get it all together; to Terry Tweed who loves to read. And thanks to Elizabeth Gershman who fell in love with Triani and whose letters kept me going with the series; to Josepha Sherman for shedding light on plot problems; and to Gordon Montador and Norman Laurila, who gave me hope. And last of all, to Jack Scovil, just for being there, and keeping that hope alive.*

1

The twin moons of Merculian cast double shadows on the grass as the air car skimmed over the ground. Cham leaned forward in the passenger seat.

"Look! I told you there's an artificial lake!" He pointed to a flash of silver as the car swooped lower.

"You sure you got enough credits to cover the fare?" the driver said.

Cham swallowed. "Don't worry, *chai*. I'm sure." He forced himself to settle back and let the seat re-form to embrace his diminutive frame.

The instrument lights threw a pale image of his young face on the curving window. He was small, even for a Merculian, being well under the normal five feet. His long, silver-blond curls framed an angelic face, the round eyes, a clear grey, outlined in black and flecked with gold. He studied his reflection a moment, then lifted a nervous hand to his hair.

"This place belongs to that famous dancer, don't it?" the driver said. "What's his name again? Jani? Tani?"

"Triani. It's his country place. He's my lover, did I tell you?"

"You don't say!" The driver looked at him more closely, his round, Merculian eyes bright with curiosity. "But you're just a kid!"

Cham grinned impishly. "I'm precocious," he said, tossing back his hair.

The driver laughed. "You a dancer, too?"

"I will be. One of these days, when you go the theatre, it'll be me up there on stage—Chamion Adino Eseris. Maybe I should write the name down for you."

"It's okay, kid. I'll remember."

Below them, the brightly lit house nestled behind its protective walls and shrubbery, covered by tinted blue domes. The air car hovered over the tree tops for a moment; then the engines cut back to a faint hum as they landed on the crowded parking strip. Cham looked eagerly towards the ornate door hanging in the wall, that led to the courtyard. As he handed the driver his card, he hoped Triani had remembered to put some credits in his name lately. Once before he had forgotten. It had been very embarrassing. This time, however, there was no acid comment from the electronic voice, just a purringly smooth 'thank-you' from the instrument panel.

"Looks like a real big do," the driver remarked, handing back his card.

Cham nodded. "It's a farewell party. The company's going to Abulon next week."

"Abulon? Never heard of it."

"You will!" Cham waved as he stepped off the small dismount platform and started towards the door.

"Good luck!" the driver called after him and the car hummed away.

Cham hesitated for a moment. Beside him, the blue shrubbery sighed and whistled with tiny night birds, their soft music soothing on the air. Luck. He shivered. Why was he so afraid his was about to run out? Taking a big breath, he reached out and held his hand under the beam of violet light in front of the shimmering gate. It dissolved to let him through.

Triani's parties were famous. There was always at least one hologram band, tables piled high with rare delicacies, Crushed Emeralds served in silver goblets and sparkling Merculian wine flowing freely from a fountain in the courtyard. But it was more than the expectation of a good party that made Cham's stomach churn with nervous excitement. This was a celebration for him. Last night, Triani had told him he was coming to Abulon too, news that flooded his heart with joy and sent his active imagination spinning off in panic. Cham longed to visit mysterious new worlds, but now that he had what he wanted he was apprehensive. Abulon had been in self-imposed isolation for centuries. All that was known about the place was gleaned from the reports brought back by the Primary Contact Team and most of that hadn't been made public. Anything could happen in such a place. The frightening possibility occurred to him that they might never get home again. Still, unlike the others, he had never been away from Merculian. It was a dream come true, and he was determined to enjoy himself.

Cham slid quickly through the brightly dressed crowd, following the music. The large, central space pulsated with sound, glittered with colour and movement. The noise beat against the twinkling lights on the domed ceiling. Most of the guests were dancers from the Merculian National Dance Company, and it showed in their lithe bodies, their acrobatic abandon. They filled the dance floor, graceful, androgynous, bathed in the insistent beat of the music. Their round eyes were bright with wine and their own inner fire. Their muscular bodies vibrated. Some had taken off their velvet or satin tunics and tossed them casually to the side.

Their smooth torsos, glistening with sweat, rippled under the many-coloured, winking lights. Some wore long, beautiful robes whose iridescent hues slid together as they moved. A few wore more tight-fitting garb, proud to show the small breasts and softer curves that came with childbirth and the nursing period. Each one was alone in his intensity, yet linked to his partner by an almost mystical union. Tactile telepaths, they had only to touch to sense each other's feelings.

It didn't take long to spot Triani. He was tall for a Merculian, and dark, with snapping black eyes. He wore tight-fitting black velvet pants that hung low on his narrow hips. His white satin blouse was tied high in front, exposing his midriff. A heavy gold chain glinted at his waist.

Cham heard the magic name "Abulon" as he slipped an arm around Triani and lifted his face to be kissed.

"Hi, sweetie. You're two hours late." Triani's lips brushed his.

"I'm sorry. I couldn't help it. You wouldn't believe what an awful time I had getting out of the city. There was—"

"I don't want to hear about it. Have you met Orosin At'hali Benvolini?" Triani turned to the smiling Merculian at his side, and Cham looked up into sherry-brown eyes. He liked what he saw there and kissed the proffered hand respectfully.

"Orosin, how the hell did you get mixed up in the Diplomatic Corps anyway," Triani went on, giving Cham an absent-minded squeeze. "You, an ambassador? You're a musician! What has politics to do with music? Are you going to make them dance to your piping on Abulon?"

Orosin grimaced. "I don't think that's what the Inter-Planetary Alliance has in mind. I'm supposed to show them what the other members are like by giving them samples of the different cultures while the Abulonians are making up their minds about joining." He helped himself to more wine. "It's *Cultural* Ambassador, Triani, with the emphasis on culture."

"I hear they're quite primitive. Let's hope they know the meaning of the word 'culture'."

"I'm counting on you to set things straight if I fail to get the idea across," Orosin replied, laughing.

"Oh, look!" Cham exclaimed. "Who's that giant pale blue person who just came in? A Serpian?"

The tall male stood at the entrance, pursing his lips disapprovingly as he looked around at the dancers.

"Yes, and I don't think he likes Merculians very much." The Ambassador smiled and shook his head. "He's on my staff, too, worse luck. He actually told me the other day how much it annoys him that the translators have selected 'he' for our third person pronoun."

"What would he prefer? 'It'?" snapped Triani.

"Who knows? I tried to explain it's not that unusual in cross-species cultural translation, but it didn't make any difference. His name's Talassa-ran something and I've never seen him smile, though I suppose there must be something he enjoys."

Triani grinned and set down his glass of Crushed Emeralds. "I'm going to find out right now," he said. He let go of Cham and started towards the Serpian.

Cham sighed. "Is that man going to Abulon with us?" he asked plaintively.

"You don't have to worry about him, Cham. He's only here because he considers it his duty as a member of my advance delegation. Besides, as a Serpian, he's taken the off-planet vow of celibacy."

"Oh." Cham twisted a blond curl through his fingers absently. "You don't suppose it will be dangerous on Abulon, do you?" he asked at last, looking at the

Ambassador anxiously. "I mean, just how primitive are they?"

"Chamion, the I.P.A. contact team has already been there. Triani was referring to the technology, not the people. There's nothing to worry about, I assure you."

Cham blushed, embarrassed by his childish question. No one else was worrying. Why should he? He thanked the ambassador, bowed and edged his way through the crowd, looking for Triani. When he found him on the other side of the room, Talassa-ran had a firm hold of the dancer's muscular upper arm and was scowling down at him fiercely.

"Please listen to me for one minute," the Serpian was saying in his thin, unpleasant voice. "You must have immunity booster shots before going to any non-Alliance planet. Why have you not complied with the regulations?"

Triani smiled up at him beguilingly through his thick, black lashes. "You're cute when you're mad, baby," he said. "But that's no way to ask someone to dance."

"I do not wish to dance. Not with you. Not with anyone. I tell you this repeatedly."

For answer, Triani threw his arms around the man's neck and rubbed his lean body up against him, laughing low in his throat. "I'm your host, sweetie. You've got to be nice to me."

The man pulled away, an expression of acute distaste on his face, his skin turning a deeper blue with anger. "This is business."

"So's dancing. I'll think about the shots tomorrow, okay?" He held up his arms invitingly. "Come on, sweetie. I can follow."

Talassa-ran turned away. "You people never have one serious thought in your fatuous heads," he muttered.

Triani shrugged. He caught Cham's eye, smiled and opened his arms. Cham melted against him. Around them, the dancers continued their joyful celebration of movement. There was no distinct break between one dance tune and the next. They all flowed together, the dancers starting in or leaving as the mood took them. Cham's arms clung around Triani's neck. His eyes were closed and his lips were smiling faintly. They moved as one, with a fluid motion, natural as thought. Others danced in groups, hand in hand, forming long, graceful lines, their feet twinkling in a complicated pattern. Bowls of marble-like candies were being passed around by small androids with metallic, silver caps. Triani slipped one in Cham's mouth, then caught sight of Talassa-ran scooping up a handful from the bowl. He glided over beside him, Cham still in his arms, and touched the Serpian's hand.

"Sweetie, I'd better warn you about those things. You haven't been here long, and if you're not used to them, they could send you around Antares."

Talassa-ran looked down at him with disdain. "Really," he drawled.

"We call them 'buzzers'. It's a common recreational drug here but it sometimes hits outsiders hard."

"How absurd." The Serpian juggled the marbles in his large hand, then popped two in his mouth as he turned away.

Triani shrugged. "Suit yourself, sweetie."

Cham raised his head and smiled as they glided back to the dance. His eyes were slightly glazed. "Give me another one, love," he murmured.

"Baby, you've had enough. I don't want you passing out on me. You better go outside for a while and get some air. I'll see you later."

Triani watched Cham's unsteady progress towards the garden, then turned to adjust a flowering rope-tree branch that had inched its way through the open door. The tree emitted a low hum as it withdrew. He would have to speak to the gardener 'droids. Perhaps they needed an overhaul.

He cast an experienced eye over the guests. The party was going well, even though that unpleasant male Serpian had shown up. He fingered the golden chain at his waist as he walked through the crowd, pleasantly aware of the warm metal links against his pale skin. Everyone was talking about Abulon. Would they recognize the importance of the dance there?

As he stopped to check the wine fountain, his understudy came rushing up.

"What's the problem, Serrin? Someone pee on your purple velvet?" He grinned wickedly, amused at the shock in the other's face.

Serrin cleared his throat. "It's that Serpian, Talassa-ran. He's really overdone it with the buzzers."

"Yeah? I warned him."

"So did I! Come on. He's in the east dome."

Triani followed Serrin through the courtyard and back into another part of the house, leaving the door open behind him.

Talassa-ran stood with one pale blue hand on the wall to keep from falling. His slate-grey eyes were unfocused, his skin beaded with sweat. Triani had a pretty good idea what he must be feeling, the way voices would fade in and out, how colours would streak in lines as he moved his head, how the music and rhythms of people's conversations would pulse inside his skin. Served him right.

"Mr. Serpian Male here figures anything we can do he can do double," Triani muttered. "How many did he have?"

"I'd say twenty. At least."

"Holy shit! Have you ever had that many all at once?"

"Never. The most I've tried was ten one wild night."

"What happened?"

"Let's just say I wouldn't do it again."

Talassa-ran gazed in fascination at the pattern made by one black curl against Triani's pale forehead. He reached out to touch it.

Triani smiled. Gently, firmly, he pushed the Serpian back on the cushions piled around the room.

"Pretty," the man said weakly, gazing up at the stars winking above Triani's head through the clear dome of the roof. He smiled with pleasure, the harsh lines melting from his face. A child-like expression came into his flat, slate-grey eyes.

"Ah, baby, you do know how to smile!" exclaimed Triani in delight. He stretched out beside him on the large cushions. "You're stoned out of your tiny mind, aren't you, sweetie?" he murmured. "I warned you, but the big man wouldn't listen to the little dancer, would he?" Slowly he ran his hand up the man's thigh. "Come on, now. Let's find out what turns you on, okay?"

Talassa-ran stirred uneasily and tried to push Triani's hand away. He ran a grey tongue over his dry lips.

"No," he said weakly, as Triani's hand slid under his tunic. "No. Please."

"Triani, he's a Serpian," murmured Serrin, watching from the open door.

"Aren't you the tiniest bit curious?" Triani asked, his hand moving in slow sensuous circles against the Serpian's chest. He smiled, feeling the surprised pleasure the Serpian experienced from his touch.

Serrin shrugged.

Talassa-ran tried to focus on the pale face hanging over him, framed by the black curls, softened by the candle light. "Beautiful," he murmured, his voice totally lacking it's usual unpleasant twang.

Triani's cheek rubbed against his, and the Serpian closed his eyes, feeling the soft skin, the warmth, the gentle friction. He smelled the scent of almonds and some flower he didn't recognize. He could hear the shiny satin of Triani's blouse sigh against the rough material of his tunic. When the warm, soft lips met his, he tasted wine and salt and sweetness... such sweetness ... And all this the Merculian picked up from his contact with the man, with an openness Serpian's usually blocked.

"See? I'm not going to hurt you," Triani murmured. "I'm used to males. I'll make you happy." His fingers were working with the belt clasp, trying to find the combination to release it.

Talassa-ran grimaced as if in pain, but his hands, moving without his volition, went to the belt, his fingers fitting into the familiar pattern to release the clasp. The heavy belt fell away.

Through the open door, the scented breeze drifted in from the garden. Suddenly there was a splash, followed by a wailing cry. Triani raised his head and listened.

"Shit. The kid fell in." As he did up his blouse, he looked at Serrin who was still watching from the door. "Just when things were getting interesting, too. He's all yours, sweetie. After all, you *are* my understudy." With a wink, he went outside and closed the door behind him. A blue privacy light flashed on.

Triani walked through the garden, heavy with the sounds of murmured conversations, to the tiny white crescent of a beach where a raft lay half out of the water. He bent down, pushed it in, and jumped lightly aboard. Standing legs wide apart for balance, he pushed off from shore, his body bending gracefully as he poled towards the spluttering Cham. He was in no hurry. Cham could swim, although in his present state it might take him a while to realize it. When he saw Triani, Cham stopped splashing about. He climbed aboard laughing, shaking back his long, wet hair.

"I fell out of the boat," he announced. "It floated away without me."

"Next time you drown."

Cham laughed merrily and stepped out of his clothes. He wrung them out with exaggerated care and dropped them on the raft. Triani watched him, watched the moonlight silvering the curves and hollows of his strong young dancer's body as he stretched out his arms to the stars. He was a statue come to life. He was beautiful. He moved suddenly to the edge of the raft and began jumping up and down, making waves that washed noisily against the shore.

Triani sat down abruptly. He could smell the sharp resin in the yellow wood. "Are you selling tickets to this show?" he called. He could hear faint laughter from the shore. In the brightly-lit garden, he caught sight of Talassa-ran, almost naked, stumbling towards the gate. His silver body hair gleamed iridescent in the many-coloured lights.

Cham stopped jumping and the raft began to level off, drifting further out from shore. "I'm cold," he said in a small, husky voice.

"Come here, lover. I'll warm you up."

Cham dropped to his knees and nestled against him. Triani held the yielding body in his arms for a moment, then cupped the small chin in his hand and raised Cham's face to his. He gazed steadily into the wide grey eyes. The gold flecks sparkled strangely in the moonlight.

"Why are you afraid?" Triani asked.

"Abulon." Tears spilled over and trickled down Cham's cheeks. "I'm sorry. It's just...I've never been off-planet before."

"Shit." Triani looked away for a moment. "Is this the thanks I get for pulling strings to let you come along?" He felt Cham tremble, felt the ebb and flow of his emotions, the fear of the unknown, the effort to overcome it, the desperate need for comfort and reassurance. "Look, I'll be right there with you. You've got nothing to worry about, okay?"

"Oh, Triani, I love you!"

"I know, sweetie. Just don't rock the boat." He eased Cham down on the gently swaying raft.

2

*B*eing an ambassador did not appeal to Orosin At'hali Benvolini. It meant leaving behind everything he loved: his family, his friends, his music and Eulio. But he could not turn down the honour shown to the family names. He gave himself a mental shake. At least he had his friend Thar-von Del with him. And the dance company was arriving next week, so he wouldn't be apart from Eulio for long. He sighed.

"What the bloody damn am I going to do if these pills don't work and I upchuck all over the place at my first Abulonian state banquet?" He looked up anxiously at the tall, pale blue Serpian beside him.

"Why wouldn't they work?" replied Thar-von patiently. "And why are you so convinced they're going to serve meat dishes?"

"They look like meat eaters to me, Von," he muttered unhappily, inspecting his image in the dusky mirror.

They were in the large, cheerless suite of rooms assigned to the Merculian Ambassador after the ceremonies welcoming them to Abulon. The rooms were high-ceilinged, but dark, lit by a peculiar combination of indirect lighting and torches. When they arrived, Orosin had placed dozens of brightly burning Merculian candles about to lighten the atmosphere, but they didn't seem to help much. There were enough fur-covered couches and chairs placed in awkward groupings to seat two dozen people. "Apparently they expect you to do a lot of entertaining," Thar-von had remarked dryly, looking around. His own quarters next door were almost cramped by comparison.

"Could you help me with this clasp, Von? I'm so nervous I can't seem to do anything right."

Thar-von leaned over the small, trim figure, his pale blue fingers working the clasp open and fitting the cloak fastening inside.

Orosin studied his reflection critically. He had never questioned his looks before: the round, smiling face; the laughing, sherry-brown eyes; the fine, red-gold curls. He wore the grey and mauve uniform of the Merculian Diplomatic Corps. The long cloak, lined with iridescent satin, hung from the clasp on his right shoulder. Ruffles of lace frothed at his wrists and a slender ceremonial dagger encrusted with jewels hung at his waist.

"Gods, Von! I look so...so.... "

"You look like what you are—an elegant Merculian diplomat."

Orosin bit his lip and didn't answer. He glanced up at Thar-von, tall and distinguished in his simple navy blue tunic with the distinctive crystal figurine on a long chain around his neck, and the silver buttons and sash that matched his hair. It was no wonder there had been that unfortunate mix-up at their arrival. Following Alliance protocol, Thar-von had stepped forward first to make the official introductions. The Abulonians had instantly concluded that this imposing figure was the Merculian Ambassador. It took a lot of talk to persuade them that such a small, pretty person as Orosin could be of any consequence. When this point was cleared up, they decided that Thar-von must be his bodyguard. "It doesn't matter, Beny," Thar-von had murmured, using the affectionate, masculine-sounding nickname he had chosen years ago for his hermaphrodite friend. But it did matter...to Beny.

The welcoming ceremonies were held in a huge amphitheatre carved out of the dull red rock. The Abulonians appeared warm and friendly. Dressed in colourful sarongs, kilts, and feathered cloaks, they packed the open spaces, waving wooden clappers to show their enthusiasm. The women were grouped together in one area, giggling and chattering to each other behind their hands. This was obviously a patriarchal society and the strutting, virile men made Beny feel positively effete. They were tall, heavily built, and dark-eyed, with deeply bronzed skin and thick, black, shoulder-length hair. They gazed at Beny's red-gold curls with lively curiosity.

At home on Merculian, no distinguished visitor would ever be exhibited like this to the stares of the public. Beny stood alone on a raised platform of rock in the middle of the open space where everyone could see him. He bowed gravely to the makers of speeches, watched with real interest the amazing riding skills of a squad of men mounted on long-haired, four-legged creatures with a lumpy, gnarled horn on their foreheads. He greeted the leaders of various clans as they paraded by with their followers and standards. There was much discordant blowing of horns by a group of musicians perched high on the cliff near the edge of the arena. Beny was thankful for his years of travel with his parents on diplomatic business when he had witnessed many strange rituals. What he was not prepared for was being the centre of attention; one lone, five-foot tall hermaphrodite amid the barbaric, masculine splendour of Abulon.

A horn sounded mournfully along some distant hallway and almost at once there was the sound of a wooden clapper at the door. It opened and a small boy bowed low.

"You are ready, lords?"

"We're ready." On impulse, Beny turned and touched Thar-von's large hand for a moment.

"Courage, my friend," murmured the Serpian. "I am with you."

They followed the boy through the high, dim corridors. Beny's hands were clenched at his side. Like all Merculians, used to almost endless daylight and the brightness of their double moons, he was terrified of the dark, and the lack of lighting here was like a frightening physical presence. He longed to touch the reassuring bulk of Thar-von, who followed the regulation three paces behind. He began to recite a familiar litany to himself: Darkness is only the absence of light. I am not afraid. One hand went to his dagger.

As the corridor curved downwards to the right, Beny became aware of the indistinct babble of voices and laughter. At last, a large, high-ceilinged hall spread out in front of them filled with smoke from the open fires built on raised platforms that were scattered about in an irregular pattern. Torches flared high up on the rough stone walls. On one side, brightly dressed women sat in groups apart from the fires. The air was heavy with the acrid smells of burning animal flesh.

Beny felt Thar-von's hand on his shoulder for a moment, heard the familiar, low voice, a whisper on the air. "It's only for a few hours. The pills will work." As they passed, men seated on the floor on rugs and animal skins waved their bare arms and made the peculiar, deep-throated noise of approbation he had noticed earlier. The firelight danced on their faces and made points of yellow light gleam in their dark eyes. Obviously, Beny thought, a race of hunters, predators. He wondered bleakly whose idea it had been to abandon him here among these savages.

Their young guide halted near the middle of the hall at a fire larger than the rest. Like the others, it was built up on a stone platform with a wide ledge running around the outside which served as a table. The Great Chief and his advisors stood to welcome them, clasping each of them in turn on the upper arm in a firm grip. Beny tried not to wince as the First Minister's steely fingers closed around his arm. He could sense he was being tested. The men's creased and weathered faces looked as if polished to a hard nut-like finish. They all sat on fur cushions or beautifully woven blankets. Thanks to the tiny sub-cutaneous two-way translators worn by the Merculians, conversation flowed easily.

It was obvious who was the Am Quarr, the Great Chief. Not that he wore any distinguishing robes or chains of office. He was simply dressed in a sleeveless brown tunic that showed off his wide shoulders and sinewy arms. It was his manner, his way of speaking, the simple assumption that he held absolute power and his every wish would be obeyed. Around his neck he wore a flat, irregularly shaped stone resembling a large cat's eye. In the uncertain light, it seemed to change colour, even texture. His deep-set, old-young eyes were full of knowledge and gave the impression of seeing much more than surfaces.

At the Chief's right hand sat the First Minister, whose name, Beny remembered, was Tquan. A streak of startling white hair swept from the centre of his forehead to his shoulders, giving him a distinguished look. It made him stand out in the sea of dark, proud faces around him. The First Minister had a leather thong around his left arm where the unsheathed blade of a small knife gleamed against his bare skin.

The Chief leaned towards Beny, nothing but polite interest in his face. "We understand that you do not eat meat for religious reasons. Is this so?"

"Yes, Am Quarr. Originally it was for religious reasons. We cherish a reverence for all life forms."

"Here we look at things quite differently, Ambassador. The life taken from an animal gives life to us as food. Therefore it is not lost, merely changed."

"It is a change we have chosen not to make, Great One."

Thar-von, at Beny's side, raised his silver head suddenly. "That philosophy is not so different from the way we think on my home planet. We, too, are still hunters, even though technology has taken away the need."

"Ah, yes. Technology." The Great One smiled and closed his eyes for a moment. "It takes more than it gives, we have found. That is why we strive to maintain the old ways, the ancient ceremonies, the legends of our people."

Beny leaned forward with interest, thinking of the Merculian storytelling art he had studied years ago. "You keep alive the old songs and legends, just as we do!" he cried delightedly. "We would be honoured to hear an example of your art."

"Quetzelan, our Dream Weaver, would be only too happy to oblige," the Chief replied.

"Am Quarr, the Lord Benvolini is himself an accomplished teller of tales," Thar-von said gravely.

Some men in the group made the distinctive growls of approval. Some waved the half-gnawed bones they were chewing. It was obvious that they enjoyed this form of entertainment, and Beny promised to perform for them soon, pleased to have discovered some common ground. He tried to avoid looking at their shiny faces smeared with fat. He took a long drink of the flat brown ale, and the clumsy horn beaker was instantly refilled. The smoke was making his eyes water. It was difficult to breathe. Far above them, he could just make out round holes in the ceiling. The smoke didn't seem to be finding them.

The First Minister leaned forward, one elbow on his knee. "You and I, Ambassador, we know that playing with words is only a game but an important game," he said, and he flashed a smile that was startling in its sudden brilliance. "And it is also something to amuse the women, no? Perhaps that is why it appeals so much to you people."

"Well, it is appealing," Beny agreed cautiously. He felt he was missing something, another meaning sliding between the words. "To us it is an art form."

"Of course. An art. Like war."

"Perhaps more like politics," Beny suggested.

"Politics." The First Minister's voice caressed the word; his dark eyes danced. His long fingers touched the naked steel against his arm. "Yes, of course. You are indeed clever. But do you not find that the absence of meat weakens the mind as well as the body?"

"Our guest has explained his position, Tquan," the Chief cut in. He held out a chunk of bread to Beny on the end of his knife. Carefully, Beny took the bread and placed it on his plate. He felt that he had lost the thread somewhere along the way and hoped he would find it again soon.

The conversation flowed on around them, talk of hunting and trading, of obscure building projects, of the festival. Beny ran down the program of exotic, alien names and assured them that the Merculian National Dance Company would be arriving next week. He thought of Eulio and ached with longing.

When he had taken on this job, he had not realized how much it entailed. For months he and Thar-von had worked steadily, setting up contacts, checking out details of transportation, preparing information packages for performers and their agents and managers. Even choosing their own staff turned out to be a problem.

Thar-von had come to him early one morning. It was obvious that he was very embarrassed. He had been closeted with the Serpian Ambassador most of the night. "Beny, I'm sorry but the insufferable woman insists we have a token Serpian on the office staff and she's chosen Talassa-ran Zox."

"Bloody damn!" exclaimed Beny, sinking into a chair. This was one Serpian male he could not abide. Zox was meticulous and precise to a fault, had no sense of humour, and thought all Merculians were slightly mad. His thin lips seemed to be always pursed together with distaste.

"There's nothing I can do about it, Beny. Believe me, I tried." Thar-von was not fond of the man either.

"What else did your charming Ambassador have to say, Von?"

The Serpian turned away. "Her usual anti-Merculian propaganda. She warned me at great length about you."

"Me?"

"She seems to have the idea that you'll try to seduce me."

"Did you tell her I tried that years ago and failed? For the first time in my life, I might add."

"No, I did not. I don't want to give her any ammunition. I'll never understand why they picked a puritan like her to serve on Merculian."

Beny had to admit that Zox was a good worker and excellent at his job of office manager. But the Merculians disliked him. Talassa-ran's humiliating experience at Triani's party had not made him any more friendly towards his Merculian co-workers, and now he insisted on reporting to Thar-von instead of to Beny.

Still, in spite of everything, the festival was taking shape. The Terran contingent was organized. Final arrangements had been made for the Medorial Chant-Singers, the Silhouette Theatre of Carpuso 5, and an Ultraati Rope Dance troupe. Zox would have his work cut out for him. Beny had just opened negotiations with Serpianus for one of their famed circus troupes. The logistics of that one would intrigue a man like Zox.

Abulonian ale was stronger than it appeared. Thar-von warned him with a touch of his pale blue hand. "Eat," he whispered. Beny tried, but the smells of the food were upsetting to him and the tastes, even of the non-meat dishes, were strange on his tongue. His stomach was queasy, in spite of the pills he had taken. The meal dragged on and on. Strange parts of unknown animals sizzled on the fire in front of him. Odd-looking scorched vegetables baked in the coals, drizzled with fat from the meat. Chunks of coarse black bread and piles of nuts were about the only things he could eat with impunity.

"Greetings." A young man dropped down beside him. He wore only a short kilt and an intricately embroidered vest. Around his neck was a necklace of rough green stones and a gold ring glinted in one ear. One slim brown hand fingered the beads as he studied the Merculian. "I am Luan of Quarr."

"The Chief's son?" Beny asked, recognizing the name from the long list he had committed to memory.

The boy nodded. "For a long time I have had dreams about an alien sun. I see a person with hair on fire and round eyes like yours."

"I guess you met the Merculian who was a member of the contact team," Beny said. He smiled at the young man, relieved to have someone to look at who wasn't covered with grease.

The boy shook his head solemnly. "I was sent to make the rounds of the sub-chiefs when they were here. It was the season of tallies. I was disappointed to miss the visitors, but I hear very few of us met them."

Beny was puzzled to hear this, but he said nothing and merely returned Luan's smile. The boy's dark eyes were shining with curiosity and friendliness.

"Are you lonely so far from your home?"

"I haven't had time to be lonely yet," Beny replied.

Luan reached out to touch Beny's hair. "We have heard strange stories about you people. Are they all small and fair like you?"

"I am quite tall for a Merculian," said Beny with dignity. "And we are not all fair. Haven't you seen my staff?"

"There is not one as good-looking as you," replied the boy, gazing at Beny with frank admiration. "You look very young to be an ambassador."

"I'm not as young as I look," laughed Beny. He considered telling the boy his age but realized this wouldn't mean anything unless he wanted to divulge a whole lot more about Merculians. He adjusted the lace at his wrists and pushed back a lock of hair with one small hand.

The boy watched him closely. He eyed the velvet clothes, the elegant slippers, the bracelets, the rings. "Have you crossed the hall to the woman's side?" he asked tentatively.

"I don't think I follow you." Beny frowned in concentration, trying to get some sense out of the words.

The boy hesitated. "Could I come and talk to you some time? Not tonight, of course. Tonight I expect to dream of you."

"You are welcome anytime, Luan."

The boy brushed Beny's thigh with his hand and Beny felt a jolt of sexual interest. Before he could react, the boy jumped to his feet and was quickly lost in the smoke.

Ah, Beny thought to himself with a smile, those kind of dreams. He glanced over at the group of women watching them from across the hall. Was growing up more difficult with two sexes?

Beny suppressed a sigh as a long procession of sticky sugar-coated pastries appeared on large wooden trays carried effortlessly by the efficient servers. Then an intricately carved pipe began making the rounds. The bowl was shaped like an animal's head, the stem long and curved and flexible. As if there isn't enough smoke here already, thought Beny. Resignedly, he accepted the pipe and put it to his lips. It was a token gesture only. He had never understood the idea of smoking. He gave it to Thar-von who proceeded to draw deeply, much to Beny's surprise, before passing it on amid grunts of approval. A peculiar smell hung in the air for some time.

"It is late, lords and elders." The Am Quarr was on his feet, now. The others were getting up in one single, fluid motion that Beny found impossible to imitate. Thar-von helped him to his feet. Beny saw the amusement on the dark faces as the men started to drift towards the women who were still chattering together on the other side of the hall. The Great Chief turned his back and began talking to a tall, spare old man who leaned on a carved staff. He had long, thinning white hair and deep-set black eyes.

The First Minister laid a hand on Beny's arm. "I see you are interested in meat after all," he murmured. "Although not, perhaps, the four-legged variety." He smiled with a flash of white teeth.

"I beg your pardon?"

"Never beg, Ambassador." Tquan raised a long finger in the air and for a moment, was all seriousness. Then he laughed and thumped Beny on the back, making him stumble. "Enjoy your evening." He stepped into the group of men. They parted before him as he strode off.

Beny glanced at Thar-von, who stood nearby, his face an unreadable mask. Beny turned away uncertainly. Life is so much more difficult when one doesn't know the rules, he thought. Straightening his narrow shoulders, he started for the door. He knew Thar-von would follow, three paces behind. He walked slowly, taking the time to sense the feelings of those he passed. There was some hostility, some ridicule, a lot of curiosity, even amusement. He quickened his pace. How long could he live in an atmosphere like this?

As he neared the doorway, he passed the Merculian office staff, who were grouped near the entrance, waiting for him. As he went by, they smiled and silently clapped their hands in support. Only Talassa-ran was not applauding.

3

*M*orning sunlight poured into the room, breaking into miniature rainbows as it shone through the cut glass edges of the round windows. There were five of them, placed high up in the wall, so that all that could be glimpsed of the outside world was the cloudless, lavender sky of Abulon. This colour was repeated in the glinting stones that studded the ceiling and adorned the base of the bed that dominated the room. On a raised platform of greenish marble opposite the bed was an oval pool, its shimmering surface in continual motion. A living curtain of blue-green leaves trailed down the wall behind it. To one side of the bed was a group of carved, uncomfortable, wooden armchairs with cushions that matched the leaves.

Beny was asleep. He looked very small in the huge bed, his red-gold curls bright against the pale green of the pillows. He stirred, uncurling into a languid stretch as he turned onto his back. He opened his eyes. As he raised his head, he found himself face to face with a large dog-like creature who stared at him expectantly with three clear green eyes. Its coat was mottled grey and brown, its hide smooth and shiny, like patent leather. Two ears stood up straight on top of its head like twin flags and a long thin tail undulated, snakelike, from side to side. It was enormous!

Beny sat up slowly, clutching the covers against him as if for protection. "Nice dog?" he said questioningly.

It moved closer.

Beny shrank back against the wall in terror. Cautiously he reached for the small communication device lying on a recessed shelf beside the bed, his eyes fastened on the creature.

"Von? Are you there? Quick! I need you!" Thar-von had grown up surrounded by all sorts of strange creatures. His mother was *the* Serpian authority on animal behaviour.

"I'm on my way!"

Beny wilted with relief. The dog hadn't moved. Neither had Beny. They stared at each other unblinkingly. The dog sat down.

A moment later the door flew open, and Thar-von strode in, a Serpian blaster in one hand.

"I don't think it's quite that drastic," said Beny in a small voice. "I panicked. It's awfully big."

Thar-von suppressed his amusement into a sort of coughing snort. He sat down on the bed and held out a hand for the animal to sniff. "Look, Ben, it's just a dog. A little unusual and large, but basically just a dog. Didn't you see them last night at the banquet?"

"No, I did not." Beny was hurt by the lack of sympathy. "I'm sorry if you think I overreacted, but I'm not more than six feet tall, and I'm not used to animals, and...he terrifies me."

Thar-von patted the animal's smooth, broad head. "I wasn't laughing at you. I was relieved that nothing serious had happened."

"It must be difficult for you, having a friend like me," said Beny thoughtfully. Thar-von began to look uncomfortable as he always did when things threatened to get personal, and Beny didn't pursue the subject. He suspected his Serpian friend might not understand his fear.

"Would you give me that robe, Von?"

Thar-von handed it to him and carefully turned his back as Beny slid out of bed. Even though he had been Beny's roommate at the I.P.A. Academy for a year, he found even the thought of Merculian nakedness disturbing.

Beny shrugged into the robe and fastened it around his trim waist with the wide sash. The deep pleats fell to the floor in graceful folds, accentuating the swell of his hips. He touched his hair uncertainly.

"What are we going to do with the brute, Von?"

"I've got one, too. It arrived while I was out on my early morning run. Met me at the door wagging its scrawny tail. I gather from the servants they're some sort of watch dogs, meant to keep us safe. They're called a 'friendship gift', and every one of us has one. I suspect they would not be pleased if we gave them back."

"Marvellous," said Beny, eying the beast uneasily. "Bloody marvellous!" He edged cautiously past it and hitched himself up onto a chair. The creature padded over at once and laid its huge head on his lap.

"I think you've made a conquest," said Thar-von with a smile. "And speaking of conquests, the Chief's son is waiting in the other room to have breakfast with you."

Beny burst out laughing. "Oh, Von! Do you suppose he thinks it's an ancient Merculian custom for the Ambassador to be awakened by a man with a drawn gun?"

"Possibly," said Thar-von. "I didn't stop to explain."

Beny gingerly dislodged the dog's head, climbed down from the chair, and went to the door. Young Luan was standing at the window, one shoulder leaning against the wall, one hand on his hip. The sad, dark eyes were dreaming.

Although not tall for an Abulonian, he was nearly six feet. He wore a loose-fitting white shirt, embroidered with multi-coloured flowers. The gold amulet on a thong around his neck, matched his earring. The dark blue pants were tucked into very shiny boots.

Thar-von leaned over Beny discreetly. "Please keep in mind that he's the Chief's son," he whispered warningly.

"Don't be a mother hen, Von."

The dog followed them into the room and lay down with its head on its paws, watching.

"I hope you haven't been waiting long," said Beny, smiling at the boy.

Luan bowed, his long, black hair swinging forward on each side of his face. "It is of no consequence, Excellency."

"Oh please, Luan! Let's drop the diplomatic protocol between ourselves. Agreed?"

The boy nodded, seeming to relax. "Sure," he replied easily.

"If you don't need me any more, Ben, I'd better go down to the office and see how Zox and the others are getting along." Thar-von opened the door and hesitated. Standing on the threshold was a stocky, bald male with strange slanted copper eyes.

"This is a personal gift to the Ambassador from my father," said Luan, stepping forward.

"A servant?" asked Beny uncertainly.

"An android," replied Luan. He handed Beny a silver cylinder with two buttons on one end. "The red one is to summon him. See? The blue one will send him to the nearest DQ."

"I beg your pardon?"

"Sorry. 'Droid Quarter. It's where we keep them when not in use. The red button will bring him to you from anywhere in the building. He also responds to voice commands."

"He's marvellous!" exclaimed Beny in delight, circling the android. "Does he have a name?"

"Dhakan 519."

"He's perfect! He looks just like a person, doesn't he, Von? Except for those metallic eyes. He's much more lifelike than the ones we have at home."

Thar-von made a noncommittal noise, bowed in the general direction of Beny and Luan, and stepped around the android on his way out the door.

Beny was lost in thought. So far, he had seen little evidence of advanced technology, apart from the shuttle port facilities, which, after all, had been prepared for them. It had been his impression that the main reason Abulon wanted to join the Inter-Planetary Alliance was to update its hardware. He had noticed a peculiar emphasis on the crude and simple aspects of life here. And now this….It was puzzling.

"My father will be pleased you like the gift," Luan said. "I hope it's all right for me to come see you like this?" He looked at Beny anxiously and fingered the amulet.

"I was just going to have breakfast. Will you join me? I hate to eat alone." Beny knelt in front of a large, blue chest set against one wall. He opened the double doors to reveal row after row of small drawers.

Luan knelt beside him and examined the cabinet curiously, running his hand over the utterly smooth surface. "This feels very strange. What is it?"

"A portable FoodArt synthesizer," Beny explained and pointed out the small console built into the back of the door. He punched in the code for biscuits, honey, and *pamayo* juice. "I hope you're not too hungry," he went on apologetically. "Judging by last night, you're used to much more substantial fare. I have a weak stomach, I'm afraid, and I find it safer when I'm travelling to stick to a few familiar things as much as possible."

Lights flashed on in front of three of the drawers. Beny stood up. and as he did so, his hand brushed the cold, wet, leathery nose of the dog, which had moved up noiselessly behind him. Without thinking, Beny flung himself at Luan who instantly put his arms around him protectively.

"It's all right," the boy said softly. "The dog would never attack you. He's trained to guard, and he's very gentle with his owner."

"Are you sure he knows I'm his owner?" asked Beny nervously.

"He knows. He will protect you, now."

Beny was beginning to feel a little foolish, kneeling on the floor pressed against Luan. A strong sexual current radiated from the boy, but what surprised Beny was the warm tenderness he sensed so strongly. Luan's hand caressed his back gently, as if almost afraid of hurting him. Beny looked up at his face, the flushed cheeks, the soft, dark eyes.

"Luan— "

"Please don't say you're sorry," breathed the boy. His hand moved up into Beny's hair.

Beny felt the soft, melting, feminine side of him reach out to the boy, responding to his touch, his dark voice, the musky, male smell that was so alien, yet so attractive. It was exactly the sort of situation Thar-von had been warning him about. It would be so easy to let go, to close his eyes, and put his arms around that strong body.... Orosin At'hali Benvolini, you are an idiot! he told himself severely. Out loud he said, "I'm getting hungry. Are you?" He pushed hesitantly against the boy's chest. Reluctantly, Luan released him.

Beny stood up and smiled as he straightened his robe. He was more shaken than he cared to admit. "I shall have to practice giving the dog orders," he said. "I can't always count on having a good-natured stranger around to throw myself at for protection." He turned away and emptied the little drawers, arranging their contents on the round table and pouring the juice into tall, fluted glasses. He curled up in a chair, both feet tucked under him, and proceeded to spread honey on a biscuit.

Luan sat down cross-legged on a stool opposite him. He sipped some *pamayo* juice cautiously, nodded approval, and finished it off. The sun glinted on the gold ring in his ear as he tossed back his long hair with one slim, brown hand.

"Tell me about yourself, Luan. What do you do all day long?"

"Oh, I'm not very interesting." Luan dropped his eyes and turned the heavy ring around and around on his thumb. "Until a few months ago, I had a tutor following me around, trying to force me to learn all about the country, its geography, administrative set-up, who heads what section, all that stuff. Boring, really. But I like meeting the leaders and sub-chiefs, like what I was doing when the I.P.A. contact team was here. And, of course, getting to know you." He gazed at Beny adoringly. "I've never met a man like you before."

Beny busied himself with the biscuits, wondering exactly how much Merculian physiology it was necessary to teach this boy. "Strictly speaking, I'm not a man, you know," he said. "All Merculians are the same sex. We're hermaphrodites. Do you understand?"

Luan blinked. "It doesn't matter. You're very beautiful, like the sun I see so often in my dreams."

Beny laughed. "Oh, Luan! I'm different, that's all."

"All the mothers of Abulon will be lined up three deep to introduce you to their daughters, just the same. No one really explained... about that."

"At least I don't have to worry about them introducing me to their sons, then," answered Beny with a twinkle. "That should save some time. Tell me, Luan, is the position of chief hereditary?"

The boy nodded, his eyes serious again.

"So, you're going to be chief when you're older."

"Not if I can help it." Luan was studying the carved table leg. "Anyway, it's not that simple. The council has to approve, and I don't think I'd ever get enough votes. I'm not the kind of person they admire. I'm not a Hunter. I keep trying to explain this to my father, but he won't listen to me, so I go to the meetings and try to make sense of what's going on. Half of it I don't understand, and the rest I don't agree with. Sometimes, when I do say something, the First Minister listens, but my father only laughs. He laughs at my dreams." He got to his feet. "I'm sorry. I didn't mean to ramble on about myself."

"It's all very interesting to me. I don't have much information about Abulon, you know. The contact team concentrated mostly on technical things, like setting up the landing facilities."

Luan stood close beside him, now, his long lashes dark against his cheek. One hand dropped onto Beny's knee. "Are you married?" he asked softly, not looking at him.

"No, Luan. I'm too young, by our standards. But I have given my love-jewel to someone at home. His name's Eulio, and he's a principal with the dance company that's coming next week."

Luan withdrew his hand and turned away. "I see." He wandered over to the window and looked out. "I should have known," he murmured sadly.

Beny watched him for a moment, a smile in his sherry-brown eyes. The boy was good to look at, tall and well-made, with the slight awkwardness of limbs not quite grown into.

Beny got to his feet and went over to stand beside him. "Don't take it so hard, Luan. You're very attractive, you know. Those Abulonian mothers you mentioned must be lined up for you, too. No?"

The boy put a hand to his hair and tugged at it nervously. "No, thanks be to the gods. Most of them have given up." He took an unsteady breath. "Look…I couldn't get any sleep last night for thinking about you. The dreams…They were different this time. I don't understand."

Beny laid a hand on the boy's trembling arm. "Hush, Luan. Don't say any more. I do find you very attractive, but it's not possible. We mustn't speak about it again." Beny reached up with his small hand and followed the line of the boy's cheek with his fingers. The skin was smooth and warm to his touch. Luan turned his head suddenly and kissed Beny's hand.

"I won't say anything more, if that's the way you want it," said Luan, his voice dark with emotion. "But I can't help feeling this way."

"You deserve more than a brief moment with a visiting alien." Beny moved away and turned to look out the window at the pink-tinged mist of the Abulon morning. "Tell me about the androids," he said, searching around for a less emotion-charged topic. "They really are quite remarkable. Are they manufactured here in the city?"

Luan waited a minute, trying to calm his breathing before answering. "I think they all come from some place in the country. It's a large operation, and it's handled by a special department under the direct control of the First Minister. I can find out more, if you want."

"Don't bother. I was just curious. Thank you for bringing Dhakan. When I take him home, he'll make me the envy of Merculian. Now I'd better get dressed. Thar-von will be expecting me in the office." He held out his hand to the boy who took it in both his own. The dark eyes under the straight black brows were bright with unshed tears.

"If there's anything you ever want, just let me know. Anything!" He raised Beny's small hand to his lips, turned it palm up, and kissed it. Twice. His lips were soft and moist against Beny's skin. He bowed formally and left the room.

Beny took a deep breath. About to step out of his robe, he paused and looked from the dog to the android, standing stock still where he had been all this time. A shiver ran up Beny's spine. "Bloody damn," he muttered. He hurried into the other room and closed the door.

4

The Merculian National Dance Company arrived in a downpour of driving rain. Because of the weather, there were no official welcoming ceremonies, nothing but bows and salutes from an honour guard and some strange bouquets of brightly coloured feathers, presented by children.

Beny's heart lifted with joy to see Eulio's small, dark-blond figure walking towards him, under the moving transparent bubble, elegant as ever in his black and silver tunic and pants. Long curls framed the fine, sensitive face, the wide-set eyes, the firm, small chin. Around his neck he wore the symbol of their relationship, a large, pearl-like love-jewel which glowed a deep purple when it touched his skin.

Triani was right behind him, holding Cham's hand. Gravely, Eulio accepted the rainbow-hued, feathery bouquet and kissed the tiny hand of the little girl who presented it. Only then did his amazing blue eyes move to Beny's face and stay there.

Triani's bouquet was offered by a little boy. Passing the alien flowers to Cham, Triani scooped the child up in his arms.

"Hi, sweetie. How about a kiss?"

The child screamed.

Hastily Triani set him down again. "Little bastard," he muttered.

"Not everybody finds you irresistible," laughed Cham.

They were all struck by the violent contrasts between the technically advanced landing facilities atop the huge, flat pyramid, and the crude, almost rustic apartments inside the building, lit by their peculiar combination of brightly burning torches and hidden-source lighting.

"You get used to it," said Beny to Eulio philosophically. "And we brought lots of Merculian candles."

Cham was delighted by everything. He had lost all trace of his fear. "It's like those recreation pods at home where it's made to look like you're back in time," he exclaimed happily. "And I love the dog they gave us! Do you think we can take him home?"

"Never mind him, sweetie. Let's try out the bed."

The newcomers were all briefed by Beny's staff on what to expect at the formal dinner that night. Even though slightly unnerved by the charged primitive atmosphere of the dining hall, the dancers soon settled down, though they stayed in groups where they had been seated and didn't stray far from each other.

It was Triani who noticed the girl first. He watched with amusement, leaning against the stone wall, one arm around his knee. It was a long time since he had seen such subtle coquetry. She was inviting, her shiny brown eyes flitting to Cham, then away. Triani nudged him. When Cham looked around, she nodded, almost imperceptibly, then demurely dropped her eyes and picked up something on her wooden plate. As she leaned forward, her long hair fell like a curtain in front of her face.

"You want a written invitation, sweetie?" Triani murmured. "Go on. She wants you."

Cham hesitated. He glanced at Beny, who sat nearby with Eulio beside him. "Maybe it's not a good idea."

Triani made a disgusted noise and pushed him to his feet. "Don't keep the girl waiting, baby. It's not polite in any situation. Trust me."

Cham slipped a buzzer in his mouth and set off across the hall. As he went, a murmur seemed to follow him, rising up behind him like a small wave of sound. He glanced back at Triani, who urged him on.

The girls welcomed him with giggles and smiles, their hands going often to their mouths, their dark eyes laughing sideways at the newcomer. As they talked, they glanced repeatedly across the room but not at Triani, who was watching them with interest.

Beny leaned across and whispered, "This doesn't feel right. Call him back, Triani."

"Why? We're supposed to 'interact with the natives'. It says so in our orientation packages."

"I get the feeling now is not the time," Beny murmured. "Look."

A tall young man was making his way across the hall. He was holding the knife he had been eating with and his eyes were fixed on Cham.

Triani jumped to his feet. "What do you think—"

Beny pulled him down as the First Minister rose and covered the distance between himself and the youth with long, smooth strides. He laid a steel hand on the boy's forearm.

The girls were now quiet, their eyes downcast, sitting without moving on their finely woven colourful mats. Cham got to his feet and looked around, confused. Then he hurried back to Triani and sank to his knees beside their ever-present watch dog.

Triani refilled his glass. "Looks like you've got competition. So, what did she say?"

"Her name's Quana."

"And? Did she proposition you?"

"Not exactly. She invited me to a picnic tomorrow."

"A *picnic*? How quaint. Just the two of you?"

"I think so. She said to meet her at the public stables at 11."

Triani threw back his head and laughed. "Good for her! She's more enterprising than I gave her credit for! Of course you're going, right?"

"I couldn't very well say no," said Cham, flustered. Now he wished he had. But he had been confused by the girls and their oblique chatter which said one thing and hinted at something else entirely. They seemed to think there was something highly secretive about a conversation that took place in the open. Then the sudden eruption of the tall young man was upsetting. The intervention of the First Minister made it seem far more important than the casual conversation he had assumed it was. The whole situation made him very nervous.

"You've never been with a girl, have you?" Triani remarked, inspecting a cube of black bread smeared with some orange substance.

"Triani, it's just a picnic." Cham glanced across the hall but the girls ignored him.

As sugared fruit was carried from group to group, the Great Chief introduced Quetzelan, the Dream Weaver, the Teller of Tales. He was a tall man with long white hair over his shoulders. His nut-brown skin was stretched tightly over prominent cheek bones and bright, black eyes glittered from deep in his head. As he rose to speak, the crowded hall fell silent. He scooped up a handful of live coals from the fire in the centre of the table and pressed it to the broad tip of his wooden staff. The Merculians gasped. Cham held his breath and clasped his own small hands together tightly, wincing in sympathy. But the regal old man showed no sign of pain. For what seemed like long minutes to the incredulous Merculians, he held the glowing coals against the wood, until a spiral of smoke began to rise from the staff. The smoke twisted and thickened, reaching out long bluish tendrils across the murky hall. Then he stretched out his hand so everyone could see the still glowing coal and slowly closed his fingers around it. His fist gradually crushed the coal. As he opened his hand, sparks flew up like a stream of fireworks, causing the Merculians to burst into applause. When quiet again settled over the hall, he leaned on his carved staff and began to speak.

His whole manner was in complete contrast to the lively, vivacious style of Benvolini, who had performed the night before. Surprisingly, after the opening pyrotechnics, Quetzelan stood completely motionless. No gestures. No change of facial expression. But it was his voice that was so unusual. Rich, dark, hypnotic, his voice drifted effortlessly through the smoke-filled hall. And as he spoke, it was almost as if another deeper shadow voice thrummed under every word. It was an odd, unsettling effect, like a muffled, barely discernable echo in the spell-bound room. When the old man had finished speaking, his voice faded away to silence in waves, like water lapping against the shore. Nobody moved. Only gradually did conversation start up again.

"Interesting technique," remarked Beny.

"I prefer yours," Eulio said, taking his hand.

"Look at them," said Triani, glancing around at the Abulonians. "They look like they just chewed a handful of buzzers or something. It wasn't that great!"

45

Cham looked around and nodded in agreement. Then he noticed Talassa-ran Zox. The Serpian was standing in the shadows, staring at Triani and the hatred in his eyes burned like acid. Cham shivered and put his arms around the dog's neck.

Cham was having second thoughts about the picnic. For one thing, he had the feeling he might have misunderstood something about the invitation. For another, he didn't like the looks of the neighbourhood. According to the scanty information the Merculians had been provided with, it didn't look the sort of place a well brought up Abulonian girl would come to by herself. Rough sheds and animal pens lined the narrow streets. One of the buildings opposite the stables had collapsed in on itself, its timbers charred and jagged.

The animal smell of the stables hung over the place like fog. The great beasts inside were called amaxes and they were shaggy and brown with bulging milk-white eyes. He backed away.

He was just coming to the conclusion that his pride would not suffer if he left now, when he heard someone call his name. A tall gangling youth with a very young face lounged through the open stable door.

"You'd better look after my sister," he said belligerently. "Beats me why she wants to go off with an alien, anyway. She's inside." He ambled off through the alley, leaving Cham to wonder why Quana couldn't look after herself. She was bigger than he was.

He walked carefully into the gloomy stable, his dainty red boots picking through the muck, his cloud of pale hair glowing in the dimness.

"Good morning." Quana was already mounted, perfectly at ease atop the huge snorting creature. She was wearing a full bright yellow garment and her long hair was hidden under a sort of cowl.

He smiled uncertainly, handed her his shoulder bag, and leapt up behind her before the thought of it could frighten him. The leap was easy enough, but he was not used to the lurching feel of the animal under him.

"May I hold on to you?" he asked anxiously, slipping his arms around her waist as they started with a jerk. He rested his head against her back, both arms wrapped tightly around her. She was a lot taller than he had realized. He was sure that she could feel his heart thumping against her curtain of hair. "Does everyone get around on these…beasts?"

"Most of the time. They can go really fast when they need to." She laughed indulgently and patted his hand. The odd shyness he had noticed the night before seemed to have vanished completely, along with the giggles.

"Don't you have any sort of air-cars for getting around in?"

"Like small ships, you mean? They say there used to be lots of them but personal vehicles aren't allowed any more. There are the flying transports for long distance travel but that's mostly for hunters or the army. Why would we need them, anyway?"

"I guess it's a pretty small city," he agreed.

After a while, he got used to the rolling, lurching rhythm of the animal. He raised his head and looked around. Behind them was the warren of back alleys and side streets that led to the stables. They were coming out of the town, climbing upwards all the time along the winding trail. The breeze caught his hair and he felt suddenly happy. It was the first time in a long while that he had been alone with someone his own age just for fun.

47

"Are you all right now, Cham?" Quana half turned, looking at him over her shoulder.

"It's wonderful," he said softly. "I've never done anything like this."

"Don't you have picnics where you come from?"

"Oh, yes. But it's quite different. Triani has a beautiful house in the country with his own lake. We like to swim to the island in the middle and eat and drink as we dry off together in the sun. He tells me about his performance the night before, who came back stage to see him, and the funny things that happened at the club afterwards. He has a great sense of humour but sometimes he can be...a little cruel." He paused, gazing over the peaceful scene around them. "He's the best dancer anywhere, you know," he added suddenly. "I'm very lucky to be with him."

He didn't tell her about the long, lonely evenings in his tiny apartment, waiting for Triani's summons, or the wild, screaming fights when his lover turned up unexpectedly and found that Cham had gone to dinner with a school friend. That didn't happen any more, of course. He hadn't had dinner with anyone else for a long time.

"Don't you have other friends?" she asked, as if reading his mind.

"I don't need any," he said.

The town was completely out of sight now. They were surrounded by fields of pale feathery grass and nodding blue flowers. Here and there, jagged blood-red rocks poked out of the blue-green sea. The only sounds came from the tinkling bells on the colourful, braided harness of their amax.

"Let's get down here," suggested Quana, pulling back on the reins.

Cham jumped. It was a relief to be on solid ground again. Remembering that he was supposed to look after

Quana, he raised his arms and she slid into them. For a moment, neither one moved. It was an interesting feeling.

"You're very strong, aren't you?" she murmured, drawing away.

Cham felt the flush in his cheeks. He tossed back his hair and laughed nervously. "I'm a dancer. I have to be strong."

They left the amax to graze peacefully and waded into the tall grass that was over Cham's head.

The dry, pungent smell tickled his nose and made him sneeze. Around him, small tricoloured insects pursued each other with high-pitched chirping noises. Two red butterflies, their delicate wings curled up at the edges, hovered above his golden head.

Quana climbed up onto a slab of rock and slipped out of her voluminous yellow garment. She wore a sort of short jumpsuit underneath.

The air shimmered with heat. He pulled off his boots and the lacy white shirt and stretched towards the sun, his hands clasped above his head. He leapt for the next rock, twirling effortlessly in the air for the sheer pleasure of movement.

"This is wonderful!" he exclaimed, as he took a bottle of Merculian mint wine out of his shoulder bag and poured them each a glass. "To picnics," he said.

She raised her glass and smiled. "It's really exciting seeing people who come from so far away. We even had a holiday when you arrived."

"I love holidays."

"Then you'll love the next one. It's called the Festival of Dreams and there's a great procession and dancing in the streets and we all get a chance to talk to the Dream Weaver."

"Could I dance with you then?" Cham asked.

49

She laughed, her hand covering her mouth as she dipped her head. "Do you always do things that get you in trouble?"

"You mean like last night? But you invited me to come over, didn't you?"

"Certainly, but I didn't expect you to actually do it!"

"You mean it was just a game?"

"In a way."

Cham shook his head. "I don't get it."

"It's all right. I'm glad you didn't play the game by Abulonian rules. Just between you and me, I was hoping you wouldn't." She smiled, looking straight at him, this time. Then she looked away.

He lay back in the grass sipping the wine and sampling the various strange delicacies Quana had brought. It was obvious she had put a lot of thought into her preparations, and it didn't matter that his palate couldn't distinguish between them. He appreciated the thought.

"Tell me about that man last night— the one who told the story. Everyone seemed really... well, I don't mean to be rude, but I didn't see what was so unusual in the story. I mean, the character was so important he didn't have a name? Can you explain it?"

"That was the Dream Weaver. He keeps our dreams alive, looks inside, and shows us what they mean. The story last night about the hunter who was lost is very old, but every one tells it differently, and only some storytellers, like the Dream Weaver or some other great leader, can make us see the images."

"Images? What images? You mean, the words he used were so powerful you could see the scenes?"

"I mean pictures, the ones he drew in the air to illustrate his words. That's what makes his stories so wonderful."

"I...don't understand. Are you talking about real pictures? Like in a hologram?"

"You mean you didn't see anything last night?"

Cham shook his head.

"Nothing at all?" She stared at him, her lips parted.

"Nothing." He remembered the low thrumming sound, the delayed echo underneath the old man's words. "I heard something strange, but I guess whatever it is doesn't work for Merculian eyes. Can you all do it?"

"Oh, no. It's a gift only leaders and dreamers have."

"We just use holograms," Cham said.

"Maybe one of my children will have the gift, like my grandfather. In ten years, I guess I'll know."

"Ten years?"

"I'll be married then, living in my husband's home, practising his ceremonials, and watching my children grow. What about you? Will you be married in ten years?"

He laughed, spilling wine on his bare chest. "We don't get married till we're around forty, and I don't think I want any children. I certainly don't want to have one myself. I think it's messy and inconvenient and you lose your figure. Besides, you have to take time off from dancing."

She looked at him, perplexed. "I don't understand. Do you mean *you* can have babies?"

"Of course," said Cham, casually. "Triani has a child, you know. Actually, he paid this other dancer to have it with him about three years ago, but he doesn't like to talk about that part. I shouldn't really be telling you, I suppose. Anyway, I won't have time for all that. I'm going to be famous some day, touring everywhere, like Triani. I just hope I have the time to do this sort of thing and know someone like you to do it with." His eyes looked into hers for a moment, then slid away. "No matter how you meant the invitation, I want you to know I appreciate it. So I made you a present. I like to make jewellery." He reached for his bag and dug out a pendant on a crystal chain. It was a silver disk with a design worked into it in tiny coloured stones.

"It's lovely! Put it on for me?" She held up her heavy hair with both hands and bent her head.

Cham fastened the chain around her neck, taking his time as he breathed in the sweet spicy girl scent of her warm body. He was surprised at the effect she was having on his senses. She was so different from Triani, from any Merculian, for that matter. He gazed in fascination at her right ear with the three green rings fitted into it and ran a small finger over the edge and around the earlobe.

"I'd love to have external ears like you," he said wistfully. "Then I could wear earrings, too."

She twisted her head around to look at him. "You don't have ears?"

"Oh, yes. But they don't stick out." He pushed back his hair to show her the thin membrane covering the sensitive inner ear. He could feel the heat from her body as she leaned close to look. "Do you want to go for a walk? I think I hear water somewhere."

She jumped to her feet and they wandered together through the tall grass onto the stony ground higher up the slope. The sound of water was louder here, tumbling over boulders, rushing headlong between narrow rocky walls. Hand in hand, they ran to the edge of the river.

Quana saw it first. "Look! Somebody's watchdog!" she exclaimed. "Poor thing. It must have gotten lost in the storm yesterday and drowned."

The animal seemed to hang suspended just under the sparkling surface of the water, its long, thin tail streaming out behind it, waving lazily with the current. Somehow its huge paws had become cruelly wedged between the stones at the bottom. Its large head hung down in defeat, the tip of its narrow black tongue showing between its teeth.

Cham let go of Quana's hand and bent down to examine the creature more closely. The leathery coat was slippery and cold to the touch. Two glassy eyes stared sightlessly at the bottom of the stream. But the third eye blazed like a jewel an inch from the forehead, bobbing about with every movement of the water. It was held there by one thin, silver wire.

Cham knelt and touched the glowing orb and its tiny wires. It came away in his hand. "It's some sort of video transmitter," he whispered, dazed.

"How do you know?"

"It's obvious. We used to make them in school." He took a deep breath. "These dogs are nothing but walking video spies!"

"I don't understand." Quana was staring from the eye to Cham's face and back again. It was clear that she knew nothing about it.

Cham felt cold horror sweeping over him. He remembered last night, the big dog so much at home in the bedroom that they had forgotten about it. But all the time it was watching as he and Triani made love for hours on that marvellous bed. He felt the heat in his face.

"What kind of people are you?" he cried, turning on Quana. "You give us a gift and then use it against us!"

"What are you talking about! They're guardians, meant to help people. Why are you so upset?"

"We are not used to being spied on! How can we trust you people after this?"

Quana drew herself up to her full height. "Perhaps you are the ones who are not worthy of trust," she said. "You're just a dancer and yet you think you're smarter than we are. You're angry because you've found out you're not."

"Just a dancer!" cried Cham, stung. He glared at Quana, then turned abruptly and started back the way they had come. She followed, easily keeping pace with him. Once in the long grass, he was forced to slow down until finally he stopped.

After a moment of silence, Quana stepped in front of him and led the way back to the rock. Together they began to collect the remains of their picnic and stow everything away in the saddlebags.

"I'm sorry," she said at last. She was braiding her hair. "I really don't understand this."

"I know," he said. He stamped his feet down into his boots. "Let's go."

When they reached the amax, she adjusted the bright saddle blanket and then vaulted onto its back, using Cham's clasped hands as a stirrup. Cham leapt up behind her. When he slipped his arms around her waist, he was stunned by the turmoil of emotions he felt from her. It was almost a relief to find she was this upset, although he knew her reasons were different from his.

The whole incident had been a forceful reminder that he was the alien here. Nothing he had read in his orientation package had prepared him for this.

"What are you going to do about...this?" she said.

"Tell Triani, I guess."

"Do you have to say I was with you? You could leave my name out of it, couldn't you?"

"But Quana, you never said it was a secret! Look, you invited me here, in front of your friends, too. If it was wrong, I didn't know!"

"You're just like everyone else! Put the blame on the female!"

"I am *not* like everyone else! You're—" He clamped his mouth shut. After a moment, he said, "Anyway, Triani knows I'm with you."

"You told him?"

"Of course! He's—" Once again, he stopped himself, suddenly aware there were possibilities for misunderstanding everywhere.

"They'll kill me if they find out I was out alone with a boy!" she exclaimed.

"But that's ridiculous! Besides, I'm *not* a boy."

"Alone with an alien is probably even worse!"

"Thanks a lot! Anyway, we were riding out in plain sight of everyone. How is that secret?

"Why do you think I went thorugh the back alleys?" she snapped. "The scenery? No one saw us."

There was silence between them for a few moments. Cham gritted his teeth as the animal lurched along with its uneven gait. His head was spinning with the possible repercussions from this innocent afternoon. "Why did you really invite me to come here?" he asked at last.

"I wanted to get to know you. It cost me a fortune to get rid of my brother all afternoon, too."

"But why shouldn't you be alone with me? Isn't there any trust between you people? Or has being under constant surveillance made it impossible for you to trust anyone?"

Quana didn't answer, but he could feel her indignation.

"I'm just trying to understand," he went on quickly. "I thought the whole idea behind joining the I.P.A. was to get to know alien cultures."

"I get the feeling you people expect this to be all one way," she said coolly. "Are *you* trying to understand?"

"I came, didn't I?" And oh, how I wish I hadn't, he thought, as they rode on in silence. He knew he would never be able to look at only the surfaces of things on Abulon again.

5

The Festival Theatre had been brought from Merculian and assembled in the middle of the Public Gardens near the palace of the Great Chief. The day it went up, a crowd gathered, chattering and laughing to see the Merculian crew patiently set out all the pieces of the building in the shape of a huge circle, as if it were some kind of a gigantic puzzle. Their amusement turned to exclamations of wonder as the outer walls suddenly began to rise upwards, the supports snapping into place in sequence, controlled by one small box with a black lever. The huge dome curved inwards and fit together with a gentle click. The triangular struts gleamed silver against the deep blue and white of the rounded walls.

As Cham arrived, workers thronged in and out under the wide arch of the entrance, putting the finishing touches to the theatre. Inside was bright with the light coming in through the translucent panels. The seats were still being assembled in gently rising tiers. The stage lights were on. The crew was checking the light tower projectors and the company's lighting designer was shouting directions as he waved his arms impatiently from the front of the stage.

Cham hurried down the side aisle. The rehearsal was called for four o'clock but he knew Triani would be here somewhere, going through his long warm-up routine, totally unaware of the chaos around him. There was plenty of time to tell him about the dog.

Cham slipped into the backstage area and saw Triani at once, poised in the glare of the working lights, colourful in purple tights and a yellow top. Cham stopped to watch. Triani's face was absorbed, the black eyes opaque and inward-looking. He stood on one leg, holding the other foot casually at arm's length above his head. He released the foot, bending the other knee as he did so. Leaping into the air, he resumed his original pose. His graceful movements were apparently effortless, totally controlled. Without warning, he fell forwards onto his hands, his legs moving slowly over his head as he arched his back, pointed his toes. Slowly, slowly his body bent until one toe touched the floor behind him. With a quick movement, he flipped over, sliding into the splits with smooth grace, his arms arched above his head. He stared at Cham. The light in his eyes changed.

"Go to my dressing room!" he hissed, springing to his feet.

Shaken, Cham turned away.

The dressing rooms were formed by brightly coloured slabs of soundproofed material, which fitted into upright metal poles attached floor and ceiling. Triani's was yellow; Eulio's, beside it, blue. Cham opened the door and walked in, glancing around at the recliner Triani always insisted on; the gleaming make-up table, its large mirror framed in light; the small, old-fashioned armchairs. There was a bar along one end of the room where costumes were hanging. A bottle of Crushed Emeralds stood on a small table.

Triani slammed the door behind him. It made no noise, only a soft hiss. "Where the hell have you been, you ass-hole? Don't you know what time it is?"

"But you know where I've been! I told you all about it. And it's not even four o'clock yet."

Triani glared at him, hands on hips. "From now on you get your ass over here one hour before rehearsal and warm up, do you hear?"

Cham nodded, backing away. He thought Triani was going to hit him.

"And one more thing, while we're at it. This is the real world, sweetie. You are just a member of the chorus; the youngest, least experienced, humblest member. Got it? You will not come to my dressing room again or even speak to me, unless I speak to you first. You will act like a profes-sional. Always!"

Cham's lower lip trembled. "You don't have to yell at me! I know how to behave backstage." He swallowed. "I'll get my things."

"They're here. I brought them." Triani tossed him the rainbow-striped bag that held Cham's rehearsal clothes. "Get changed."

"Here?"

"Just this once."

Triani flung himself into a chair, one leg over the arm. His yellow top was damp with sweat. He pulled it over his head and rubbed his chest as he watched Cham turn away and begin to undress.

"You've got a great little body," he remarked.

Cham didn't answer. He was deeply hurt by Triani's scalding anger. He always found it difficult to adjust to these drastic swings in mood. As he reached for his bag, strong arms embraced him from behind.

"Got a smile for me, baby?" Triani's fingers traced the outline of Cham's lips and ran caressingly over his smooth chest. Cham stood still and felt a sudden stab of resentment. A sob caught in his throat. How can you do this to me? he wanted to say. But he knew he wouldn't. He knew he would yield unreservedly to Triani's driving need, as he always did. The sob escaped in a whimper. Then, his body singing from Triani's touch, he turned around and lifted his face for a kiss. He could feel Triani's desire all through the body pressed against him.

"Oh, love me, Chami," murmured Triani as he sank to the floor with Cham in his arms. Their smooth, naked bodies tangled together for a few moments before Triani pushed Cham onto his back, the long curls spilling out on the floor. He knelt above him, stroking the soft inside of his thighs until Cham's whole body quivered with longing. Silvery moisture dampened his pubic hair as his desire for union exploded, and he reached out with a cry.

Suddenly, urgently, Triani slammed into him. Cham clung tightly, his eyes closed, tears caught on his lashes as the assault went on. When Triani lay still, Cham opened his eyes again and smiled. He felt Triani's long, shuddering breaths all through him, felt the withdrawal of his sex, the softening of his nipples, the thumping of his heart. Cham let his own sex emerge at last, seeking union with his lover.

Triani ignored the signal. "Look what I have to do to get a smile out of you," he said.

"Rough, isn't it?" Cham pulled his face closer and kissed the side of his mouth.

Triani ran his long fingers through the pale, gold hair. "Come on, baby. We can't lie around on the floor all day. Time for work."

"But....." Cham's voice trailed off. Triani was already heading for his private shower. Swallowing his hurt and sexual frustration, Cham got to his feet and followed, resignedly.

When they were dressed, Cham sat at Triani's make-up table brushing his hair and watching his lover in the mirror. His heart felt painfully full of tenderness in spite of what had just happened. He wondered if he would ever understand Triani. The story of the drowned dog would have to wait now. He dropped the brush in his bag and stood up. Triani was right behind him. His hand caught the back of Cham's neck, his fingers in the long hair.

"It's not going to be easy in there, baby," he said. "Don't let me down. And don't ever let them see you cry." He brushed the soft cheek with a kiss. "Knock 'em dead, sweetie. You can do it!"

Cham felt his heart turn over. At that moment he would happily have died for Triani. He reached for his hand, raised it to his lips, gently sucked the tips of the fingers, one by one. His eyes never left the loved face.

"Shit. You're one sexy kid."

Cham kissed the inside of Triani's wrist, turned without a word, and went out the door.

Cham was the first one back at their apartment. He was trembling with the effort at self-control. He poured himself a tall glass of Merculian mint wine and stood by the window, his forehead resting against the cool glass. Every few sips he would close his eyes and take several deep breaths. If only Triani would come home. To keep busy, he washed in the small pool that was constantly filling with warm water, dressed in a pale blue robe, and put on the gold collar Triani had given him for his birth day. He laid out some of the Merculian delicacies they had brought from home on the long, low table and placed silver candles down the middle.

He put two furry cushions on the floor, side by side. He shut the dog in the bedroom. With everything done, he knelt in a corner of the huge sofa that nearly filled one wall, both small hands clamped tightly around the riot of fruit carved along the back.

Today was the first time he had danced with the company. He was physically and mentally exhausted. It wasn't the dancing that had done it but the constant emotional drain of feeling hostile eyes on him, knowing they were just waiting for him to make a mistake, ready to pounce if the star's little darling made one slip. No one said a word but their resentment and jealousy were heavy on the air.

Triani had warned him. "You're not going to be popular, baby." But Cham hadn't expected hatred. It wasn't just because of his relationship with Triani, although that was a big part of it, but because of his extreme youth and talent. Now Cham wondered if he could take this kind of constant pressure.

No one had befriended him. The only bright spot had come during a break, from an unexpected source. Cham knelt alone in the wings, adjusting a slipper when a comforting arm was draped over his shoulder. Surprised, he looked up into the wide blue eyes of Eulio Chazin Adelantis.

"Remember, you're on that stage because the director of this company thinks you're good enough."

"But Triani asked him, *chai*."

"Triani got you an audition. You got yourself the rest of the way. Remember that, Chamion."

Cham smiled for the first time. "Now I know why *chai* Benvolini loves you so," he said shyly.

Eulio flushed slightly and got to his feet. "Don't get cheeky with me, child. And don't let them get you down."

After the rehearsal, when Cham went to the dressing room he shared with three others, they all stopped talking. They made him so nervous he didn't want to change in front of them. He pulled his red pants over the tights, got into his boots, and shrugged into the lacy shirt. He wanted to scream at them, to make them acknowledge him but he was afraid he would cry if he said anything at all. He picked up his bag and left. As the door closed, he heard one of them say loudly, "They share a bed, why can't they share a dressing room, for god's sake! Why crowd us?"

Cham stared at the carvings of the alien fruit. Why do they want to hurt me? he wondered. When he felt the touch of Triani's long fingers on the back of his neck, he let out his breath in a sigh.

"It was rough, baby. I know." Triani sat down close behind him. "I couldn't get away any sooner. I'm sorry." He caressed the pale flaxen curls. "You've got to let it out. Don't let them chew you up inside. Come on." His hand moved soothingly over Cham's back.

Cham gulped and, with a sudden twist of his body, buried his face in Triani's neck. All during that awful rehearsal he had longed for these arms around him, for the comforting strength of Triani's body against his. Finally he let the tears come.

Triani rocked him gently in his arms. "The bastards," he muttered and kissed the top of his head. "I'm proud of you, Chami. You did good out there."

Cham clung to him for a long time as the tension gradually drained away.

Finally Triani said softly, "You okay, now, lover? I'm starving."

Cham laughed a little shakily and wiped his eyes. "Do you want some wine?"

"You go wash your face, sweetie. I'll pour it."

When Cham came back, he sat on the cushion beside Triani and took a sip of wine. "I've got something to tell you," he began.

"Baby, it'll never be as bad again as it was today."

"I don't mean the rehearsal. Something happened at the picnic."

"You laid the girl."

"Be serious." Cham looked at him reproachfully. "This is really weird. While we were walking in a field, we found one of those big watch dogs drowned in a stream. His middle eye had come out. Except it wasn't an eye. It was a video camera."

Triani stared at him, his glass half way to his lips. "Shit! Those bloody sneaks! Talk about invasion of privacy!" He jumped to his feet and looked around for his boots. "Holy shit! If I'm going to be in the porno business, I'm sure as hell going to get paid for it! Where can I find the Chief? And where's that shitty dog now?"

Cham was on his feet, clinging to his arm. "Please, Triani! It's ten o'clock at night! We can't go to the Great Chief now! It's pitch black out there! The dog is in the bedroom," he added.

"Well, he's not going to be there tonight," muttered Triani, sitting down and picking up his wine.

Cham knelt beside him. "You don't have to say anything about the girl, do you? I mean, it's not really necessary and besides, I think she'll get into a lot of trouble if her parents find out she was alone with me."

"Well, well! If it isn't the Merculian Menace!" laughed Triani. "What do you care anyway? It was her idea."

"I know, but still…." Cham sighed. "Everything I do here seems to come out…wrong."

Triani made a sound of annoyance and tossed off the rest of his wine. "Come on. We'll tell Benvolini the whole thing and see if he can keep her out of it. He's the ambassador. It's his problem."

Cham was not looking forward to a recital of his private picnic in front of Benvolini and Eulio. It occurred to him that not only Quana might get into trouble over this, but there was nothing for it but to take Triani's hand and follow him to the Ambassador's apartment.

Even before the door opened, they could hear the music.

The android who stood there had his name on a silver disk around his neck, spelt out in the Merculian alphabet because Eulio found it hard to remember.

"My masters are occupied, lords," he said solemnly, holding the outer door open with one large hand.

"So I hear." Triani pushed the door further open and sailed in, his black velvet robe brushing lightly against the android. Someone was playing the Merculian pipes, and, judging from the results, it could only be Eulio. His mother, a well-known maker of the instruments, had taught him at an early age. Wild and achingly sweet, the clear notes sounded from the other room. A high, crystalline soprano sang along with the instrument, weaving a counter-melody around it. The voice hesitated, stopped. Laughter filled the sudden space before they started over again. Triani said, "This is urgent. Call *chai* Benvolini at once."

The android did not move. "I cannot, lord. They said not to disturb."

"Oh shit," said, Triani. He marched past the anxious android and thumped on the inner door with his fist.

The music stopped. The door opened.

"What the bloody damn..." Beny was holding a tall glass. His turquoise tunic hung open and his feet were bare. Behind him, Triani could see Eulio sitting on the raised platform by the pool, one bare leg dangling in the water as he held the gilded Merculian pipes close to his chest. His lavender robe was bunched up around his thighs. He leaned his head against the wall and squinted up at Triani. He was a little drunk. He always maintained he played better that way.

Triani spread his hands placatingly. "Hi, Benvolini, sweetie. I'm sorry to bother you. I really am. But this is important. Cham has something to tell you."

"At this hour?"

"I know. It's late. Dhakan, why don't you take the brute for a walk, okay sweetie?"

The android remained impassive. He didn't move.

"He looks like he wants to pee. Don't you think so, Benvolini?" Triani went on. He gestured with one hand and touched Beny's arm for a moment, holding the contact.

Beny's pupils dilated slightly. He fastened his tunic, picked up his belt from the floor, smoothed his bright curls. "Dhakan, Triani's right. Take him out, please."

The android bowed at once, grabbed the dog by its collar, and headed for the door.

"This had better be good, Triani."

"But what do they want, darling?" Eulio complained as Beny helped him to his feet. When nobody answered, he scooped up a bottle of wine and followed them to the other room. He sank languidly into a sofa and delicately crossed his ankles. "If you hauled yourself away from your sweet, juvenile games at this hour, Triani darling, it must be important indeed."

"Watch it, baby!" Triani scowled at him but Eulio only laughed.

"Not now, you two," said Beny, wearily. He moved behind the sofa where Eulio lay. "What's this all about? What have you got to tell me, Chamion?"

Cham cleared his throat. His round grey eyes flicked to Triani, then back to the ambassador as he told his story. Wringing his hands in his earnestness, he begged him not to reveal Quana's name. At last he showed him the green lens of the video eye.

The ambassador's face turned a flaming red.

Eulio lay unmoving on the sofa while the color slowly drained from his cheeks. "God's teeth, Orosin!" He reached for Beny's hand.

Beny sank down beside Eulio. "I suspect we're not the only ones they've been watching," he began calmly, studying the inlaid pattern of the wooden floor. "I've seen many of these animals around in the short time I've been here. The bedroom aspect is probably nothing but an unexpected fringe benefit for them. I'm sure that's not the reason for this elaborate scheme. They want to study us, our habits, our way of speaking to each other, what we talk about, and what we say about them behind their backs."

"Audio-visual teaching aids, sweetie?"

"Something like that. By the way, Chamion, did you tell Triani your plans about the picnic with the girl?"

"Of course, *chai*. Last night."

"With the dog watching? Then I'm afraid the identity of your friend is already known."

Cham pounded the arm of his chair and swore.

"It's not your fault," said Triani.

Beny got to his feet. "Thank you both for coming to me with this. Just keep the bloody damn dog out of the way for now, and I'll tell the others to do the same. Tomorrow we'll have the video eye disconnected."

"Anything to oblige." Triani draped his arm over Cham's shoulder. "Come on, child. Playtime."

6

"Are you positive this is important?" Thar-von's voice crackled sharply from the small communication device in Beny's hand.

"Bloody damn, Von, don't make me give you an order!"

"I'll be there in five minutes."

Eulio had fallen asleep on the sofa. Beny woke him up. "Go to bed, *chaleen*. This will take awhile."

"I'm sorry I can't stay and help, but I'm so very tired."

"So am I," muttered Beny. He helped himself to one of Eulio's short-term stimulants and went back to the other room to pace.

Thar-von arrived fully and impeccably dressed in exactly five minutes. He bowed.

"What's the matter?" asked Beny warily.

"I fail to understand why every Merculian crisis has to occur close to midnight," he replied, his voice tight.

Beny was shaking with fatigue. As a Merculian, he needed many more hours of sleep than Thar-von did. He found it very difficult to keep his objectivity, and the stimulant played havoc with his nerves. He turned away from the man he had considered a good friend for years and sat down on one of the many fur-covered chairs.

"I do not control the times of the crises," he said as calmly as he could. "I apologize if I have inconvenienced you. Sit down. Please."

Thar-von took the chair opposite him and bent his head to listen as Beny carefully related Cham's story.

"Does that rate Serpian approval as a genuine crisis?" he finished acidly.

Thar-von blinked. "As I see it, the main problem is that they did not inform us before hand. Otherwise, I can see the watch dogs as a fine invention. They could take children to school and bring people home safely late at night. They could do guard duty and crowd control. Mine goes running with me early in the morning. Now I will feel doubly secure."

"I'm happy for you," said Beny sarcastically. He clamped down on his feelings of anger, suspecting it was because the Serpian had no reason to be upset or embarrassed as they had. He looked at him consideringly. "Where do you keep your animal?"

"It sleeps at the foot of my bed."

Beny thought he spotted a flash of amusement in the navy blue eyes. "You smug, self-satisfied bastard," he muttered.

"Would you care to repeat that, Ambassador?"

"No!" Beny looked about helplessly for a moment, wondering what had happened to their old, easygoing relationship.

"If I may be frank, Orosin, I understand perfectly why you are so upset about this invasion of privacy. You are worrying about aliens watching your undoubtedly bizarre love-making rituals."

Beny's face grew red with fury. "That remark is uncalled for! Just because you Serpians are forced to take a vow of celibacy—"

"That is irrelevant. Tell me, if the dog had not been in your bedchamber last night watching you and Eulio disporting yourselves, would you be this upset? Would you not simply have waited until morning and written a letter of gentle diplomatic complaint?"

"Damn you, Von!" Beny stared at the Serpian. Thar-von had never talked to him like this. When he thought he could trust his voice again, he went on. "It's more than that. We have diplomatic immunity. Our apartments are supposed to be a little piece of Merculian in the wasteland of Abulon. It is *our* laws that should apply here. That's what makes what they have done so serious."

"Please remember that these people are not used to dealing with I.P.A. member states. They do not know the ins and outs of intergalactic law. They are simply trying to protect important visitors from harm."

Beny ran his fingers through his thick curls and looked at the ceiling. His hands were shaking.

Thar-von studied him. After a minute's silence, he got up and came over to sit beside him. "Are you on stimulants?"

Beny nodded numbly.

"Can I get you something to drink? I know you always get thirsty when you're on those things."

"You're not my servant, Thar-von. I can get whatever I need myself." He sniffed miserably. "What do you suggest we do?"

"I don't think we should make a major issue of this."

Beny wiped his eyes. "We have to make an official complaint of some sort, Von. But I agree. No big commotion. What about a letter to the Chief explaining that we appreciate the good points of the system but would have preferred to have been informed."

"That sounds good. But no mention of the bedroom aspect, I think."

Beny nodded. "All right. And tell him we're disconnecting the video transmitters."

Thar-von rose to his feet. "I will draw up the document and bring it in for your approval and signature in the morning." He bowed and withdrew.

Beny sat staring at the door after he had gone. His whole body was vibrating with tension. It was bad enough to discover they had been spied on by aliens without feeling he had been judged and found guilty by a friend for some crime he was unaware he had committed. He twisted the material of his tunic around in his hands. This was the kind of situation that could explode into major danger. He knew that. Just as he had sensed the danger in the apparently innocent meeting of Cham and that girl in the dining hall. Look where that had led! Here he was, deserted by the one person he had counted on to be there for him on this project, the only male he had ever trusted entirely.

When he couldn't stand it any longer, he steeled himself to face the shadowed corridor and knocked on Thar-von's door. "I'm coming in," he shouted.

Thar-von sat beside the darkened window drinking *siva*, the fiery orange Serpian liquor. He had relaxed enough to undo the top three buttons of his tunic. As Beny came in, he turned his head but didn't get up.

"For God's sake, what have I done to get you so mad at me? Tell me!"

"I'm sorry," said Thar-von in a flat voice. "I don't know what's wrong. Maybe it's because, for the first time, you outrank me."

"I don't believe that! There's not a jealous bone in your whole body. There must be something else."

"Talassa-ran Zox. It's ridiculous, but I feel honour bound to spring to his defence all the time, just because he's a Serpian. He does seem to get along well with the Abulonian men, though. I think they have discovered they share a passion for gambling."

"It's hard to imagine Talassa-ran having a passion for anything."

"Well, he does. It's the real reason he's no longer a raider."

"I didn't know he ever was one."

"You never read the files. Anyway, I spend most of my time these days ironing out problems between Zox and your Merculian staff."

"*Our* Merculian staff, you mean."

"No matter how I try, it keeps coming out as two Serpians against all you Merculians."

"But it's not like that! It's *never* been like that!"

"I've never worked so closely with you and your people before, Ben. Do you realize that five times in three days you overruled my orders?"

"So that's it. I don't even remember."

"For instance, the break-in at the theatre. I started an investigation, and you cancelled it, without consulting me."

"Oh, Von, that was just a waste of time and effort. You said yourself nothing much was missing, only a few bits and pieces of hologram equipment and some other odds and ends that made no difference to the production staff and aren't dangerous or anything. It was probably just souvenir hunters."

"I doubt it. If you had consulted me, I would have told you my theory that the very fact of the odd choice of things to steal might prove significant. Without an investigation, we will never know."

Beny sighed and sat down beside his friend on the recessed window seat. "Why didn't you say something? I'm sorry. And those other times, too. I guess I forgot to check with you. Please, please tell me right away if something like this happens again. I'm new at this, too, you know." He shook his head sadly and was silent for a moment. "Von, do you know how I feel here with you, seeing the admiration and respect in the Abulonians' eyes when they look at you? When they look at me, its only curiosity, puzzlement, sometimes even pity. You're athletic. You can talk about hunting and…and marathons. They don't want to talk about music or painting, and they don't seem to have any theatre in our sense of the word. If either one of us has the right to be jealous, it's me. They feel a natural affinity with you. Now I find out they even like Zox! It hurts, Von. It really does."

Thar-von looked at him gravely. "I didn't realize," he said. "I'm sorry. They have no right to feel that way about you." His lips quirked in a half-smile. "One of them certainly doesn't."

"You mean Luan, the Chief's son?"

Thar-von nodded. "He follows you about like a dog. Every time I drop into the office, he's there, just looking at you. It must be embarrassing."

"They say it's good to have friends in high places."

"If Eulio weren't here, would you…respond to his interest?"

"Eulio *is* here." Beny sighed. "What's gotten into you tonight?" It occurred to him that the vow of celibacy might have a lot to do with it. Thar-von handed him the *siva* and he took a sip, coughed and handed it back. He looked up into his friend's strong, gentle face. "Oh, damn, Von! Please don't be mad at me any more!" He flung his arms around Thar-von's waist and kissed his cheek. "Please?"

The Serpian tensed, then smiled down at him tolerantly. "Remember the first time you did that?"

"How could I forget! You threw me across the room."

"You took some getting used to."

"You took the trouble to try, Von. I'll never forget how you came to my rescue that time at the academy when those Lanserian thugs were beating me to a pulp. You looked out for me after that."

"Ben, please. That's ancient history."

"Maybe. I just want you to know it's not forgotten."

"Understood." Thar-von sipped thoughtfully at his drink. "I apologize for what I said about you and Eulio. I had no right to say any of that."

"That's all right, Von. I shouldn't have mentioned your celibacy vow, either."

Thar-von nodded. "I'm beginning to think I no longer support the concept of purity of the race," he said quietly.

"I never understood it but I thought it was a basic Serpian tenet."

"It is. There are historical reasons for it—so many cases of monstrous birth defects in the past—but nevertheless...."

"What's changed your mind?"

"Abulonian women." He paused and Beny could feel the sigh. "Even the female androids in this place arouse me. Perhaps I am losing my mind. Could it be as simple as that?"

"I thought Serpians don't do that sort of thing."

"We don't, as a rule. The strain is telling on me, I guess."

Beny nodded, his head on Thar-von's chest. He was listening to the peculiar double thumps of the Serpian's heart and wondered if there was any Abulonian woman in particular whom his friend found attractive. He knew better than to ask, however. He could sense that Thar-von's unusual excursion into the personal was at an end, for now.

"What do you think of the Chief, Von?"

"The Am Quarr is a ruthless man. He does not trust us, but I think he is acting in good faith, as he understands it."

"I guess so. What about the First Minister?"

"The difference between the two, as I see it, is that the First Minister thinks he has a sense of humor," Thar-von remarked dryly.

Beny smiled. "Maybe we just don't understand Abulonian jokes." He paused. "Sort of like Merculians with Serpian proverbs," he added.

"'The beasts do not change their shape when the light seeps out of the forest'," Thar-von said, his voice dropping into the sing-song pattern he used when quoting.

"Exactly," Beny said, with a smile. "You just proved my point."

7

"*L*et's hit the high spots, baby, if there are any in this wilderness." Triani flung his arm over Cham's shoulders. Together they strolled around to the back of the flat-topped pyramid-shaped complex where they lived and stopped to look around. The narrow walkways that led off in several directions were damp from a recent shower. In the shadow of a clump of spiky bushes, a small boy was watching them.

"Which way do we go?" asked Cham, looking down first one lane and then another as they twisted out of sight among the jumble of wooden buildings.

"You want some action?" The boy had sidled up to them and was looking at Triani with hopeful, dark eyes.

"You got it, kid. Just lead the way."

The boy turned to his left and started confidently down the cobbled walkway. Every few steps he glanced back over his shoulder, shading his eyes in the bright sunlight, to make sure they were following. His narrow brown face looked older than the rest of him.

"On the way, baby, pretend I'm blind and make me see what you see." Cham looked up at him questioningly. "An artist must be very observant. You have to know how a person holds his head while talking or listening, how they move, the way they sit on a chair or sip a glass of wine. You must know the subtle differences between the sexes. All of them. You never know what role will come your way. Open your eyes, lover."

"I'll try." Cham sounded doubtful but he looked about him intently as he started to talk. "Ahead of us stretches the winding street which has been swept clean by squads of shiny-headed androids. Some of them are just finishing now. They never raise their copper eyes from their work. They all wear the same baggy brown pants and tunics. They have no expression at all."

"Good. What about the buildings."

"They seem to be shops— workshops, I think. They're dim and narrow and go back a long way from the street. Some of them are open all the way through and you can catch sight of colourful gardens out the back door." He stopped speaking. Quana was across the street, walking beside a tall, gaunt woman whose black hair looked as if shellacked to her skull. Between them walked a large green-ish watch dog. Quana looked right at him, then her eyes slid aside and she turned away, with a scared expression on her face. The smile died on Cham's lips and he kept on walking.

"Cut you dead, eh sweetie?"

"She's in trouble because of me. Maybe if I explained to her parents...about us, I mean. Do you think that would help?"

"Explained what? That you're perfectly capable of laying their precious daughter, who appears to have the hots for you, but you don't feel like it because you're living with a 29 year old letch who exhausts you every night?"

"Aw don't. Please." Cham hung his head and scuffed his red boots on the uneven paving stones. "It's not like that."

"Don't be so sensitive, you'll live longer." In spite of the glib words, Triani was aware of the pain in the beautiful face and hated himself for being the cause of it. He grimaced briefly. "Look, if you want to make up with your stiff-necked girlfriend and her parents, why not send them tickets for opening night? Holy shit! Is this the best you can do for us, kid?"

The boy had stopped at a dim doorway of a place that looked like some sort of a café. He was gesturing them inside, a wide grin on his face.

"I don't think I want to go in there," said Cham, hanging back.

Triani shrugged and flipped a coin to the boy. "Suit yourself." He disengaged himself from Cham and went through the open door. After a moment, Cham followed. When he looked back, the boy had disappeared.

Inside, three men stood around a rectangular table with a recessed top, playing an intense game. They were using black and white counters and what looked like large, spongy triangles. A fat man with a thick neck was keeping score with the help of some sort of an abacus. They were obviously gambling. Stacks of paper cards with writing on them changed hands at intervals. Discordant music came faintly from a battered speaker at the back of the room. The men were drinking the native brown ale and wiping the foam from their mouths with the back of a hand. Only one man was smiling but he didn't look friendly.

They paused to look up as Triani walked in. A man with a blue earring in his misshapen ear, was wearing one of the distinctive figurines carved from blue crystal that Serpian men often wore. The fat man nodded. The one with a scar running the length of his cheek looked him up and down insolently, a faint smile on his lips.

"You're one of them dancer Merculians," he remarked.

"Well, well. You don't miss much, do you, sweetie." Triani put his hands on his hips and grinned up at the man. The others laughed and Triani, encouraged, came closer. He propped one foot on a stool, rested his elbow on one knee, and leaned over to study the table. "Playing for pennies, boys?"

"Hardly. You want in?"

"What are you playing for?"

"Whatever you've got." They were looking at the flashy rings he wore.

Triani could feel their interest but there was no expression in the dark, impassive faces. "How do you play?" He looked at the fat man who cleared his throat and launched into a complicated explanation of an essentially simple game. "I usually play cards," said Triani doubtfully. In fact, he stayed away from games of chance because he found it difficult to know when to stop, especially when the stakes were high. "On the other hand, this looks like the only game in town. Deal me in, or whatever you say."

Cham examined the room, the stained bar at one side, the dusty pictures of tall men with their arms on one and others' shoulders. He wondered if there was anything here he wasn't seeing, anything hidden just below the surface. He moved back beside Triani and stood patiently, watching and waiting. Gradually he became aware that the men were staring at him. One reached over to touch his hair.

"Hands off," said Triani, not taking his eyes off the game. "He belongs to me."

"You're on a winning streak. Why not put him into the pot? We don't want any more of your damn credits."

"You want him that much?" Triani laughed. "Find your own lover, sweetie. This one's not for sale."

Cham pushed back his hair nervously. These men were serious. The fat one was looking uneasy as he watched Triani take a long pull at his ale.

"What have you got for me of equal value?" Triani cocked an eye at the man with the scar who hesitated, then reached inside his vest. He glanced at Triani's rings, two of which were already on the table.

"You look like someone with an eye for gems." He held out his hand. In his large palm gleamed three enormous *mantino* stones, flashing fire in the sunlight coming in the open door.

Triani held one to the light and checked it with a practised eye. "Flawless," he murmured.

Cham felt a sudden chill in the pit of his stomach. He knew Triani's weakness for precious stones. He laid a small hand on his arm. "What are you doing, love?" he whispered.

Triani slipped an arm around his waist and gave him a quick hug. "You're flawless too, baby." He turned back to study the table. "On the other hand, I can't lose."

"But obviously they think you can," said Cham, worried. "And besides, it's the first time you ever played this game."

Triani drained his glass. "This is ridiculous." He backed away from the table.

"Look here, fellow. You can't pull out in the middle of a game. One more go. All or nothing." The man's fists rested on his hips. He towered over the Merculians.

Triani moved back to the table. "I didn't say I was welshing! Back off, mister!"

"Nobody welshes on us." The men exchanged glances.

Triani took Cham's hand a moment and toyed with the ring on the middle finger. Cham was frightened, too frightened to sense what Triani was trying to tell him. Tears welled up in his clear grey eyes. He didn't say a word.

Triani turned back to the table and rested his hands on the raised edge. His black eyes studied the game intently.

Watching him, Cham felt cold all over. He sensed violence in the air. He saw Triani tense and spring, heaving the table over and knocking the fat man off his stool. Counters, triangles, chits, and beads scattered over the floor.

"Run, Cham!" Triani sprang at the man with the scar, kicking out with his powerful legs.

Cham stood rooted to the spot in horror. He couldn't believe what was happening. Suddenly he was grabbed roughly from behind. The breath rushed out of him as he was thrown over a man's shoulder. As the man started to run, Cham fainted.

Triani was not a coward. Although he had the instincts of a street fighter, he had very little experience. The other two were obviously trained. The only thing in Triani's favor had been surprise and the powerful muscles in his thighs. They hadn't expected a Merculian to fight.

Several men and women gathered in the doorway to watch. "A hundred to one on the little guy," someone shouted, but no one took him up on it.

Triani didn't last three minutes. By the time the Officers of Concord arrived, the three men had disappeared, taking the money, rings, and other valuables with them. Triani lay on the floor, unconscious, blood on his pale face, his red silk tunic torn to shreds.

The fat man told his story, bobbing his head, rubbing his pudgy hands together. He was a witness. Triani had attacked a man without warning in an effort to get out of paying a gambling debt. Nobody mentioned Cham.

Triani came to in a small cell. He looked up into the wizened face of an old man who was rubbing his stubby

chin anxiously. "Who the hell are you?" He tried to sit up and
was hit by a searing pain in his shoulder. "Oh, shit! I'll have to take a double shot of pain killer to dance with this."

The man laid a cool, dry hand on his forehead and smoothed back the black curls. "Hush, now," he said softly, as if to a sick child. "How do we feel?"

"I don't know about you, sweetie, but I feel like shit. Where am I?"

"In jail, young one."

"Why? Did I kill one of the bastards?"

"Oh my dear, no. Here. Drink this." He handed Triani a tall pottery mug of steaming liquid.

Triani wrinkled up his nose in disgust. "What the hell is this? Rat piss?"

"Hush that talk now and drink it all up. It'll take the ache out of your bones." The old man patted his shoulder.

Triani looked at him quizzically, shrugged, and drank the potion. He pressed the heel of his hand against his forehead, trying to clear his thoughts. He looked around the bare cell. There was no door, just heavy, old-fashioned bars across the opening. There was no window, either.

"Where's Cham?" he asked, sudden panic constricting his chest.

"No one was brought here with you."

"Oh God! They took him! They've got Cham! I must talk to someone in authority. Now!"

"The Chief of Concord is not here at present. Who is this Cham person?"

"He's my...my ward. They kidnapped him! Oh shit!"

"Hush that talk, now. He is just a child, do you mean? He was with you at the bar?"

"Yes, yes. He is quite young and...very beautiful."

"Well, then, no one will harm a hair of his head, will they?"

"Man, what are you on? It's not his head I'm worried about!" Triani's laugh was harsh. He swung his feet to the floor and tested his legs. "Who's in charge here?"

The old man stood up and patted Triani's shoulder again. "There was no one at the bar with you, young one. You need rest, now."

"Look, old man, I'm a Merculian citizen! I demand to see my Ambassador! That's my right!"

"Oh, but I'm afraid you're an accused criminal, you see. You have no rights. Just rest awhile and someone will come to talk to you in good time." He laid his palm over a panel in the barred doorway, and it silently slid open.

"Wait!" Triani sprang across the room but the bars clanged to in his face. "Damn you!" he shouted after the slowly retreating figure. He pulled the remains of his tunic together and tucked them neatly into his pants. He glanced at his hands, checking for broken fingernails. "Shit! They even took my rings," he muttered. He went back and sat down on the hard cot and thought about the Serpian crystal figurine hanging around the neck of the man with the blue earring.

8

"*I* have been in jail all night! *All night*! Do you realize that? Me, Triani, star of the Merculian National Dance Company, languishing in a filthy alien cell! Why? Just tell me that, will you?"

"I will, if you give me a chance." Beny felt at a distinct disadvantage sitting behind his desk. He stood up. "We only heard this morning. The instant we heard, we acted."

"You sent Thar-von Del! That's acting? Why didn't you come yourself?"

"Because I thought he could handle it better."

"He doesn't have your authority."

"He has their respect!" Beny sat down again and wished he hadn't admitted this last fact. "Triani, you broke their law. They had every right to put you in jail. At least he persuaded them not to press charges."

"And what about Cham?"

"According to their law, no one is officially missing until three nights have passed."

"I thought we were operating under our laws here?"

"Only in our private quarters."

"You're telling me no one is going to do one damn thing! You're going to sit on your ass— "

83

"Triani!"

"Okay, okay. I'm sorry. Shit." He finally slumped down in a chair and covered his face with his hands.

Beny tried to think of something comforting to say. He picked up a message cube, stared at it, put it down again.

After a moment, Triani raised his head. "You're not going to like this but I have to say it. I don't trust Thar-von Del."

"I know you've never liked him."

"That, too, but in this case I mean 'trust'. One of the men who took Cham was wearing a Serpian pendant."

"What?"

"Those figurines are unmistakable. They're nothing like Abulonian ornaments. Where else would he get one?"

"Be careful what you say, Triani."

"Serpians aren't known for their generosity, either. Those things are worth a lot of credits."

Beny felt around on his desk for the communications device, found it under a pile of order forms, and called Thar-von. "Don't let your anger run away with your good sense," he said to Triani.

"I knew I couldn't expect any support from you. He's your friend, after all. Just remember I'm the same species as you are, even if I wasn't born with a gold chain around my waist. That should mean something."

"What should it mean?" asked Thar-von, closing the door behind him.

"I want to know why one of the men who beat me up and kidnapped my lover was wearing a Serpian figurine around his neck."

"Good taste," said Thar-von unperturbed. "If you are accusing me of something, please do so. I am very busy."

"You bastard!" shouted Triani. "Don't you have any heart?"

Thar-von drew himself up to his full imposing height and looked stonily at the wall above Triani's head.

"Sit down, both of you." Beny tried to get some sort of control on the situation. "Triani, ask Thar-von a polite question, and he will answer it."

"Do you still have the Serpian pendant you brought with you?"

Thar-von looked startled. He glanced at Beny who nodded. "No," he said.

"What did I tell you!" cried Triani triumphantly.

"Where is it?" asked Beny.

Thar-von had turned a dark blue. His hands were clenched at his sides. "Must I answer this?"

"Under the circumstances, yes."

"I gave it to a lady I met at the reception two nights ago."

Triani looked at him in astonishment. "You? Ice-water Del?"

"Has it occurred to anyone that I am not the only Serpian on the planet?"

The Merculians exchanged glances. They had both forgotten about Zox.

"I think you owe Thar-von an apology, Triani."

"I hate to admit it but I guess I do. Sorry, okay?" Thar-von finally turned his navy blue eyes on Triani. "So I'm not very good at it," said Triani nervously.

"You could practice," suggested Thar-von.

Beny came around his desk and slid a hand under Triani's elbow. "If you want us to accomplish anything, you have to give us a chance. This is my job. Go away and let me get on with it."

Triani paused at the door. "Find Cham," he said. "If you don't, I will." He swept out the door, leaving Beny to close it behind him.

"I resent what just happened here," said Thar-von at once. "Why did you force me to divulge something personal that was none of his business?"

"Von, I apologize, but Triani is difficult to handle. It was the fastest way to make him see how false his accusation was. I need some sherry. What about you?"

Thar-von gestured no with his hands and sat down. His face was expressionless.

Beny pulled one of the big chairs over beside him and climbed into it, resting the sherry on the wide arm. He could feel the tension in Thar-von's body across the space that separated them. "The fact that you're my friend makes this even more difficult," he said. "I know how Serpians regard personal questions but I have to ask, Von."

"Wait." Thar-von clasped his hands together, his fingers interlocking. "It will be less painful for both of us if I tell you. This is, of course, privileged information."

"Of course." Beny sprung the privacy lock on the door and settled down to listen. Past experience had taught him that it didn't have to be much to qualify as 'privileged information' to a Serpian but just the same it was serious to his friend.

Thar-von bent his head and began to talk. "I noticed her the first day we arrived, sitting in the Banquet Hall with the other women. She is more...beautiful.than any lady I have ever seen. Everywhere I went, she was there. At first it wasn't so bad. Then, when the company came, you spent all your spare time with Eulio, and.... I keep thinking about her. I can't sleep because of her. I feel as if she knows this, watching me with the wonderful dark pools of her eyes. And then, her brother introduced me to her at the reception. I made a fool of myself."

Beny took a sip of his sherry. "Go on."

"She makes me feel weak with longing," Thar-von said quietly. "She is intelligent and charming. She asks a lot of interested questions about us. And the sound of her voice—" He broke off abruptly. "Forgive me. You do not want to hear this."

"Von, my dear friend, I think you are in love."

"No!" Thar-von shot out of his chair and strode across to the recessed shelf where Beny kept the sherry and the *siva*. He poured himself a tall glass of the orange liquor. "No," he said more calmly. "It cannot be."

"Why do you say you made a fool of yourself?"

"I touched her."

Beny tried to interpret what this could possibly mean to a Serpian. "You kissed her?" he ventured.

"I wanted to, very much. I touched her hand, but then her brother came back. That's when I gave her the figurine."

"Where did you meet this brother of hers?"

"He spoke to me one day in the Public Gardens when I was walking to the theatre. He's some kind of a soldier and he drops into the office now and then just to talk. He seems to like me." Thar-von threw himself back in his chair and stared at the ceiling. "I wish I hadn't lost my head with Xunanda."

"You didn't do anything too drastic, Von."

"I gave her the figurine. That means a lot to us. I was trying to show her how I felt even though I couldn't express it physically. Obviously she didn't care about it or me. She must have given it to a friend."

"Von, you yourself pointed out just a few minutes ago that you are not the only Serpian on the planet. How can you be sure the one Triani saw in that bar was yours?"

Thar-von took a slow, deep breath.

9

"*I*'m Triani from the Merculian National Dance Company." He flashed his knowing smile at the bony woman, who stood at the door in the bright sunlight, squinting down at him.

"Oh," she said doubtfully. "You want something?"

"Naturally, sweetie. I didn't come all the way over here and climb up all those steps for the good of my health." He glanced back at the four flights of stone steps that had led him to what he had assumed was the main door of the house.

"Well, what is it?"

"I want to see Quana. Is she in?"

The woman looked at him uncertainly. "Well, I don't know. I guess you'd better come inside." She stepped back reluctantly, and Triani sauntered past.

"You're all heart, sweetie," he remarked, looking about him.

"Wait here." She went off down the dim hall and opened a door into sunlight. "It's one of those weird Merculian fellows," he heard her say. There was the sound of running bare feet.

"Cham!" The girl's dark eyes were bright, her cheeks flushed. She stopped dead in front of Triani.

"Sorry to disappoint you." He noticed she was wearing the pendant Cham had made for her. "He's not the only weird Merculian around."

"You're Triani." She held out her hand, palm up, in greeting.

He bowed, turned the hand over, and raised it to his lips. He didn't let go. "Why are you afraid of me? I wouldn't harm the proverbial fly."

"I'm not!" she said indignantly and pulled her hand away.

Triani grinned. "So. Cham didn't tell you Merculians are touch telepaths." He wondered how much else he hadn't told her.

"Is that true?"

"I don't lie, sweetie."

"Why did you want to see me?" She led the way to a group of uncomfortable carved wooden chairs and sat down, leaning slightly forward, her back very straight.

"May I close the door?"

"No. It is not allowed."

Triani shrugged. "I caught sight of you in the doorway of the bar yesterday morning just before I blacked out. It was you who told Benvolini I was in jail, wasn't it?"

"I'm afraid I don't know what you're talking about," she said haughtily.

"Oh, cut the crap, sweetie! Of course it was you. I only wish you'd been quicker about it. I've kept you out of it, by the way."

"Why?" she asked, surprised.

Triani looked at her steadily. "Cham was very anxious that your name not be mentioned. He thinks of you as a friend, Quana, even though you cut him dead in the middle of a public street in front of me."

She dropped her eyes. "I'm sorry. I really am. It's just that…sometimes I'm a coward. Where is he now? Wouldn't he come with you?"

"I was hoping you could help me find him." Triani was walking around the small room looking at the charcoal murals, examining the carved wooden animals placed at intervals along the waist-high shelf. A shadow fell across his face.

"Quana-la, you did not tell me you had a visitor." There was a hint of reproach in the clear, rich voice.

The girl jumped to her feet, flustered. "I'm sorry, mother. This is…Triani. He's with the Merculian National Dance Company."

"Well, how nice," said the woman, smiling graciously.

Triani bowed low over her hand. Then he gazed up at her calm, dignified face. He could feel her strong disapproval but there was no hint of it in her manner. Bitch, he thought and gave her a dazzling smile. "I am delighted to meet you, madame. I only hope I have not offended in any way by coming here without an invitation."

"Not at all. It is not usual, but you are a stranger here, and you are welcome in our home." She sat down and folded her hands. "I was not aware that you were acquainted with my daughter."

Triani smiled and waited for Quana to be seated, a custom he had noted somewhere in his travels. Then he sat down opposite her mother, one long hand over the other on his knee. "Actually, it is Chamion who knows your daughter, madame."

"Ah, yes. He is that sweet-looking boy with the long blond hair."

Triani nodded gravely, wondering how Cham would appreciate the description. "He wanted you to have tickets for opening night tonight but was unable to deliver them himself." He handed over the sphere of round tickets he had managed to pry out of Nevon.

"That was thoughtful of him. One hears such strange stories about theatrical people."

"There is a great deal of malicious gossip in the galaxy," remarked Triani thoughtfully.

"You are a close friend of this Chamion?"

"Much more than that, madame." He was aware of the girl's sudden tension and smiled. "I look after Chamion, you see."

"Ah. Just as I thought. So he is like a son to you."

Triani raised a hand to the gold medallion he always wore around his neck. "I have a child of my own who is three years old. Would you like to see him?" He reached into his waistband and withdrew what looked like a flat piece of rigid plastic. He held it out and squeezed the sides lightly. With a faint click it opened up into a clear cube, lit from within to show the figure of a tiny child in brief red shorts. His little feet bare, hands clasped behind him, he was smiling out at them impishly, a tangle of black curls down his back. Triani's long fingers touched a green button at the side of the cube and the figure sprang to life, bowing low from the waist and laughing as he almost lost his balance. The child's laughter held the sound of a tinkling music box as he stood erect again, his cheeks bright with color, his black eyes sparkling with fun. He threw back his curls with a toss of the head. "My name is Giazin Triani Orlato," he announced in a lisping treble, "and I'm going to be a great dancer just like my daddy when I grow up." He arched his back, raised his little arms, and skipped around in a circle. With a final unsteady bow, the image vanished.

"That's wonderful! And he's so cute!" Quana was still gazing at the cube in fascination. "Cham told me something about him."

"He looks just like you," said her mother politely.

"So everyone says." Triani was looking fixedly at the tiny figure that had reappeared. "But he won't have a childhood anything like mine. Not if I can help it." He collapsed the cube with a snap and returned it to his waist pocket.

"Is your wife here with you?" asked Quana's mother.

Triani blinked, going over the question in his mind before answering. "The child's maternal parent and I are no longer together," he said at last and folded his hands.

The next hour went by with excruciating slowness as they sat together sipping sweet flower tea, nibbling sugared fruit slices and making polite conversation. Triani was unfailingly charming and attentive. He found it exhausting to nod and smile as he held back his frustration at not being able to talk openly to Quana as he wished. He told them entertaining tales about Giazin's childish exploits and much edited versions of his own adventures with Cham. Finally, in spite of his ambiguous sexuality, his flashy rings and exaggerated gestures, he won the approval of Quana's mother. She left them alone while she went to see to the ordering of the evening meal.

Triani went limp. "Shit!"

Quana collapsed in her chair laughing and pressing her hands to her mouth to stifle the noise. "You're a marvellous actor!" she sputtered.

"Thanks, sweetie, but I can't take much more of that. Is she coming back?"

"I don't think so."

"Quana, did you notice anything at all while you were at the door of that bar?"

She frowned at the floor, thinking. "I went back to look for Cham. You know, to say I was sorry. By the time I got there, two men were hitting you, and I didn't see Cham anywhere. The men you were fighting with were hunters."

"That means trained killers, doesn't it?"

"Well, I never thought of it like that before, but I guess it does. Did they take Cham? Why? What does it mean?"

"Search me, sweetie. How do you know they were hunters?"

"Because the top joint of the fourth finger of the left hand was missing."

"I've noticed that before here. Who do they work for? The Chief?"

"Some of them do. Once they're trained, anyone could hire them, I guess."

Triani studied his rings for a moment in silence. "They kept looking at Cham...wanting to touch him. Do you think they might be perverts?"

She blushed and turned her head away. "I never heard any stories like that. They're just hunters. soldiers." She hesitated before going on. "I think one of them may be my uncle."

"What?"

"Hush! I'm not sure. I didn't get a good look at him, and I haven't seen my uncle for three years. That's when he ran off to join the rebels in the hills. He's a lot younger than my father. We don't mention his name in this house any more. He's dead to us, now."

"Which one was he?"

"He wore a blue earring and what looked like a glass figure on a chain around his neck."

"You mentioned something about rebels in the hills. Do you mean there's a revolution going on here?"

"Not really. It's just a few people who aren't happy with things the way they are. There's always someone like that around."

"Not kidnapping peaceful alien visitors off the street, there isn't. No one told us anything about this."

"It's not of major concern. I don't even know if that was my uncle, Triani."

"Well, thanks for telling Benvolini about me being in jail, even if it did take you awhile."

"But I did it at once. When they arrested you I was afraid they might not tell your people right away, especially if politics was involved, or they thought it was. And I was worried about Cham. So I went directly to the festival office and talked to that blue man who was there. He said he was in charge of the staff. I told him everything and he said he'd take care of it."

"And this was right afterwards?"

"That's right."

"Well, well. Do tell. Look, I'd better go before your mother gets back. Just one more thing. What's your uncle's name?"

She hesitated for the first time, twisting the thin material of her sarong between her fingers.

"Quana, sweetie, I've got to find Cham. He might be able to help."

"His name's Akan, but I don't know how you can find him."

"Thanks. I'll find him. You know something," he went on with a grin. "Your hair really turns me on."

She looked at him, alarmed, and stepped back a pace. "Ah...thank you for coming."

He laughed and stepped out into the late afternoon sunshine. The narrow, steep street below was crowded with android servants carrying baskets balanced on their shiny heads. It was a strangely silent crowd. No one laughed or talked or even exchanged glances. Triani paused.

"Quana, if you find out anything...anything at all that might help, please let me know, okay?"

She nodded.

Triani leap down the long series of steps, his black curls bouncing, his red sash streaming out behind him. When he reached the bottom, he looked up and waved.

Early that evening, Triani slammed through the stage door and strode rapidly down the narrow corridor towards his dressing room. Fabrin, the stage manager, jumped out of the way as he went by.

As usual, Triani was very early. He laid out his make-up with his customary almost fanatical neatness. He spent some time checking through boxes of shoes and tried out several pairs, looking for just the right feel of pliancy and suppleness. Using all of his considerable will power, he kept his mind rigidly to schedule, surrounding himself with the myriad small rituals of his art. He went through the long series of warm-up exercises he always used before a performance. He showered and got into his costume tights. Finally he sat down at his dressing table to make up. That was when his control broke. His eye fell on a card tucked into the side of the mirror with all the notes and interstellar telegrams of good wishes for opening night. It was the rough drawing of a three-eyed dog with a wide, leering grin on its face. Its head rested on a bed. Written in Cham's large, ornate writing was the caption: "Can any solo be this good?"

Triani pushed the card into a drawer, jumped to his feet, and flung open the door of his dressing room. He grabbed a young member of the chorus who was just arriving.

"Find Nevon and tell him I want him," Triani hissed, holding the young dancer's arm so tightly he winced with pain. "Now, asshole!" He released him, slammed the door and began to pace as he fought back the waves of loss and guilt and worry.

When the director arrived, his broad face creased with anxiety, Triani took a handful of his brown tunic and backed him up against the wall. "No one in that shitty damn audience knows a thing about Cham! They should be told! This was supposed to be his opening night, too. And they refuse even to look for him!"

"I know, dear, I know." Nevon laid his capable hands on Triani's shoulders. "I'm going to tell them myself before the curtain goes up. The company is offering a reward."

"Thanks to you, no doubt."

"Everyone is contributing."

For just a moment, Triani rested his forehead against Nevon's substantial shoulder. "He trusted me, Nev. He was afraid, and I said I'd look after him."

"Stop blaming yourself, darling. You didn't let him down."

Triani turned away abruptly and sat down to finish his make-up. Nevon watched him for a moment.

"You were always so damned independent," he said, shaking his head. "I'll make the announcement now."

During the performance, Triani could shut out everything. Once the curtain came down, the pain was back. He was surprised to find how far Cham had crawled inside his private, secret space. Cham's almost ethereal beauty haunted him. The uncertainty gnawed at him constantly, not knowing what had happened, imagining what might have happened....

After the show, Triani spent a long time getting out of his make-up and changing into his street clothes. He sat at his dressing table, staring into the mirror, seeing Cham smiling up at him as he had so often, the big gold-flecked grey eyes so trusting and full of love. He sighed wearily.

The great dog lay at his feet, the third eye covered with a thick coat of metallic paint. Triani was glad to have the wide collar to hang on to as he stepped out into the night. There wasn't far to go, but it was dark, the shifting shadows making the way unfamiliar. The Merculians usually went home in a group, carrying torches, and making a party of the whole experience. Tonight Triani did not feel like a party. "I bring disaster to anyone I let get close to me." He thought bleakly of the pretty, vivacious Savane with whom he had had a short, but stormy relationship, ending with the birth of his beloved child. The baby Triani had wanted ruined Savane's career, and all the money Triani sent could not compensate for being relegated to the ranks of a second-rate company in the provinces. And then there was Lucius. Triani swallowed hard and blinked back the unaccustomed tears angrily. And now the pattern was repeating itself with Cham, gentle, loving, trusting— 'Shit! What's wrong with me? It's my fault! It's always my fault!'

He tightened his grip on the dog's collar as they came abreast of a shadowy figure leaning against one of the stunted trees that lined the boulevard. The dog growled low in his throat, but Triani shushed him and patted his head. He had recognized Luan, gazing up at the lighted windows of the Merculian apartments, high above him.

"How can you pick out Benvolini's window from this distance, sweetie?" asked Triani, curiously.

"It's easy," replied the boy.

Triani studied him. It was hard to make out his features in the shadows. "Listen, I don't want to go home alone tonight. You want to come with me?"

The solemn dark eyes looked back at him a moment. "I know what it's like to be lonely," he said. "I'll come."

"You don't mind standing in for someone else?"

"Not if you don't."

Triani slipped his arm around the boy's waist. "So long as we understand each other, sweetie. I hope you're not under age or anything." It occurred to him he didn't know the rules in this place.

"I won't make any trouble for you."

"I was thinking of your father."

The boy shrugged. "He doesn't care what I do."

When they reached Triani's apartment, the emptiness hit him like a physical blow. He hesitated, unsure for a moment how to continue. He offered Merculian sherry to Luan who tasted it with caution and finished it with pleasure. Triani started lighting candles. He knew there was no point. They wouldn't be staying in this room for long, but it gave him something to do while he organized his thoughts.

Luan was watching him with sad eyes. The three strings of amber beads he wore glowed against his dark skin. "I was there tonight, in the theatre. You're a terrific dancer."

"I know." Triani took a drink of his wine. "What part did you like the best?"

"Oh, I couldn't pick just one part. It was all…wonderful. And you—you're pretty sexy, in a different sort of way."

"That's why you came home with me."

"Partly. I heard the announcement, too. I thought you might be lonely."

"You're all heart, sweetie."

"Perhaps I made a mistake."

"I don't think so. I'm good at more than dancing." He ran one hand across Luan's bare chest and felt the desire throbbing just under the skin. "You're just dying to lay a Merculian, aren't you?"

"I guess we both know that."

"I don't know what to make of you, Luan. One moment you're all awkward youth and the next you come on total self-assurance."

"I'm the son of the Great Chief. For as long as I can remember, people have tried to use me to get to my father. You're doing it now."

Triani nibbled at his ear. "Relax, baby. Don't be so uptight."

"It's no use," Luan went on. "I can't help you. I want to, but I can't."

"Can't, or won't?"

"I have no power."

"You've got to have more faith in yourself, sweetie. Come on. Let's go to bed."

Triani undressed with his usual care, folded his clothes neatly and put away his shoes. He felt numb. He didn't want to think about what he was actually doing. Maybe it wasn't such a good idea. He looked at the boy who lay naked on the bed, waiting. "Do you mind if the lights are on?" he asked.

Luan shook his head.

Triani lay down beside him feeling very small and unusually vulnerable. He wished Luan would take him in his arms and surround him with his young, masculine strength. Instead, Luan sat up and studied the Merculian's smooth, muscular body with frank interest. Triani felt a stab of annoyance.

"What's the matter, sweetie, don't you like what you see?"

99

"I…ah…." Luan hesitated, threw back his hair. "I didn't know what to expect."

"Now you know, baby. For you I am a woman, okay? Isn't that what you want?"

Luan shook his head slowly, his dark eyes fixed on Triani's face. Gently he laid his hand on the small, shell-like fold of skin that nestled like a snail in the crisp, black hair that curled thickly between Triani's legs.

"Ah-h-h." Triani reached for Luan's head, guiding it gently, firmly, twining his fingers in the long coarse hair so different from Cham's. He trembled as he felt the boy's warm mouth opening against him. Luan's tongue began to caress the delicate, fluted membrane that covered the core of his masculinity, and Triani closed his eyes as the first melting waves of pleasure swept over him. He felt the gradual emergence of his sex as it opened out slowly, like a flower unfolding from a bud.

Luan drew back, watching in delighted fascination. "Wonderful!" he breathed as he stroked the flexible stalk that pulsed gently in his hand. "You're really something," he murmured, and took Triani in his arms, kissing him hungrily, his mouth, his eyes, his hair, his hard, smooth body. With a sudden movement, he flipped the dancer onto his stomach, pressing his open mouth into the warm neck.

But Triani twisted around onto his back again, his agile body slippery with sweat from his exertions. "No! This is on my terms!" His black eyes glittered as he fastened his powerful legs around Luan's waist. "Now!" he said with an abrupt movement of his hips.

Luan was taken by surprise. He felt himself grasped, engulfed, pulled deep inside Triani. He cried out, his back arched, his head thrown back. Then he collapsed, gasping for breath. Triani pushed him off.

"Are all Merculians like you?" Luan asked finally, rolling onto his back.

"We're all made the same, if that's what you mean. I'm just more muscular than Benvolini." Triani smiled at him lazily. "Have I taken away some of the glamour?"

"Oh no!" exclaimed Luan. "It's really...exciting." He propped himself up on one elbow and studied the small figure beside him. "I don't think that was much fun for you, though, was it? Tell me what you want me to do."

Triani shook his head. "Just don't leave me tonight, sweetie," he said, moving closer to the boy. He slipped his arms around Luan's waist. "I don't want to be alone."

"Tri-ani." Luan said the unfamiliar name carefully, almost tenderly, as he embraced the small figure beside him. "Nobody wants to be alone."

10

The next morning, Luan was very talkative. He sat cross-legged on the bed beside Triani, eating biscuits and honey and drinking fresh *pamayo* juice brought from Merculian.

"It's nice waking up with someone, isn't it?" he said.

Triani nodded absently.

"You know that kidnap thing with your flaxen-haired beauty is probably political, don't you?"

Triani sat up alertly. "No, I don't. Tell me about it. And don't get crumbs all over the bed."

"Well, my guess is that Yonan has him in the mountains somewhere. He wants to embarrass my father in front of the Alliance, and he's found the perfect way to do it."

"You mean someone took him for ransom?"

"If it was money you would have heard already. I think it's Yonan. He'll get in touch eventually and spell out exactly what he wants."

"Who is this Yonan?"

"He's the rebel leader. He and my father hate each other. Yonan could have been elected to the council and then stood a chance of being in line to be chief, or at least a minister. He's from the right clan, like a lot of the advisors, but he wouldn't wait. Instead, he tried to overthrow my father and found he didn't have as many followers as he thought. Some say he was betrayed. I don't know, man. That was five years ago, and he's been fighting in the hills ever since."

"Why didn't anyone tell us about this?"

Luan shrugged. "My father thought he could keep it quiet."

Triani jumped out of bed. "Cham was kidnapped because your shitty father wanted to keep things quiet? Is that what you're telling me?"

"Don't shout at me. I'm trying to help." He smoothed the bed invitingly.

Triani climbed back in and sat down again, chewing his nail thoughtfully. "What's this Yonan character like?"

"I don't know, man."

"Stop calling me 'man'! You should know better than that by now."

Luan was carefully brushing the crumbs onto the floor. "We hear only the bad things about Yonan, like the bombings and the android raids, but he can't be all bad. A lot of people admire him, even the First Minister, in a kind of a way. Then again, it might be one of the splinter groups who took your friend."

"Holy shit! What's going on in this place? Civil war?"

"Not really. There aren't that many of them."

"More than enough to raid and pillage," Triani muttered. "And we were told it was safe here!"

"It is. Usually. I really don't know all the ins and outs of the rebel thing. It's kept pretty much under wraps."

"I bet." Triani added sherry to his pamayo juice and took a long drink.

"You know, I'm glad you picked me up last night. I was really aching." Luan laid his dark head on Triani's shoulder.

His long hair fanned out over his chest. One brown hand slid down between Triani's legs. "Let's do it again. Please," he pleaded.

"You help me, I'll fuck you. Agreed?"

"Hmmm." Luan's tongue began making circles on the Merculian's smooth chest. Triani let his body go limp as Luan slipped a strong arm around him and lifted him further down on the bed. It was a long time since anyone had handled him as easily as this. Triani closed his eyes and let himself drift, feeling the urgent hands, the hot breath, the fluttering beginnings of pleasure. He didn't hear the knock or see the door open.

Eulio stood there staring at Luan's dark body entangled with Triani's pale limbs.

"You don't believe in letting the bed get cold, do you?" he said in a voice tight with anger. He turned and slammed out the door.

"Shit!" Triani jumped up and grabbed an orange robe from its carved peg on the wall. He was trembling with rage. "You stay put, Luan. I've got a few choice words to say to that prying bastard!"

Triani stamped out the door and along the corridor to Beny's spacious apartment. He flung open the door unceremoniously. Eulio spun around as he came in.

"What the hell do you think you're doing, bursting into my bedroom like that, you bastard!" shouted Triani.

"It never occurred to me that you'd have anyone with you! I thought you were asleep."

"Then what did you want? A change of pace, sweetie? Is that it?"

"How dare you!" Eulio stamped his foot. "I thought you might be interested in a message about Cham. Remember him? Or has he been replaced already?"

Triani hit him hard across the face. Eulio fell back on the sofa, his mouth open in disbelief, tears of shock and pain in his eyes.

"Stop!" Beny stood in the doorway, fastening his belt, his reddish curls damp from the pool. "If you ever touch him again, Triani, I'll knock you cold. You've gone too far!"

Triani sank down on a fur-covered chair, his head in his hands. "God, Eulio, I'm really sorry! But you shouldn't have said that. You don't understand this."

"You're right," Eulio agreed. "I don't understand."

"I'm not like you, sweetie. I wasn't born with a gold chain around my waist and a title in front of my name. I wasn't even born on the right side of the law. I was the product of illegal self-insemination. It's not just for fun that I only use one name."

"I thought it was for publicity."

"You were wrong. I've been a hustler since I was twelve years old. By the time I was Cham's age I had picked out a lover with enough clout to get me guest spots dancing with the best company on Merculian."

"But that's ours."

"You said it, baby. My lover was Nevon Deliris Bantino, the then up-and-coming young director everyone was raving about. I used sex then, and I'm using it now. I'm going to find Cham and this is the only way I know how. My name means nothing to these people. Sex is all I've got."

Eulio picked up a small box from the table and handed it to Triani. "Do you want a tranq stick?"

"Thanks. You said something about a message. Tell me about it." He glanced at the Ambassador.

Beny was still standing in the doorway trying to deal with the anger that flowed through him. "The personal history is informative, Triani, but it does not excuse your actions. You are behaving like an animal. You do realize that

I could bring charges against you for this? You could be suspended from the company." Triani dropped his eyes. His long fingers tensed on the arm of the chair. After a moment of silence, Beny came into the room. "Don't let it happen again."

Triani clenched his jaw. "Okay, Benvolini, what does it take? Me on my knees? Shit! Just let me know so we can get on with it! The message, remember?"

"Talassa-ran Zox found it this morning when he went to open the office. Cham's yellow fringed sash was with it."

"What does it say?"

"We don't know. We need someone to transcribe it." Beny looked at Triani thoughtfully. "Is Luan still in your apartment?"

"As far as I know."

"Wait a minute, Orosin." Eulio put a hand on his arm. "*You're* not going in there, are you?"

"If necessary." Beny sat down and studied his toes in their brown, beaded boots. "How many Abulonians do we know whose loyalty we can count on?"

"I'm not sure we can count on Luan," said Triani.

"You can't do this," whispered Eulio. "It's not fair. We don't know what's in the message. We could be asking him to go against his father, perhaps to be a traitor."

"For God's sake, Eulio, this is war!" exclaimed Triani. "There's a secret revolution going on here! This is no time for bleeding hearts!"

"He's right, *chaleen*. We have to find out what's in that message. How do you want to work this, Triani?"

"Give me the damn thing. I'll take it in to him."

"How will we know what he says is really what is written there?" asked Eulio.

"We have to trust somebody," said Triani.

FROM: YONAN of Quekar, leader of the People's Technical Revolution Party
To: OROSIN AT'HALI BENVOLINI of Merculian,
Ambassador - Inter-Planetary Alliance

Your Excellency:
We are not diplomats. We are soldiers. We look to you and your Council of United Planets to help us show our people the errors of the Great Chief and his stiff-necked, reactionary advisors in turning back the clock and stopping the forward motion of progress. They have made our once great nation into a police state where slavery is secretly the norm and privacy no longer exists.

The last time we tried to get in touch with one of your people, our runner was completely discredited, publicly shamed, and secretly executed. We have been forced to seek other means to gain the ear of the Alliance. To this end, we have now in our hands the Merculian CHAMION ADINO ESERIS of the National Merculian Dance Company. In exchange for his life, we demand:

1 A meeting with a representative of the Inter-Planetary Alliance.

2 The right to broadcast an uncensored video message to the people

3 The reinstatement of the People's Technical Revolution Party as the official opposition.

4 Amnesty for all members of the Revolutionary Army and their supporters.

Time does not stand still.
THE WAY AHEAD LIES FORWARD!

11

"*V*on, how do you think the Chief is going to react to this?" asked Beny anxiously, checking his wrist chronometer.

"Did Luan give you any hints when you talked to him?" Thar-von was methodically checking through a pile of message cubes on the desk.

"He said this sort of thing had happened before and the hostages were killed because his father refused to deal with Yonan. But surely he sees this is different. I can't believe he'll just stand by this time!"

Triani spoke up from the corner. "It's your job to make sure he doesn't 'just stand by' this time, okay?" He tapped his foot impatiently.

Thar-von smoothed the fine silver hair over his high forehead. "Let me repeat, Ben, that I do not approve of letting Triani come to this meeting. Things will be difficult enough without him there."

Triani tossed his head. "Del, sweetie, it's like this. Either I come to this meeting, or I don't go on stage tonight."

"He has an understudy, does he not?" remarked Thar-von with a shrug.

Triani smiled. He looked at Beny, a mocking light in his black eyes. "Did Eulio ever tell you how he feels about my understudy?" he asked sweetly.

Beny winced. This is blackmail, he thought angrily. But the inevitable chain of events that would follow Triani's refusal to dance was something he didn't want to contemplate right now. "Let him come, Von."

"Could you at least tell him to keep his mouth shut?"

Triani stood up and adjusted the gold medallion around his neck. "Why don't you try addressing me in the second person for a change, Del? Or do you Serpians know anything about polite conversation?"

"This has nothing to do with polite conversation," Thar-von said, turning to Triani for the first time. "This is diplomacy. Remember, you are just an observer at this meeting. Keep a sharp rein on that quick temper of yours. No comments. None at all. Understood?"

"You won't even know I'm there, sweetie."

"Make certain of it."

The meeting was held in a small room overlooking a garden in the Chief's palace. Imperial Hunters, armed with a glittering array of knives, lined the halls and stood guard outside the door. There was nothing in the room but a large table surrounded by stools, carved from some rock-like material. The Chief sat waiting for them, his First Minister on his right, Luan on his left. Beny almost missed a step on seeing the boy. It had not occurred to him that the Chief would have his son present. The boy's sleek dark head was bowed, his long lashes downcast, his hands folded on the table in front of him, like the others. He had changed to blue beads and a white vest embroidered with flowers. He didn't raise his eyes as they sat down.

"Ambassador Benvolini, I am desolate," the Chief began. "You are in my country less than two weeks and already we have offended you with the gift of watch dogs, made you ill with our food, and allowed one of your countrymen to be forcibly taken from you. What can I say to express my sorrow? What can I do to right the wrongs?"

Beny smiled graciously, sketching a gesture in the air with one small hand. "Great One, the dogs were merely a misunderstanding, and the food you could not have known about. All we are concerned with here is Chamion Adino Eseris who was taken by rebel hunters and is now in the hands of someone called Yonan. Can you explain this to us, Chief?"

The Am Quarr raised his eyes to the dim ceiling and lifted his hands in the air, palm upwards. "Let the Gods be my witness, I knew nothing of this! I cannot tell you how sorry I am that this has happened. Yonan commands a small but well-drilled and fanatical force of rebels hiding in the hills. They raid and pillage the surrounding towns and villages but rarely do they venture into the capital."

"Three of them did this time, sir," Thar-von said quietly.

"Are you the one involved?"

"I am." Triani leaned forward tensely.

"How do you know the men who took this person are rebel hunters?" the Chief asked. "You are a stranger to our customs and have been here even less time than the Ambassador."

"They are missing the top joint of the fourth finger, left hand."

"But so it is with the hunters who are loyal to me."

"Oh, come on! Surely *your* men don't attack and carry off helpless aliens!" said Triani heatedly. Thar-von laid a warning hand on his arm.

"The barbaric exploits of the degenerate anarchists always distress our Chief," remarked the First Minister gravely. There was no sign now of the flashing smile. "It is most unfortunate that you have become involved in our internal problems."

"That was the point, wasn't it?" asked Luan in his soft voice.

"It is a pity that my only son shows no desire to be Chief," his father said dryly. "Those uncouth savages could have no real grasp of your Planetary Alliance, Ambassador. They are isolationists who are against mingling with anyone from another culture, let alone species. They claim it will only weaken us. It is a good thing that they have no real following among our people."

"It is also a possible reason for taking your friend," the First Minister said. "To frighten you away, no?"

"That is highly unlikely, sir," said Luan, softly. He was looking steadily at his father, ignoring Tquan.

"No one gave you permission to speak," the Chief replied, not looking at his son.

"But sir —"

"Be silent!"

Luan's sad brown eyes flicked to Beny for a moment and then dropped again.

"That is not the reason they give, Great One." Beny was watching closely to see the man's reaction.

"You have been in contact with them?" The Chief's evident surprise gave Beny some satisfaction.

"We received a message from him this morning, along with the sash Cham was wearing at the time."

"And how was this missive delivered?" asked the First Minister.

"It was left in our office." Beny nodded to Thar-von who produced the original copy and handed it over to the Chief.

"It must have required a considerable amount of time and effort for you to transcribe this," said the First Minister. Beny said nothing. Slowly Tquan turned his head and stared for a long moment at Luan. The boy flushed, his eyes fixed on his gold ring. For the first time, Tquan smiled. "Perhaps intergalactic politics is more appealing to your son, Am Quarr. I have always said he has talent."

The Chief made a noise of annoyance.

Beny cleared his throat. "We want Chamion back, Great One. He is one of ours."

"Of course. That is entirely understandable." The Chief scanned the writing rapidly, making a sucking noise through his teeth. "They demand a great deal. Far too much." He passed the paper across to his First Minister.

"Great One, this does not look like the work of degenerate anarchists to me," said Thar-von in a reasonable tone. "Nor do they seem to be trying to frighten us off. Quite the contrary, wouldn't you say?"

"Lord Del, we have vast experience dealing with these people. We have tried to take them at their word and time after time have found them to be utterly faithless." The Chief sighed. It was obviously a great sadness to him.

"They wish a hostage of greater importance, lords, such as the Ambassador. Do you not see this?" The First Minister leaned forward suddenly. The white streak in his hair seemed to glow. "It is a trap."

Luan rose to his feet. "May I speak?" His father nodded, his face without expression. "As your son, sir, I am in a position of prominence. I have also had some experience with politics, having sat in on many meetings and conferences as part of my training. I know a fair amount about the situation. For these reasons, I volunteer to be the representative they wish to meet."

"But, Luan, what do you know about the Alliance?" asked Beny gently.

"You could teach me, lord."

The Chief smiled, his eyes openly mocking.

Luan flushed. Nervously fingering the rough blue beads around his neck, he continued, "I have a very good memory for detail, Ambassador. You could give me the power to sign in your name whatever you agree to in advance."

A muffled explosion of sound burst from the Great Chief. When Beny glanced at him, he winked. Startled, Beny realized the First Minister was speaking and hastily turned to listen.

"I fear that the impetuosity of youth has not considered all sides of the question. I admire the motives—"

"Hah!" The Chief interrupted him. "Surely you realize that this oh, so heroic, gesture on the part of my son is a hollow one? There is no question as to who goes. There is no question of anyone going!"

"But Father— "

"Enough!"

Luan bit his lip hard and sat down.

"Bastard," muttered Triani under his breath.

"I will not deal with terrorists," the Chief went on calmly. "They must be made to realize that acts like this accomplish nothing. We will not be threatened. They must know this."

Beny felt his stomach lurch. His hands were shaking. "You are talking about a life. Does this mean nothing to you...sir?"

"I am sorry, your Excellency. You must see that there can be no exceptions."

"But Chief! You do not understand!" Beny leaned forward intently, both hands now clutching the edge of the table. "This is not just an internal matter, as you seem to think. Chamion is a Merculian citizen and subject to the protection of Alliance law."

"Ambassador, it is you who does not understand. Abulon is not a member of the Alliance as yet. You are merely visitors to our planet and subject to our laws, just like everyone else."

"I don't believe this!" muttered Triani.

"Is there any chance of a move by the military to rescue Cham?" asked Thar-von.

"I am afraid that is out of the question. Because of the terrain, that would entail a full scale army operation which might escalate to a civil war. We can not run that risk, however minimal."

"They are very well positioned and defended," the First Minister added.

"But I thought you said it was a small force!" exclaimed Triani, unable to restrain himself any longer.

"Relatively speaking, it is," said the Chief as he turned towards him courteously. "Their exact numbers, however, are unknown to us. It would not do to underestimate them."

"'It would not do'! Shit, man! This is not a theoretical tactical manoeuvre we're discussing here! It's a life! A young, vibrant life full of joy and talent— "

Thar-von pulled him down roughly and bowed his head to the Chief. "This person is understandably disturbed, Great One. He is very close to the hostage. If his conduct has offended, I apologize on behalf of the I.P.A."

Beny ran his fingers through his thick curls and gazed earnestly at the impassive face of the alien leader. He tried hard to keep his voice level. "Sir, this planet was represented to us as friendly and safe, as it seemed when the original I.P.A. contact team was here. The Alliance will not be pleased to find that this was a false impression created for their benefit."

"Do not threaten us, Ambassador."

"It is not a threat, merely a reminder. As is the fact that the one whose life you are playing with is a scant few years younger than your own son."

The Chief looked at him coldly. "I fail to see the relevance of that remark, your Excellency. If the hostage were my son, my position would be exactly the same."

Beny felt a cold shiver, like ice water trickling down his spine. He got unsteadily to feet. "You cannot turn your back on life!" he exclaimed desperately, hanging on to the edge of the table. "Can you not find it in your heart to compromise? Just this once? Just a little? Is what they ask for so much when compared with a life? I beg you—"

Thar-von rose swiftly, breaking in on the flow of words. "Unfortunately our time is up, lords. It is with reluctance that I remind my Ambassador of a prior commitment."

Beny closed his mouth and tried to mask the surprise he knew must be on his face. He trusted Thar-von implicitly. "My regrets, gentlemen." He bowed with as much dignity as he could muster and swept out of the room, followed by Thar-von and a confused Triani.

"What the hell was that all about?" sputtered the dancer when they were outside the door.

Thar-von's strong, capable hands held an elbow of each Merculian and propelled them firmly along the corridor towards the main gate. "Didn't you see the storm clouds gathering, Ben? An emotional appeal is the last thing to use with that man. He was about to cut you off, to insult you by walking out of the meeting. That would have made things much worse."

"How could anything possibly be worse?" exclaimed Triani hotly.

"Thanks, Von. I should have seen that coming. I remember Tquan himself warned me the first night we were here, never to beg. Now I know what he meant."

"Let's look at it from their point of view," Thar-von went on. "Chamion made himself conspicuous right from the beginning. He broke away from the group to approach a

young unmarried girl without an introduction. More seri-
ouously, he then went with her alone outside the city, with
no adult companion. And then he discovered the secert of
the dogs' third eye."

"But none of that's his fault!" cried Triani, stopping suddenly and pulling away from Thar-von's grasp.

"I know that. I'm merely pointing out how it might look
to them. He made himself a target."

"What the bloody damn can we do next?" asked Beny.

"Regroup and come in for another attack," said Thar-
von stolidly.

12

The afternoon sun beat down relentlessly on the narrow path, wilting the jagged leaves of the large purple flowers and bringing out a thin sheen of perspiration on Luan's dark shoulders. He climbed slowly, kicking up the dust with his boots. He was in no hurry to reach the arched opening in the hill above him. The rough blue stones of the necklace were warm against his chest.

He paused and rested one hand on his knee as he looked down over the city ruled by his father and his small circle of advisors. There was no movement visible on the shimmering roof gardens or in the steep narrow streets. He noted with pleasure the luxuriant red and yellow striped flowers spilling out of tubs and boxes everywhere, in front of windows, at doorways, even around the perimeter of the shuttle port atop the flattened pyramid in the distance. He had lived in this ancient city all his life, secure in his privileged position with few demands made on him.

Until now.

Suddenly, people expected him to act, to make decisions that might alter the whole course of his life. He was not ready. His mind kept turning over and over the humiliation of the noon meeting. He heard again his father's laughter, saw the pity in the eyes of the First Minister. He needed someone, but he had always been a loner. And so now he climbed the Mountain of Dreams, hoping to talk to Quetzelan, the Dream Weaver, in his retreat far above the city. He had no secrets from the All-Seeing One.

How many times had he climbed this hill, his eyes often blinded by tears? Once he had tried to die on this path by slashing his wrists with a hunter's knife. For a long time he lay among the dusty clumps of grass, staining the flowers red, until Quetzelan found him. He had wanted to escape the pain of memory, to erase forever the picture of the life-less body of his only friend, his lover, dead from a hunting accident. Since that day, almost two years ago, Luan had refused to have anything to do with hunting. It was nothing but a stupid game with death. It put man on a level with the animals he killed. It did not prove a thing. But the Hunter Code was cherished by his people. Turning away from it marked him as different, even more of an outsider. At times, he felt that his entire world rejected him—except for the Dream Weaver.

Quetzelan's cave went deep into the side of the hill. Luan stopped at the opening and bent down to take off his boots. There was no guarantee that the old man would appear. Sometimes the main chamber of the cave remained empty. Luan prayed it would not be so today.

In the dim light inside, he could just make out the shal-low pool of water in front of him. A torch burned beside it, the steady flame reflected in its quiet surface. Luan walked through the cold water and reached up to pass his hand through the flame, thus cleansing body and soul. He paused a moment to let his mind clear and then continued deeper into the hill. Before him, the cave opened into a dim pas-sage through which he continued, his feet cushioned by the deep white moss. The air got colder as he advanced towards the light. The tunnel at last opened up into a cavernous hall, which arched high above his head and became lost in uncertain shadows. The old man sat on a throne-like chair, the arms made of the carved heads of animals. He did not move as Luan came towards him and dropped to one knee in silence.

At last, the old man spoke. "What is your dream, Luan, my son?"

"It is the same as ever, All-Seeing One. I wish only to live with one I love in a small dwelling place with a large garden and to create beautiful growing things never seen before. Is that so much?"

"A peacock would find it difficult to live with the pigeons for ever, my son."

Luan bent his head. "All I want is to live my own life, my own way."

"You see a new image in your dream, do you not?"

"I see the sun. Again." Luan paused, then went on, in a rush. "I want to help the Merculians. No one else must die. My father is…wrong about this. But he *is* my father."

"The image appears unclear?"

"Yes…No! I know what it means, now. I must help. The rebel demands are not that impossible. At a meeting between my father and the Merculians, I offered to go myself and talk to them. My father laughed at me. He thought I was only trying to impress the Merculian Ambassador."

"And were you?"

Luan raised his head and looked into the old man's eyes. "It's true that I would like to make an impression on him. But that's not the reason I made the offer."

"You think it would be possible to talk to these rene-gades?"

"Yes, I do. They want to talk, lord. How can anything be accomplished if there is no communication?"

"It is true that dialogue is necessary for understanding." The old man fell silent. He reached over and dropped a few twigs into a large brass bowl at his feet. As he scattered a handful of fine powder, a blue flame ignited the contents of the bowl with a hissing noise. A sharp, pungent odour drifted into the cavernous room. The old man leaned forward and placed his large, twisted hands on Luan's head, the touch firm but gentle.

"You are my dream-son, Luan. You are brave and lithe as a young forest animal. But you are too accepting of other's views, too quick to think them right and you wrong. You are an intelligent young man, born to be a leader. Soon you must decide the path you will follow. Will it be the one chosen by your father?"

"No! His ways are not mine. I do not wish to become like him nor have I any desire for power over others. And....and I do not want to be married. My father is not thinking of me at all in this matter. He only wants grand-sons!"

"That is not surprising. You are his only son." The old man paused. His eyes were fixed on nothing as he stared above Luan's head into the cloud of fragrant smoke. "May I ask if a wife would seem so out of the question if you had a Life's Companion by your side, as your great grandfather had? A triple marriage is not unheard of among our people. Perhaps it would suit you better. Or perhaps you would pre-fer a male union, like your uncle Kuandar. You are the only one who can choose your way of life, my son. But it is not wise to live alone." The old man paused, stroking the long dark hair thoughtfully. "Your father is a hard man, I know, but he has loved you all your life. There is much affection in his laughter."

Luan remained silent, his eyes fixed on his heavy gold ring.

"Your father is one kind of leader. You, Luan, could be another; one who does what he believes is right for him, one who does the things that will work for him, a leader not afraid of new ideas, not a follower of the rules made by others, not a weakling, but a man to admire! A Dreamer, who has the power to lead!"

The words thrilled through Luan's mind. He was on both knees, now, the old man's hands gently pushing him down, his head very near the fragrant smoke. He swayed slightly and put a hand on the wooden rim of the bowl to steady himself. Images were beginning to form in front of his eyes, swimming towards him through the smoke.

"Tell me what you see, Luan."

The boy sank to the ground, gazing steadily at the incense. Tears ran down his cheeks. "I see the Merculian Ambassador holding my hand and leading me to the rebel stronghold. His hair is on fire like the sun, and he looks at me with eyes that care. I will do anything for him! I mean— almost anything. I will transcribe messages and write the letters for them in Abulonian script, but I will not betray my father. I cannot!"

"You are confusing the man and the office."

"I can't help it! It's a separation he does not make himself." Luan wiped his eyes with the back of his hand, like a child. "I see the Merculian Ambassador with his arms full of flowers. He is laughing and happy, and he wants to be with me. We find a secret cave together which no one knows about but us." Luan looked up at the old man, longing in his eyes. "Maybe if I help to get the young dancer back from the rebels, he will let me hold him in my arms. Is this the way?"

"You know the answer to that, my son. Continue."

Luan turned back to the incense. "Ah! The cave is gone, now, and the rebel camp is in the distance. I hear someone calling my name. A light Merculian voice. Is it the Ambassador?"

"Luan, my dear boy, he is an alien, neither a man nor a woman. Can you picture him living with you in your house with the flowers?"

"I…No, lord. But, I am so alone!" He covered his face with his hands. In the silence, the Dream Weaver sat motionless. Luan sighed and looked once again at the smoky basin. For a moment he thought he saw a pair of round black Merculian eyes looking at him intently. "That young dancer should not die because of my father," he said, his voice growing hoarse. "I must try to get him back, if only so I can sleep again. But the shapes I see now are not clear…. not clear….Perhaps I am not a Dreamer, after all."

There was silence again, hanging in the cave like dark draperies around the shoulders of the Dream Weaver. Time passed. Luan heard a strange thrumming and looked up. The old man's voice seemed to come from far away, although he was right in front of him.

"It is time, my son. It is time for you to prove to yourself what I have always known. Do you trust me?"

"Completely."

"Hold your right hand over the brass bowl."

Luan obeyed, watched the blue smoke curl against his skin. It clung to his flesh coating his hand with bluish-green luminescence. He watched it, fascinated.

"Now, plunge your hand into the brass bowl and pull out a handful of the sacred fire."

Luan swallowed. Sweat broke out on his forehead. He felt the cool trickle of it under his arms. Taking a deep breath, he thrust his right hand into the brazier. Heat seared along his arm, and he jerked back. At the last minute, he remembered to close his hand around the pain. Through traitorous tears, he looked up at Quetzelan and he opened his mouth to speak. Far away, he heard a distant thrumming.

"...a campfire...trees...a rushing river.... moonlight on the water....Everything is whirling together and I cannot... cannot.... A cat's-eye. I see my father's cat's-eye, high above my head."

"Touch it, Luan. Reach out and touch it!"

Instinctively he held out his hand, still clutching the remnants of the coal, to the image he saw floating near the roof of the cave. It was close...very close.... Puzzled, he looked down and saw below him the carved throne, the brazier, the old man watching. Everything was bathed in an odd bluish light, which shimmered in the dimness. At that moment, he realized he felt no pain, and that the thrumming noise was his own voice, speaking in the voice of a dreamer, telling the beginnings of a tale. But he couldn't hear his own words. He looked down and felt the panic rise in his throat. His blood pounded in his ears, drowning out the voice. In alarm, he opened his hand, trying to catch on to something, anything, that would keep him safe. The small piece of coal fell to the ground—and so did he.

Luan cried out in fear as the hard stone floor rushed up to meet him. The cave swirled around him. He felt the solid rock against his knees, felt the painful indentations in his flesh. His dark head sank low on his chest as consciousness slipped away, and his body crumpled against the old man's knees.

Quetzelan smiled. "Do not fight it so," he murmured. "You *are* a Dreamer. Soon it will become clear to you, dear child."

The sun was slanting low in the sky when Luan at last emerged from the cave. He stood on the path swaying, blinded by the light as he tried to bring his mind back from the tangle of dreams. He rested against the rough surface of the rock behind him and breathed deeply, trying to steady himself.

What had happened this afternoon in the cave? It had been so different this time. It had been more than the caring touch of the old man's hand on his head, guiding him to see the way, make his own choice, try to understand. Was it a dream? A vision? He could still hear the echo of Quetzelan's voice, feel the odd thrumming deep inside himself as he opened his mouth and began to tell the story he now couldn't remember. He saw the cave spread out below him, shimmering in that unearthly blue-green light....

Luan shivered. Was that part merely a dream, too? Or did he really have the power to travel, as if in a dream, as Quetzelan could? As all the true Dreamers could. He raised his right hand and stared at the red mark on his palm. It throbbed, but the skin wasn't blistered. Tentatively he touched the burn with a finger and winced.

"Hi, sweetie. What's the matter? You look kind of wasted."

Luan blinked. "I'm...fine. I guess I fell asleep up here."

"Sure you did." Triani laughed.

"What are you doing here?"

"I followed you."

"Why?" asked Luan, stunned. He sat down beside the path, his arms around his knees. He didn't want the Merculian to see how unsteady his legs were.

Triani sat down beside him. "Ever make it in the grass?" He stroked Luan's arm.

"Not now, man."

Triani shrugged. "You were pretty impressive in that meeting today. Did you mean what you said?"

"I meant it, but I sure wouldn't call it impressive. Neither would my father, as you saw."

"I would. You made me feel I can count on you."

"Wait. Give me a minute." The world was rushing back at him too fast, too soon. Luan closed his eyes and stretched out both arms on either side as he filled his lungs with air, held it for a long moment and then expelled it with a loud explosion of sound. He repeated this process several times until the images in his mind had receded. He felt calmer now. He knew what he had to do. He opened his eyes and stood up. As he looked around him, the dazzle had left the world.

"Is all this some kind of religious thing?" asked Triani with interest.

"In a way. Do you have a plan?"

"You're a real pro, sweetie." Triani stood on tip toe and kissed his cheek. "I want to go back to that bar and see if I can find out something. Do you know someone named Akan?"

"What clan?"

"How would I know? He's Quana's uncle, and don't ask me what clan she belongs to."

Luan nodded. "Let's go."

Triani soon admitted it wasn't as easy a place to find as he had expected. Luan was the one who eventually discovered the nondescript bar, even though it was not the kind of place that interested him. He did not share the national passion for gambling, another thing that set him apart from his countrymen.

As they went in, the fat man looked up from the abacus he was working with behind the counter. His mouth opened slightly in surprise, whether because he recognized Luan or because Triani was with him was difficult to decide. There was no one else in the room.

"Business not good these days, sweetie?" Triani climbed up on a stool and leaned on the counter. "Word must have got out you beat up your customers and steal alien kids."

"I don't want any trouble," said the man, looking from Triani to Luan and back again.

"Neither did I, but I got it, didn't I?"

"Look, I'm sorry about what happened. But what can I do? I just own this place, right? They hang out here all the time—"

"Who is Akan?" Triani interrupted.

The fat man seemed to turn even more pale. He licked his lips. "He's a player. He doesn't talk much, but I know he's one of them."

"You mean he's one of Yonan's men?" asked Luan.

"Well, now, I don't know for sure." The man was looking more and more uncomfortable. "I mean, if I did I'd report him, wouldn't I?"

"Tell us about him."

"I don't know. He's a player, like I said. Lately he's been winning big from that alien fellow who comes here a lot. Big blue guy. I don't know what you call them."

"A Serpian?" exclaimed Triani, amazed. "Zox! You mean Talassa-ran Zox?"

"Yeah, I guess. Sounds something like that. Is this any help?"

"I don't know. It explains where Akan got the figurine."

"The Serpian sold your young friend to pay off his debt," said Luan.

"What?" exclaimed Triani, stunned.

"If these men are subversives, they don't want money, they want power," Luan explained. "They got their hostage by winning heavily from the Serpian and exacting your young friend as payment."

The fat man poured a small glass of thick yellow liquid and pushed it towards Triani. "On the house," he muttered.

"I still don't get it," said Triani, reaching automatically for the drink.

"How did you find this bar in the first place?" asked Luan.

"A young boy came up to us and…."

"Exactly. In other words, someone paid him to bring you here."

Triani swallowed the drink without another word. "I'm going to kill that son of a Serpian bitch," he said.

By the time they got back to the Public Gardens, the sun had dropped out of sight, plunging everything into gloom. The festival office was closed, and Zox was nowhere to be found.

"I'll walk you to the theatre."

Triani nodded. "It's lucky for Zox I have to dance tonight," he muttered darkly, as they made their way the short distance along the boulevard.

"You can talk to him tomorrow." Luan smiled above the Merculian's head.

"Talk isn't what I have in mind for the Serpian bastard," Triani growled. "Are you going to watch the show?"

"I think I'll wait for the program change. I'll be at the Gala."

"See you later." Triani disappeared through the stage door.

Luan walked back through the gardens. He didn't want to go home, back to the fortress-like palace, permeated with his father's autocratic presence. Besides, now that he was alone, he still felt shaken by the afternoon's experience in the cave. He wanted to think. Almost automatically, he turned towards his favourite spot.

The low-hanging moon silvered the branches of the trees along the path to the reservoir. Somewhere in the night, an animal called out shrilly. Luan walked slowly, trying to decide how much of a contribution he could possibly hope to make to help right the wrong against the Merculians. Even if nothing was accomplished, he decided, he would at least feel better about himself.

Massive, twisted *kahadari* trees surrounded the reservoir, their shadows grotesque in the moonlight. He stood for a long time gazing out over the motionless expanse of water, his hands on the rough wooden rail. He didn't notice a man come and stand beside him, only gradually becoming aware of his quiet presence. Luan turned his head and looked up at the tall figure, the clear-cut features pale in the moonlight. His black hair fell straight and gleaming to his shoulder blades. A rough gold nugget dangled from one ear. Luan turned back to the water. Suddenly he found it difficult to breathe, and although the air was cool, he felt a glowing warmth all over. The man's hand moved and covered his on the railing. Luan stood motionless, his heart pounding. He turned his hand, moist palm upwards, and entwined his fingers with the stranger's.

"The moon makes a silver highway across the water," remarked the man, and his voice was a low whisper in the stillness.

"Twice I tried to take that highway as an escape," replied Luan, admitting to a total stranger what no one else knew.

"That is never an answer." The man looked at him sternly. "Don't do it again."

"I don't want to. Not now." Luan turned towards his companion, tightening his fingers around the strong hand. "Why have I never seen you before?"

"I've been away."

Luan gazed into the deep dark eyes and knew he could easily get lost in them. He felt the man's other hand move to his waist. In sudden panic Luan moved away slightly and turned back to the water. Oh gods! Please don't let me make a mistake! he prayed fervently. Who was this man? Did it matter? He could feel the quiet, strong presence at his side, part of the night and the moonlight. He had seen no recognition in those great, dark eyes. Nothing but a possible answer to his own hunger and loneliness. He wanted to keep his identity a secret as long as possible. Let this be an encounter of souls where for once who he was played no part. He could take the man back to Triani's apartment. It was the only anonymous place he could think of. He let out a long breath and started back along the path, still holding the man's hand. From somewhere came the nagging thought; was this all an act? Had this man been sent by someone because he was strong and tall and good-looking, with a face Luan had seen in his dreams? Even the voice went straight to his heart. He pushed the thought away. He remembered the image he had glimpsed in the Dream Weaver's cave, the moonlight on the water, the whisper of a soft voice on the air. He could almost smell the incense. They were walking very close together, the man's long hair brushing Luan's cheek. They didn't speak another word.

If his guest was surprised by the alien objects in Triani's apartment, he asked no questions. He followed Luan into the bedroom, undressed, and immersed himself in the pool. When his head broke the surface of the water, he threw back his long slick of hair and reached for Luan at once. He slid his arms around the boy and kissed him, tasting him as if he were a rare delicacy. Luan felt like crying as the man's body strained against his, releasing emotions long held in check.

"Let's go to bed," he whispered.

An hour later, the man got up, prepared a long-stemmed pipe and brought it back to the bed. He offered it to Luan.

"I don't want this to be a casual, nameless meeting," he said, watching Luan pull at the pipe. "I want to be with you again."

"It's like I've known you all my life. I've never felt this way before." Luan handed the pipe back. His moment of decision had come. He took a careful breath. "My name's Luan, of Quarr."

The dark eyes flickered once. He couldn't read the expression. "I am Marselind." Luan waited for the rest. Marselind pulled at the pipe before continuing. "I cannot lie to someone who has touched my naked heart. My clan has disowned me."

"It was a minor offence?"

"Not in your eyes. If I tell you, I put my life in your hands. Do you demand this?"

Luan studied the man's face. "You're telling me you are with the rebels."

"Yes."

"No!" Luan turned away, cold with shock. How could his dream image have betrayed him?

Marselind got up and started to put his clothes on. "I will leave now. It is the only way."

"Wait."

"You are going to call the guards?"

"There are no guards. As you have probably gathered, this is not my place."

"No, it's mine," came a voice from the door. "Or at least I thought it was. Look, guys, you're both gorgeous, but I don't go for threesomes, okay?"

"Triani!"

"Make your choice. Either him or me, sweetie, but hurry up. I'm exhausted."

Luan got into his clothes quickly. Marselind stood quietly by the door, his dark eyes watchful.

"I came to the city to see you dance," he said.

"Well, I don't do it in my bedroom. You'll have to buy a ticket and come to the theatre like everyone else."

"I intend to." Marselind bowed and followed Luan out the door.

13

"Ambassador Benvolini, I must speak with you on an urgent matter." Talassa-ran Zox, the Serpian office manager, manoeuvred himself in front of the door so that it was impossible for Beny to leave.

"I would appreciate it if you would take this up with Thar-von Del, as is your custom," said Beny, adjusting his tunic.

"But Excellency, Del-k'sad is not here."

Beny glanced up at the man, suppressing his irritation. "What is this urgent matter?"

"Excellency, I try to do my appointed tasks well, observing all the— "

"I have no complaints about your work," Beny broke in impatiently.

"I am relieved to hear that. But you must know that some of my Merculian co-workers continue to find fault with me, even though they are not as conscientious as I. Sophisticated hardware is left unattended. Power-source packs are allowed to deteriorate. Security codes are completely ignored. I have even found some inaccuracies caused by carelessness, which could seriously throw off important calculations, as you know. Yet all these shortcomings could be corrected."

"Then do so," said Beny crisply.

"But sir—I mean, Excellency, the prejudice I encounter at every turn makes this very difficult. They reduce everything to the personal."

The word 'prejudice' acted as a red flag to Beny. He rubbed the palm of one hand with his thumb. "I understand the problem, Zox-k'sad," he began, using the Serpian form of address. "But I feel that perhaps you do not. This is precisely why the choice of key personnel for a test project such as this is of prime importance. There is always more than meets the eye in these cases, as a man of your experience well knows. Your position here is no less one of diplomacy than mine, and we are evaluated in much the same way, on many levels. The inter-personal level is of major importance in the diplomatic corps. Do you follow me, Zox-k'sad?"

The tall Serpian blinked twice as he digested the possible meanings of this speech as applied to him. "You called this operation a test project," he said.

"Indeed. When, to your knowledge, was a Serpian male sent out as manager with a group of Merculian office workers by the I.P.A.? Your embassy has faith in you."

"I see." A look of satisfaction spread over the Serpian's face. "But it is not easy."

"Nothing of merit is ever easy," replied Beny smoothly. "Are you capable of handling this?"

"I am, Excellency." Zox bowed and was moving away when the door burst open behind him.

"You fucking bastard!" cried Triani, springing at the Serpian.

Zox raised one hand and brushed him aside. The Merculian staggered and fell.

"You are my witness, Excellency. That was an unprovoked attack, a prime example of what I was just talking about."

"Unprovoked? You shitty traitor! What the hell—"

"Enough!" Beny pulled Triani to his feet and shoved him into a chair. "There will be no more screaming histrionics from you in this office. Is that understood?" He sat down behind his desk and slipped one of the flat, yellow tranquillizers Eulio had given him under his tongue.

Zox stood ram-rod straight, his feet apart, his hands clasped behind his back. Triani slumped in his chair and stared at the ground, rubbing his arm where it had hit the floor. His eyes looked smudged with fatigue.

"What have you got to say?" Beny asked the dancer, trying to sound sufficiently fierce.

Triani told him briefly what he had learned the day before from the fat man at the bar, then added his own interpretation.

Beny looked at Zox for his rebuttal.

"Losing at games of chance is not a crime," said Zox coolly. "I freely admit that I was forced to give up my crystal figurine pendant in payment of a debt. The rest of what he says, about me having anything to do with the kidnapped dancer, is a complete fabrication."

Beny looked at him consideringly. The Serpian was a senior member of his staff who had already hinted at prejudice against him on the part of the Merculians. Triani's unsubstantiated story played right into this complaint.

"I'm not going to apologize," said Triani suddenly, almost as if reading Beny's thoughts. "That man hates me. He would do anything to hurt me."

"Why?" asked Beny innocently.

For a moment, the Serpian's slate-coloured eyes blazed a deep blue. "That is untrue," he said quietly.

But for the first time, Beny began to wonder. "I don't think anything more will be accomplished now," he said in a conciliatory voice. "If you would return to your duties, Zox-k'sad, I would appreciate it."

The Serpian bowed and withdrew.

"He *does* hate me," Triani said. "I don't know why, but I know he does, even though I can't pick up any signals through that thick Serpian hide."

"If you're right," said Beny, "your recent behaviour is certainly not going to change the way he feels."

"How would you feel if you had reason to believe someone supposedly on our side had sold Eulio to the enemy?"

Beny felt the words like a blow in the stomach. "Frankly, I did wonder at one point if they were after Eulio. To an Abulonian, blond Merculians probably all look alike."

"If we're being honest here, you're the one they should have been after."

"Of course. But I rarely get time to go beyond this office or my own apartments. Therefore, Eulio is the next choice."

"Well, someone slipped up. It's Cham they've got." Triani toyed nervously with the rings on one hand. "You didn't see the way those big hulking males looked at him," he said softly.

"What you saw was curiosity."

"And you know where that leads, don't you? You do know our history, what happens to Merculians taken prisoner by—"

"That's enough. I don't need you to remind me of the danger. I've come too close myself to ever forget. On the other hand, Cham is a political hostage. It would hardly—"

There was a loud crash, followed by a rumbling noise. They could feel it under their feet. They looked at each other.

"Holy shit! Is it a quake?"

"I don't think so." Beny rushed to the window. "I can't see anything here. Let's go next door." They rushed down the hall to Thar-von's office on the other side of the building. Several people were crowded around the window already, including two Abulonian runners.

"What is it?" asked Beny. The crowd parted to let him through. Clouds of smoke billowed over the north part of the city.

"They hit the reservoir," said one of the Abulonians.

"Yonan," whispered the other one.

"Let's hear it for those peace-loving revolutionaries," muttered Triani between his teeth.

Beny stared at the ragged stain of smoke smudging the lavender sky. I think it's time for plan B, he said to himself. He turned away from the window.

"Where are you going?" asked Triani.

"To do my job," answered Beny as he started off to find Luan.

14

*A*pplause rose out of the darkness in waves, breaking over the small figures on stage, who stood hand in hand, bowing to the audience. The Merculian National Dance Company was a huge success. Ever since Cham's 'disappearance', as the official bulletin put it, interest in the alien dance group had increased tremendously. Line-ups for tickets started early in the morning, and prices soared.

Tonight was a gala event, and everyone was there. The Great Chief sat in the middle of the gilded balcony surrounded by his six daughters. Luan was with him, Marselind by his side. The Chief had even brought his wife, a short, rotund lady with beautiful liquid brown eyes. It was her opinion that the little Merculians all looked as if they needed a good meal. "They must eat like birds, dear," she murmured to her youngest daughter. "No meat! Can you imagine?" She shook her head uncomprehendingly. Nearby sat Quana with her parents, shaking her wooden clapper with enthusiasm. She had good reason to be pleased with herself for engineering this second visit to the theatre. Even with Triani's help, it had not been easy to get the tickets. The Merculian office staff, who never missed a performance, were jumping up and down, shouting themselves hoarse and throwing garlands of flowers on stage. Talassa-ran Zox looked at them with lofty disdain. He was glad that it was so obvious he was not one of them.

Triani looked out over the sea of faces, his artificial smile stretched painfully tight across his face. The lights sparkled on the multi-coloured spangles of his costume and made his black eyes glitter as he stepped forward with Eulio to accept the bouquet of feathers. Pink. Cham's favorite color. Triani blinked. There were pink feathers in his dressing room from some unknown admirer. When they had arrived, Triani sat down at his dressing table and started to drink mint wine. He felt that he was beginning to come apart, slowly, painfully. He wanted to keep it private. He dreaded sympathy.

When Nevon came into his dressing room this evening before the performance, Triani didn't even turn around. The director looked at him for a moment, sighed, and shook his head. "I know I don't mean anything to you now, dear one, and probably never did, but I still care about you. I can't stand by and let you kill yourself with guilt right in front of my eyes. Just because you never get drunk doesn't mean this stuff is good for you." He picked up the bottle and put the stopper back on.

Triani sat motionless, one slender hand holding the fluted glass. Nevon sighed again and gently touched the soft black curls. "Oh, Anni," he murmured. "Won't you even look at me, darling? After all these years, don't I at least get to comfort you?"

Triani moved his eyes to meet Nevon's in the mirror. His lips felt numb. "I always thought I was incapable of these feelings."

"So you used to tell me years ago," said Nevon. "Are you all right, dear one? If you can't go on tonight, I'll understand."

"I'll go on." Triani threw back his head and finished the wine in his glass. "I'll always go on, Nevon."

Triani turned now to face Eulio and kissed his hand, the ritual sign of respect for a good partner. Eulio smiled graciously and returned the gesture, realizing as he did so that Triani was only partly aware of what he was doing. In the state his partner was in, Eulio found it hard to understand how his dancing had become even more brilliant than usual. Triani had always created an atmosphere of excitement and magic on stage, but now he projected the charged feeling that every breathtaking leap and spin might be his last. They joined hands and bowed again, backing up to take their place in the centre of the line of dancers.

Without warning, the lights went out.

There was a collective gasp from the Merculians, whose instant response to unexpected darkness was terror. Eulio's grip tightened painfully on Triani's hand. Instinctively the dancers moved closer together. The Abulonian males automatically clapped their hands to their weapons, although most wore only the short broad knives that were more for show than use. The women froze, uttering no sound.

Suddenly a low roll of drums sounded from above their heads. A murmuring rustle came from the audience as everyone twisted around in his seat, looking for the source of the noise. On the right hand side of the theatre, halfway up the wall, appeared the hologram image of a small blond Merculian. Triani caught his breath and swore. Several Abulonians screamed. They had never seen a hologram.

When the din died down, the image began to speak.

"My name is Chamion Adino Eseris, and I am from Merculian." He bowed low, one foot pointed, one knee bent. His hands gestured gracefully in the air as he straightened, adding extravagant flourishes to the movement.

On stage, the dancers muttered amongst themselves and glanced towards Triani. They had all been trained in the language of mime, although its significance was lost on the Abulonian audience. Triani had, of course, caught the desperate words that came to him from the fluttering gestures. 'Come rescue me, my love, for I am dying.'

Triani stifled a sharp cry as Cham continued. "The People's Technical Revolution Party has allowed me a few moments to speak to the Great Chief of Abulon. So far, I am well and unharmed. Yonan has promised to send me home if the conditions are met. He is a man of high ideals and an iron will. For my sake, pay attention to his words. Please. My life depends on it."

In the dim theatre, Thar-von was writing down what Cham was saying on the backs of programs, using a peculiar-looking Serpian shorthand of his own invention. Beny sat tensely beside him, one hand on his friend's knee, trying to calm his jumping nerves. He stared with concentration at the young Merculian face hanging above them. He didn't seem drugged, and he certainly wasn't tied up in any way. There were no guards to be seen. But he looked very strained and thin, and there was something about the voice that didn't sound quite right. The image flickered, stabilized, flickered again, as if the person responsible was unfamiliar with the equipment. The break-in, Beny thought suddenly.

In the semi-darkness a messenger bent over him.

"Your presence is requested, Your Excellency."

"Where?"

"In the High Council Advisory Room, at 11:45."

Beny scribbled a note on a message cube and sent the boy off to find Talassa-ran Zox.

When Cham finished speaking, a powerfully built, hawk-nosed man wearing the red and white headband of the rebel party took his place. A low growl swept through the audience, accompanied by the clank and clash of metal. Beny squeezed closer to Thar-von. The Abulonian's dark eyes were bright and quick and he stood forward slightly on the balls of his feet.

"I am Yonan of Quekar," he began with easy assurance. "There are many who seek to discredit us. The Great Chief of Abulon encourages these lies. Why? Because he does not want you to know the truth. We are men and women, just like you. We want what's best for ourselves and our families. He is the one who has forced us to take up arms. What happened when we tried to change things peacefully? We were thrown in jail! Is this the way of peace? Is this the way to make Abulon a better place for our children? No! If diplomacy will work, we would prefer it. But change will not happen if we do not fight! If sacrifice is needed, we will have sacrifice. If battles are needed, we will have battles. And we will persevere. Is the life of this innocent alien youth the price you are willing to pay for the truth? We do not enjoy the ritual of death. It is the Great Chief of Abulon who wields the knife at midnight!"

"What do you think?" asked Beny, looking at his aide.

"That man is a damn fine speaker," said Thar-von quietly. "It's no wonder the Chief wants to keep him muzzled. Apart from that, I wonder who had the expertise to use Merculian equipment."

"Bloody damn," remarked Beny, without enthusiasm.

The festival office was lit up as if for a party. Acting on Beny's scribbled orders, Talassa-ran had unlocked the doors and switched on the auxiliary lighting system. Now he stalked about, making sure people didn't tamper with anything, although what these primitives would make of such sophisticated equipment was beyond his imagining.

Most of the dancers were there and all of the office staff. Luan was there, too, sitting on a desk watching Marselind, who leaned casually against the wall, one eye on the chronometer. Triani was hunched up in a big chair, massaging his ankle. He had pulled a muscle during the last part of his solo and the pain gave him something to concentrate on. Eulio paced back and forth between the rows of desks, chewing on a tranq stick, and hitting his thigh with his open hand. They were all waiting for Beny and Thar-von to come back from their meeting with the Chief and the First Minister. Luan had not been invited.

People had been dropping in and out since the office opened its doors an hour ago, offering sympathy and advice. Their words were often vague but always kindly meant. A few left without saying anything on seeing Luan there.

When Quana arrived, with her young brother, she went hesitantly over to Triani and touched his arm. He glanced up impatiently.

"Shit!" he muttered through his teeth. "What the hell are you doing here?"

"Hey! Watch how you talk to my sister!"

"Oh, shut up," said Triani wearily.

"I want to help Cham," she said to Triani, ignoring her brother. Her voice wasn't very steady. "I'm trying to trace my uncle. If I can find him, maybe he can stop all this."

"Before midnight?" asked Triani dully.

Quana started to cry. "Yonan can't kill him! He won't! He sounded so reasonable, so rational! Men like that don't kill people, do they?"

"No. They pay others to do it for them." Triani pulled himself to his feet. He felt very tired and old. With one finger he brushed the tears from her cheek. "I don't understand you people. To me, you're primitive and violent. This man you call reasonable has killed before. He did it again this afternoon, or haven't you heard? He blew up the reservoir. An old man and two children were killed. Is this rational?"

Marselind covered the space between them in three strides. "That was not the work of Yonan!" he said hotly.

"So you say. Who the hell are you anyway, smartass?"

Luan stirred uneasily. He was relieved when the door opened and Beny and Thar-von came in. Beny looked exhausted, his face pale and blotchy from fatigue and worry. Thar-von went around the room ushering out the people who in his opinion didn't belong there.

Beny sank into an armchair Eulio brought for him with a sigh. He held out his small hands, palms up. "I'm sorry. The bloody damn man won't budge." He looked over at Luan. "You know your father very well. Let's hope you are equally right about plan B."

"Now?" asked the boy.

"Now."

With one smooth motion, Luan unfolded himself from the desk and stood up. He was carrying a small, grey box. "I'm betting my life on this," he said simply and handed the box to Marselind.

The tall Abulonian took the gadget and moved to the centre of the room. He paused and looked around at the expectant faces, obviously used to commanding attention. "Triani has asked me who I am," he began. "My name is Marselind, and I am one of the captains of Yonan. I brought the hologram here and activated it in the theatre tonight."

A gasp of astonishment from Talassa-ran. He turned toward the Serpian coolly. "Yes, sir. There is much about us that you do not know."

"You got that right," muttered Triani.

Marselind continued: "Luan was afraid that his father would not back down on any of the points relating to the release of the hostage. He made a secret agreement with the Ambassador that if this proved to be the case, the Merculian would send his own I.P.A. representative to Yonan as a go-between. This person has yet to be appointed. When that is done, I will signal the camp, and we will leave immediately, before the Chief decides to close down the city."

Triani sprang at Marselind fiercely. "You dirty, rotten, bastard son of a bitch!" he shouted. "You don't give one god damn about anyone! That so-called deadline didn't mean sweet shit, did it?"

"But they won't hurt him now, Anni, don't you see?" Nevon tried unsuccessfully to calm him down. "They won't do anything till they meet with the representative."

Triani swung around to face Beny. "I demand to be the one appointed, Benvolini!"

"Triani, you're about as diplomatic as a terraforming bulldozer." said Beny patiently. "You may go along but not as my representative. And Von, it's no use volunteering. You're just as official here as I am. It can't be anyone attached to this office." Beny ran both hands through his reddish curls distractedly.

Eulio came out from behind Beny's chair with an air of purpose. "I'll go."

"Wait a minute," cried Nevon. "What about the program?"

"Use the alternative cast with Alesio and Serrin," said Triani. "That's what understudies are for."

"I'll go," Eulio repeated. "I have a title, and that gives me the right to speak for my government."

"It hardly gives you the right to speak for the I.P.A., *chaleen*."

15

Two very large and shaggy animals stood blowing and snorting in the moonlight, their breath smoking in the cool night air. Marselind and Luan stood beside them, holding the braided bridles. Nearby, Triani waited beside Nevon. Now that they were actually about to do something, Triani was feeling more relaxed. Eulio, on the other hand, was shivering with cold, nerves, and apprehension as he looked up at the huge animals.

Beny slipped his arms around Eulio's waist and pulled him close. "You know I can't go, dearest," he whispered, his mouth in the blond hair. "I would if I could."

"I know, love."

"Have you got everything? Your pills? A sweater? Legwarmers?"

Eulio nodded and hugged him.

"I love you," said Beny and kissed him on the lips. He was aware of the others waiting patiently in the shadows. Eulio's hair gleamed silver in the moonlight. For a moment, a shocking memory flashed through Beny's mind of another time when Eulio had made a valiant and unexpected gesture that nearly ruined his life. "No!" Beny breathed and held him closer.

Eulio gently pulled away. "This is different," he whispered. "I'll be fine."

Beny turned an anxious face towards Luan.

The boy met his eyes and nodded. He helped Eulio to mount, then leapt up in front of him. Triani was already sitting behind Marselind, his arms wrapped securely around the man's waist.

"You're a big boy, aren't you, sweetie?" Triani remarked appreciatively.

"I thought you only go for the young fish," countered Marselind, urging the animal forward.

"That depends what's in the sea, doesn't it?"

"Not to me," said Marselind curtly. "And see that you keep your hands where they belong."

"Ah, sweetie, don't get mad," Triani cooed softly.

Eulio was hanging on for dear life. The rocking, swaying motion already made him feel sick. "Does one get used to this?" he asked breathlessly.

"Sure," said Luan. "It'll only be for a few hours and then we'll camp for awhile."

"Thank the gods!" said Eulio with feeling.

Both Merculians had taken pills to keep them awake, since this was far past their rest time. Eulio glanced over at Triani. His pale face looked tired and dissipated in the fitful moonlight. His dark head rested against Marselind's broad back, the black eyes staring. Eulio shivered and pulled his long coat around him.

There were no lights in the windows of the silent houses they passed, and they met no one in the streets. To one side, they could see clearly the ruins of the reservoir.

"I suspect my father's agents did that," said Luan.

"Possibly. It certainly wasn't Yonan." Marselind's voice was firm.

"I don't suppose the precious man ever blows up anything, does he?" snapped Triani irritably.

"Of course. The Waterfall Bridge, for example, just last week. There was no loss of life."

Eulio and Triani exchanged glances. Eulio didn't care who blew up what. His body was already aching with fatigue and he had cramps in his legs because of the cold. He pulled out a pain-killer and swallowed it. "How much further?" he whispered.

"We're not out of the city yet," Luan replied, patiently.

Eulio sighed. After a while he felt himself slip sideways and snapped awake with a jerk. Luan felt it, stopped the animal, and traded places with him. "This way I can hang on to you in case you fall asleep," he explained, his strong arms encircling the slight Merculian protectively.

Sitting in front proved even more frightening for Eulio. It was impossible to avoid seeing the countryside lurching towards them. The shadows of the trees danced threateningly in the breeze, bringing back nightmare memories he thought he had banished for good. "I'm not a very brave person, you know," whispered Eulio, cowering against the young Abulonian.

"Yes you are," said Luan seriously. "You volunteered to help. You did what you had to do."

Eulio grimaced into the darkness. "I did it for Orosin," he said. "I did it for love, not because it was my duty. Typical Merculian reaction, I suppose."

They were in the forest now and Eulio's terror increased. Both his small hands clutched fiercely at the woolly neck of the beast under him. His body tense and rigid with strain, he pushed against Luan. Even the air smelled different in the menacing darkness.

Finally, they came to a break in the trees and turned off the trail into a small clearing. Luan slid down and pulled

Eulio into his arms, setting him on the ground with great care.

"We can catch a few hours sleep here," said Marselind, prying Triani's arms from around his waist.

"A few hours!" cried Triani, waking up.

"By that time the sun will be up and the going will be a lot easier."

The Merculians looked at each other in consternation. Then Triani shrugged. "Well, you insisted on coming, sweetie."

"You can't be centre stage all the time," muttered Eulio crossly.

Marselind was unloading the saddlebags, his movements calm, unhurried. Casually he tossed a flat green rectangle to each of the Merculians. "Self-inflating sleeping bags," he explained briefly. He removed the colourful blankets from the animals' broad backs and then suspended their food bag from a low-hanging branch of a tree. "Good night," he said courteously and went over to join Luan. They stood talking together for a moment before taking off their boots and crawling into the sleeping bag together.

"Nothing to it," remarked Triani, watching.

Eulio sniffed. "Have you ever slept outside in a forest before?"

"Of course not, asshole."

"Don't be vulgar." Eulio stared numbly at the green bundle in his arms. With stiff fingers, he started untying the tabs.

Triani soon had his spread out on the ground and was trying to figure out how to get inside. He discovered a pillow and fluffed it up.

"Oh, the joys of nature," he muttered.

Eulio burst into tears and dropped his bundle on the ground.

Triani sighed. "If you wouldn't take so many pills, your brain wouldn't go numb," he remarked.

"At least my brain isn't pickled in alcohol!"

"Look, sweetie, which one of us is doing all the work around here?" Triani looked at Eulio, standing there helplessly, his face wet with tears, shaking with cold and fatigue. "Oh, shit!" He spread out the bag full size on top of his. "Come on, baby. Get in here with me." Eulio stared at him blankly. "Come on! You're safe with all those clothes on. It's the only way to get warm. Trust me, for once." Eulio wiped his eyes on his sleeve. After a moment's hesitation, he sat down and worked his way into the sleeping bag beside Triani.

"You're awfully bony," he complained, wriggling around to find a more comfortable position.

"At least it's warm bones." Triani pulled the sleeping bag up under his chin and put a cautious arm around Eulio. There was no reaction. Triani chuckled softly. "My, my! What a fascinating story to tell the folks back home! My night under the alien stars with Eulio Adelantis."

Eulio jabbed him in the ribs with an elbow. "Shut up." After a moment he said, "Triani, do you ever think about what happened on the *Wellington?*"

"Never," said Triani firmly. "I've blocked it all from my mind."

"I thought I had, too," murmured Eulio.

In two minutes they were both asleep. The forest sighed around them. Now and then a pair of curious eyes gleamed from the branches. The moonlight was cold and glittering where it was caught in the dew on the grass. Gradually the sky lightened. It seemed only moments later that someone was shaking Triani by the shoulder.

Marselind grinned down at him. "Sun's up," he said cheerily. "Time to get going."

Luan had started a fire in the middle of the clearing within a circle of rocks. There was the smell of cooking meat on the air. Eulio moaned and snuggled closer. Triani considered various dramatic ways of waking him up but dismissed them all. Finally he laid his mouth close to the fine membrane covering the sensitive inner ear and whispered a few words.

"You're disgusting!" cried Eulio, wide awake.

"I love you too, sweetie."

They crawled out of the bag. Eulio stood up, rubbed his eyes, and yawned. "Oh, I'm so tired!"

Triani was trying to roll up the sleeping bag. After watching him for a moment, Eulio knelt down beside him. He wasn't much help. The bag kept slipping away from his fingers and unrolling again.

"Along with that title, it's a pity you didn't inherit any brains," snapped Triani.

Eulio pushed him over and jumped to his feet. "What's that awful smell?" he asked, looking around, his nose wrinkled in distaste.

"Some diplomat you are, Conte Adelantis. That's meat. You should be able to recognize it by now. And watch who you're pushing around!"

Luan was coming towards them, the gold ring in his ear catching the light. He looked relaxed and rested. Baggy leggings were stuffed into his scuffed boots, and he wore a long knife at his belt as well as a hand weapon of some sort. As he smiled at the Merculians, Triani realized he had never seen him look happy before.

"Congratulations," said Triani, grinning up at the boy. He glanced over at Marselind who was squatting over the fire wearing the red and white headband of the rebels.

Luan blushed and kicked at a pebble with his boot. "Thanks."

"You mean you two are a couple?" Eulio was confused. "I thought if you're a man you get together with a woman. Isn't that the idea of two sexes here?"

Luan shrugged. "If that's what you want. You can choose anyone you like for your Life's Companion."

"Is that like being jewelled? Like Orosin and me?" Eulio touched the jewel, glowing deep green at his throat.

"I guess so. We swear vows to each other."

"So do we."

"Well, Marse and I haven't had time to talk about that yet." He knelt down and with a few deft movements rolled up both bags and fastened them securely. "I'm sorry we had to get you up so soon. I know you need a lot of sleep but we have to avoid the patrols and the safest way is through the forest. Unfortunately, it's also the longest." He handed Eulio a small blue box. "Here's your breakfast, compliments of the Ambassador." He went back to the fire.

Eulio watched him go, turning the box around and around in his hands. "Isn't that interesting. What happens if you want a baby, do you suppose?"

"How should I know. I guess then you choose a woman."

"But then you end up with three people, Triani. I don't think I'd like that." Eulio sat down on the blanket and opened the box. "It certainly wouldn't work for Merculians. Things are complicated enough with one sex, don't you think? I couldn't handle two."

"You don't have to. Anyway, it's not the first time we've seen something like this. Don't you ever pay any attention on tour off planet? Give me one of those biscuits."

Eulio passed over a biscuit and dug out a cylinder of pills at his belt. "Here. We'd better take one of these, too."

Triani looked at the small triangular stimulants suspiciously. "This doesn't look like your usual," he said.

"It's stronger. You don't want to fall off your beast, do you?"

Triani shrugged, threw back his head, and swallowed the pill. "This is going to be hell."

He was right.

For hours the sun stabbed at their tired gritty eyes making them feel as if they were crossing a desert instead of the rocky field. When they came to a stream, they jumped down and drank greedily, cupping their hands in the clear water. Luan gave them a canteen to fill and helped them mount up again. The Merculians shared one of the animals, this time, Eulio sitting in front because he was shorter. Luan assured them that the animal was a docile creature who would follow its mate without urging. He and Marselind rode ahead, talking quietly together, obviously enjoying their closeness.

"It's nice someone's having a good time," muttered Eulio.

After a while, they helped each other off with their tunics and tied them around their waists. It was getting hotter and hotter, but the other two didn't seem affected.

Suddenly their mild amax gave a wild, fierce snort and broke into a gallop, heading off the path through the dense forest. Eulio screamed. Triani pushed him down hard against the creature's neck, hanging on to the beast's long, shaggy wool. They both closed their eyes. The ground shook with the pounding of hooves, and the air was filled with high, wild snorting. Eulio felt his fear rise in his throat. Triani's body was pressing him down, and he could hardly breathe. He fainted.

Triani was very much aware of what was happening but he was powerless to do anything about it. He looked over his shoulder to see if the Abulonians were following, but the wild plunging of the animal made it impossible to see anything but a blur of trees, sun and leaves. He turned back just as the animal veered off the trail and pounded through the dense undergrowth. Triani raised his head again to get some idea of where they were going. A low-hanging branch knocked him to the ground. The great beast plunged away. Triani sat there stunned, feeling as if his backbone had been rammed up into his head. Shakily he got to his feet and followed the trail of broken branches. There was no sign of Luan or Marselind.

In front of him, the forest opened up, and the ground stopped. It seemed as if the land had caved in suddenly, plunging down to meet the ribbon of water that curled through the dense greenery below. The stream was fed by a noisy waterfall that tumbled and splashed nearby. Nothing stirred in the warm air but a wide-winged bird, spiralling slowly downwards against the lavender blue of the sky. Far below, in an open stretch of rock and bare, red earth, a patch of bright royal blue caught his eye. Eulio! The sun glinted on the gold bangles on his wrist. "Ah, shit!" Triani was looking for a way down when the ground gave way beneath his feet. He clawed desperately at the empty air as he fell, landing with a thump on his backside, sliding uncontrollably towards the small, sprawled figure of his partner. The sky tilted crazily. Everything went black.

16

*B*eny stood at the window wringing his hands. In the open space below, the Imperial Hunters were engaged in some complicated and mystifying manoeuvres, but Beny wasn't aware of them. He felt as if things were closing in on him. If everything continued to move ahead on schedule, sixty-five Terrans would be arriving in three days. A week ago, he would have been delighted that all his careful planning for the festival was working out so smoothly. Now he couldn't let it happen. He couldn't take the responsibility of letting more innocent people come to this place expecting a safe environment. He should have made a move sooner.

He paced around the room one more time, ending up in front of his desk. His hand was shaking as he punched in the combination for the bottom drawer. It slid open silently, revealing the flat red communication device that was for emergency use only. It took two voice prints and three codes to activate. It had never occurred to him that he would have to use it.

He shut the drawer again, unable to face making the call just yet. It made him feel as if he had already failed. Everything that had always been considered a plus to him before, seemed a definite minus here: his height, his soft androgynous good looks, his slender build, even his talent for music. Damn this place! It was worse than the I.P.A. Academy! It had taken disaster to make him fully realize that the term 'Ambassador' was more than a courtesy title, as he had thought. Abulon was an important posting and what did he have to report? One terrorist kidnapping; both the stars of the Merculian National Dance Company out in the woods on a dangerous and uncertain mission; his office manager close to revolt, and the contempt of the Great Chief because he wasn't doing one thing about any of it.

The door opened softly and the First Minister appeared, his dark face split by a wide friendly grin. "I am going against all the rules, no?" he said cheerfully. "I would not let them announce me. This is just an informal visit. Why stand on ceremony?"

"No reason at all," Beny stammered, staring at his unexpected guest. "Sit down. Would you like something to drink? Eat?"

"No, no." The First Minister waved his hand, dismissing the suggestion and began to prowl around the office, inspecting and touching the strange devices Beny took for granted. "You have so much equipment. So much amazing technology. It must be a fine place, where you come from."

"We think so, Excellency."

"Please. My name is Tquan. Perhaps some time you will explain to me how these things work—what it is they are all for."

"Certainly. But I thought you were not in favour of technology?"

"Although we support our Chief, we do not all think as he does. Besides, there is always curiosity, no?" He winked and sprawled his long frame in the easy chair opposite the desk. Then the smile faded from his face. "I am sorry for all this unpleasantness. I wanted you to know that you have my sympathy." He paused, watching Beny, his face somber now.

"Thank you," murmured Beny, unsure what was expected.

"I also wanted to warn you." He stopped, glancing at the closed door. "We are alone, no?"

"Quite alone," Beny assured him.

"The Chief's son is an impetuous and inexperienced youth. I am very fond of him, you understand, and he has many good qualities, but he tends to be erratic, ruled by his heart, rather than his head as a good leader must be. He is just a boy. Do you understand what I am telling you?"

Beny felt a cold thrill of fear. Had he been too trusting? Had he sent his jewelled lover into a trap? "I appreciate your coming here," he said warily. "It is good to know our worries and anxiety for one of our group are understood on more than an intellectual level." Even as he heard the words coming out of his mouth, he cringed at their meaninglessness.

But the First Minister seemed satisfied. He rubbed his hands together. "It will soon be our Festival of Dreams, a major celebration for us. Ordinarily, I would insist that a distinguished visitor such as yourself be our honoured guest, but as things are.... Of course, all may be well by then, no?"

"Let's hope so."

"So." The First Minister sprang from his chair, his cheerful grin restored and reached across the desk to give Beny a friendly thump on the arm. "Just so we understand each other," he said. "And if there is anything you need, anything I can help you with, you have only to ask." He winked again, waved and was gone.

"Bloody damn," muttered Beny. He glanced down at the closed drawer, more convinced than ever that he would have to contact the I.P.A. But not now. His ears were hurting with tension. He needed a break.

Turning away from the crowded desk and the soft, reproachful hum of the computer, he slipped out the back door. He had never been in this narrow passage before, but he was sure it led up to the shuttle port area and sunshine. He had to get away for a while, to sit quietly by himself in the open air and think things through. As he followed the rough, dusty passage upwards, he was startled to see someone coming the other way. With a sinking of his heart, he recognized the Chief.

"Are you looking for a peaceful corner, too, Ambassador?" He smiled his strange, lopsided smile.

"Sometimes one has to get away," Beny agreed warily.

The Chief pushed open a low door sunken into the thick wall. "This is my private place, hidden away back here in this unused passageway. Would you care to join me for a pipe or some ale?"

Beny bowed, trying to master the consternation he felt as he preceded the man into a long, narrow room. The walls were painted a deep green and the rough wooden floor was bare. In the middle was a beautifully carved table covered with dust. On top was a large glass case holding pipes, bottles, and three glasses. Two deep chairs were placed by the wide window, which looked out high over the roof tops of the city.

"Sit down. Relax. No one is allowed to disturb me here." He was collecting pipe and tobacco and filling two glasses with the strong frothy ale.

Beny stretched out with calculated care. He thought it was much too early in the day for anything stronger than hot chocolate, but he willed his limbs to relax, his face to look serene. The Chief settled down beside him and handed him one of the glasses. Beny nodded his thanks, noting the many tiny wrinkles in the Chief's nut-brown face, so in contrast to the bright wary young-looking eyes.

"I must commend you on the impressive program you have lined up for us. We are all looking forward to the arrival of the Terrans, especially my son. He has always been fascinated by Terrans."

"Is that so?" Beny carefully inspected his glass.

"Let us hope their visit will be...uneventful." The Chief was working with the long-stemmed pipe, holding the bowl in his hands, tamping the greenish tobacco gently. "Do you think my son would make a good leader?"

"He speaks well," said Beny cautiously.

"He will be of age soon. If he were more experienced, I might be tempted to resign. I don't really enjoy the game any more."

The game! Chamion's life just a game! Beny closed his eyes tightly for a few seconds and then opened them again. "I thought he didn't want to be Chief," he said quietly.

"No one can turn down power, Benvolini."

"Some can."

"I doubt it. I'm willing to bet that new friend of his can't. He's a clever man, that Marselind. And he comes from a good family, too," he added.

Beny had to smile in spite of himself. "Chief, you sound just like my parents when I brought Eulio home for the first time."

The Chief laughed. "I guess parents are the same all over."

"Probably."

"It seems just yesterday that I appointed Quetzelan, the Dream Weaver, as regent in the event of my death. Now Luan is nearly of age. The boy has a natural instinct for politics. It's in his blood and eventually he will see that. Maybe he already has." He smoked for a while in silence.

Beny swirled the liquid around in his glass thoughtfully. He hadn't wanted this meeting, but perhaps he could use it to his advantage. "You know, Chief, it isn't my place to say this, but it seems to me that you and this Yonan aren't really so far apart. You both want what's best for your people, after all. It's just the means you don't agree on."

The Chief leaned back and watched the smoke curl up to the ceiling. "I never questioned what my father was doing when he was in power for so long. He was afraid of machines. He said we Abulonians were never meant to be a nation of button pushers and weaklings. The two were synonymous with him. Hunters are looked up to for their bravery, courage, and strength. He couldn't see technology and physical prowess going together. So he turned back to the old ways. In our culture, physical prowess has always been what makes us superior to others."

Beny turned his head sharply. His mild, sherry-brown eyes hardened. "You consider yourselves superior to others?"

The Chief looked at him, surprised. Almost at once a shutter dropped over his face, making his eyes blank. "The word I meant was 'stronger'," he said easily. "We have a strong army, a strong population. Most of our young men are trained as hunters, even if they choose not to serve. Let me get you some more ale." The Chief rose and refilled Beny's glass as well as his own. "What do you think of this building? This whole place is a monument to my father, blending our ancient culture with modern niceties, or should I say necessities? But he did not look ahead. Now, when things break down, there is no one to fix them. We are too dependent on the androids. When they break down, what will we do? We need the Inter-Planetary Alliance."

Beny was thinking of the high technology watch dogs, the smooth-running facilities of the shuttle port, even the air-circulation system in this building. It was a puzzle he thought it best not to comment on. He decided to stick to politics. "You realize the I.P.A. might turn you down when they find out the...ah...precarious state of affairs here?"

The Chief lifted his shoulders in an elaborate shrug. "It was a gamble, like everything else. I thought the obvious advantages of the move would appeal to the people and weaken Yonan's support. This time I lose."

Beny felt something snap inside. "You don't give a damn, do you?" he cried. "Are you made of ice? Have you no heart? No soul? Cham may be dead right now, and all you talk about is power! Games!" Beny slammed the glass down so hard it shattered on the floor. Uncaring, he stood up and made for the door.

"Can you find your way back?" asked the Chief courteously.

Beny didn't trust himself to say any more. He bowed and went out into the narrow passage. He closed the door behind him and leaned against the wall for a moment to collect himself. I'll have to resign, he thought. I'm never going to make it in the Diplomatic Corps.

When he arrived back at his office, it was already eleven o'clock. Right on cue, the android Dhakan came in, carrying the tray of hot chocolate Beny always enjoyed at this hour. The Merculian smiled at the android absently and reached out automatically to steady him as he stumbled on the uneven floor. The smile faded from Beny's face. The round eyes filled with shock. He had never touched his android servant before. He stared at Dhakan in disbelief.

"I have done something wrong, master?" asked the android, looking at Beny intently with his shiny copper eyes.

Beny jumped up and flung his arms around the stocky android, closing his eyes in concentration. It was true! He sensed surprise, fear, and finally...compassion?

The android hesitantly put his arms around Beny. "You miss master Eulio?" he asked. "You wish me to...comfort you?"

"Oh my god!" Beny backed away, breathing fast. "I should have known! I should have guessed before. But I've been so busy!" Beny continued to stare at him. "What does 'android' mean to you?"

"One who serves without question, master. What have I done wrong?"

"Nothing! Nothing at all! It's not your fault, Dhakan." Beny sat down behind his desk and put his head in his hands. Dhakan hovered over him anxiously. "Call Thar-von Del for me, please."

It seemed incredible to Beny that he had never noticed before. Now that he knew, he remembered little details that should have alerted him: Dhakan's very eagerness to please, the times when he seemed actually tired, the fact that he and Eulio covered their nakedness when he came in, something it didn't occur to them to do at home in front of androids.

I wish I had known about this before my little chat with the Chief, Beny thought now, rearranging the piles of paper on his desk. It might have given me the courage to say a few more things that should be said. The words of the Chief echoed in his head: 'What do we do when the androids break down?'

Dhakan opened the door and stood aside for Thar-von to enter.

"That confirmation has finally come through from Serpianus," Thar-von said, dropping into a chair.

"Forget Serpianus."

Thar-von raised one silver eyebrow.

Dhakan poured the hot chocolate.

"Sit down, Dhakan," said Beny, taking one of the tall two handled glasses.

"But master!" The coppery eyes looked almost panic-stricken.

"Just sit down. Please."

Dhakan sat, straight-backed and stiff, one large hand on each knee.

Thar-von stretched his long legs out in front of him and looked from Beny to the android, puzzled.

"Have you ever thought much about the androids here, Von?"

"Other than admiring their lifelike qualities, no. I've had far too much to do. Why?"

"That's just it. We've all been too busy." Beny got up and went over to Dhakan. He took the android's hand in his. He drew the ceremonial dagger he always wore and passed the tip across the outstretched palm. Dhakan looked up at him, pain and confusion in his eyes. He didn't try to withdraw his hand. Thar-von stared at the ribbon of blood oozing from the cut. He got to his feet to examine it.

Dhakan said, "Are you punishing me, lord?"

Thar-von was angry. "That wasn't necessary!"

Beny wiped the blood away and curled Dhakan's thick fingers around his soft scarf. "Did that hurt?"

"Yes, master."

"I'm sorry. If you were a real android, that wouldn't have hurt. Do you understand?"

Dhakan shook his head. He looked frightened.

Beny poured a glass of sherry and handed it to him. "Drink this."

"But master, it is not allowed."

"I say it is."

Dhakan took the glass and sipped the wine obediently. Beny perched on the corner of the desk, watching. "Listen,

Dhakan, an android is supposed to be a machine that looks like a person, a machine that you turn off and on. You are flesh and blood, not circuits and wires. You eat and sleep, don't you?"

"An android is just a computer that looks like a man," said Thar-von. "Do you understand?"

"No, lord. I am an android, but I am not a machine like that." He pointed to the console. "You never talked like this before, master." He looked reproachfully at Beny.

"How did you find out?" asked Thar-von.

"I caught his arm when he tripped. I felt...emotions."

"Now we know what Yonan means by slavery. They must come from breeding farms."

"I come from Xenuam Plantation. You wish to go there?"

"Yes," said Beny.

"No," said Thar-von. "We have enough to deal with, Ben. We can't afford to get mixed up in this. Send a report to the I.P.A., and leave it at that."

"They won't do anything, Von!"

"You, of course, are going to free the slaves single-handed."

"Don't make fun of me."

"You're being unrealistic."

"It's one of my more endearing qualities."

"That depends on the point of view. How do you summon Dhakan?"

"I just..." Beny held up the small, silver cylinder and pushed the button on the end. Dhakan turned his head and looked at him inquiringly.

"It must be some sort of electrode implanted in the brain." Thar-von shook his head.

"Does it hurt when I push this?" Beny asked anxiously.

"No, master. I just know you want me."

"Would it wake you up if you were asleep?"

"Of course. It's the summons."

"Von, I'm resigning from the bloody damn Diplomatic Corps!"

"Don't you think you'd like to wait till Eulio gets back?" asked Thar-von with a smile. "And you seem to forget, in your reforming zeal, that we're here as cultural ambassadors only."

"Everyone seems to forget that." He glanced over at Dhakan who was slouched back in his chair with a wide grin on his face.

"That's very nice juice, master," he said happily.

"Isn't it?" agreed Beny.

"If that's how alcohol affects him, I can see why it's not allowed. Well, this is your show, Ben. What's next?"

"For one thing, there go any chances of I.P.A. membership. It's not a matter of semantics any more."

"I wonder where they came from originally? They're physically quite different from the other Abulonians."

"Well, there's one thing I can do. I'll send Dhakan over to the company's doctor to get the implants removed." He called in one of the Merculian office staff, gave him his instructions and sent the happy 'android' off in his care.

When they were alone, Beny collapsed into his high-backed chair. He felt very small against the huge leather cushions. "I think something's going to happen at the Festival of Dreams," he said. He told Thar-von about his unexpected visit from the First Minister and the strange warning.

"It seems a reasonable enough precaution," Thar-von pointed out. "He is in charge of security, among other things."

"Maybe. But the Chief didn't even mention it. Besides, I picked up something...odd. I don't know how to explain it. Sort of like a premonition." He shook his head. "On the other hand, I don't know how to read the man. He certainly seems friendly enough. I may be completely wrong. One thing I do know, I can't put this off any longer." He took the red communications device out of its special drawer and looked at Thar-von gravely. "It would be totally irresponsible to let any one else come here when we know things aren't safe. It makes me feel like a failure, calling in the I.P.A. like this, on my first mission, too."

"Let me remind you that you did not apply for this post. You would only be a failure if you didn't make the call."

"I should have done it sooner."

"'A boat leaves no wake before the prow'," Thar-von remarked.

Beny paused and looked at him curiously, recognizing another obscure Serpian proverb.

"Hindsight gives one perfect vision," Thar-von explained. He joined him by the desk, and they took turns laying their right hands on the sensitive panel below the row of buttons. A light flashed on and a low hum came over the speaker.

Beny cleared his throat. "Ready?"

Thar-von nodded.

One after the other, they gave their name, title, and identification number, followed by the complicated series of passwords that would open the top priority channel to I.P.A. Headquarters.

17

Triani came to with a loud buzzing in his ears. His back was burning all along one side, and his left arm felt as if it were no longer part of him. Carefully he opened his eyes. Everything was red. He blinked. Turning his head, he brought the rest of the hillside into focus. There was something wrong about the angle. A moment of concentrated thinking revealed the astonishing fact that he was upside down.

The process of righting himself was a slow one. It was also painful. Everything was bruised, but nothing appeared to be broken. His ribs felt as if they had been separated and then put back together again. His shoulder was streaked with blood and dirt where the shale had broken the skin. He sat up carefully and looked about him as he rubbed the circulation back into his arms. Eulio lay a little further down the steep hill, one arm flung out.

Triani suddenly froze. He held his breath, feeling the cold sweat of terror break out on his skin. His hands tingled. A long blood-red snake, with black and yellow markings, was coiled near Eulio's motionless arm. Its flat, ugly head wove back and forth above the Merculian's golden skin as if fascinated by the gleaming bracelets.

Triani found it difficult to be rational when confronted with even the thought of a snake. Now he found it difficult to think at all. Without being aware of what he was doing, he started inching backwards up the hill. His movements dislodged bits of earth and stone which rattled down the hillside. The snake raised itself up further and stared about malevolently.

"Holy shit!" he breathed, wiping the sweat out of his eyes. Something had to be done but he was far from sure that he would be able to do it. The very idea of him going any nearer the snake made him feel faint.

Eulio stirred. The snake drew back, hissing. Triani watched, his breath harsh and painful in his chest. He was paralyzed with fear. Eulio moaned and moved his arm. The snake hissed louder. Triani screamed. The noise seemed to push him into action. Grabbing a rock, he sprang down the hill. The snake slithered quickly away. Triani swore and threw the rock after it.

He crouched, shaking, beside Eulio's still figure, waiting as gradually his heart slowed to normal, and he could think again. He leaned anxiously over Eulio's unconscious body and felt his legs and arms and back with his long, sensitive hands, checking for broken bones. Carefully he turned him over and pillowed the blond head on his rolled up tunic. He ripped a sleeve out of his own top and went, crab style on the steep hill, over to the rushing waterfall. Gently he sponged the dirt and blood from Eulio's cuts and gashes and laid a cool cloth on his forehead. "Come on, you shitty Merculian aristocrat! Wake up!" he muttered between clenched teeth. His own shoulder was throbbing painfully. He wondered what he would do if the snake decided to come back.

Finally, Eulio stirred. His eyelids fluttered, opened.

"Well, it's about time," said Triani, leaning over to shield him from the bright sun.

Eulio raised a hand in a vague gesture, his eyes confused, searching. He touched Triani's head and his expression changed from confusion to fear. "Triani? Is that you?" His small hand moved hesitantly over Triani's face. His lips trembled. "I can't see! Oh, gods! I can't see!" His arms went around Triani's neck. "Don't leave me! Please don't leave me alone in the dark!"

"I'm not going anywhere, baby." Triani stroked Eulio's back. "Can't you see anything?"

Eulio shook his head. He was trembling uncontrollably. "What happened? Where are we?"

"I was knocked off the shitty animal and you were thrown down this hill. I fell down after you and here we are." There was no point in mentioning the snake. "Our guides will come for us soon, and then—"

Without warning, Eulio threw back his head and screamed, striking out with his fists at Triani. "Oh god! What will I do? I can't dance like this? I'll never dance again! I'll never see Orosin's face! Or my family! Oh, help me! Somebody! Please!"

"What the hell do you think I'm trying to do!" cried Triani, attempting to catch his wrists. "Stop hitting me!" He shook Eulio hard. "Ah, shit!" he muttered as his partner burst into tears, staring sightlessly at the sky, his hands clenched tightly against his chest. When Triani tried to comfort him, Eulio shoved him away.

"Why? Why did this have to happen?" he sobbed. He pushed his knuckles into his mouth and hunched his shoulders as he bent over on his knees, rocking back and forth, back and forth.

"Come on, baby. Stop that. There's no use asking that question about anything." Triani gently took his hands away from his face and wiped away the tears. This time Eulio didn't push him away. "Besides, who says this is forever? Merculian medicine is wonderful, you know that."

But Eulio didn't seem to hear him. "I won't even be able to get dressed by myself...or see the colours...or go to the theatre. Oh Triani, I'll never dance again!" He was beginning to shake.

Triani winced. Never dance again.... If he couldn't dance, he would die, simply cease to exist. Dancing was everything to him. He felt a sudden hot surge of dark emotion and instantly blocked it, shielding Eulio from any telepathic contact. His partner needed all his strength to handle his own emotions.

Triani turned Eulio's tear-stained face towards him. "Listen to me, Eulio. Listen!" He gentled his hands, his voice. "You *will* dance again. You will. You might not be able to do solos, that's all. But who wants solos when you can dance with me?" Triani was rubbing Eulio's back soothingly, rocking him gently in his arms. "It'll be alright. It will! You and I touch-dance like a dream. We know lots of numbers for the two of us already, and you're good at choreography. Very good. And Nevon likes your work. You could use Orosin's music, too. Oh, baby, solos aren't everything. You'll still be able to dance, and that's what counts. That's the important thing."

Triani could sense Eulio beginning to calm in his arms, starting to really listen as his panic subsided a little. As Triani glanced around to make sure the snake was nowhere in sight, he went on automatically patting Eulio's back, making soothing noises. Sometimes it helps to be a parent, he thought wryly. He wished the two Abulonians would hurry up.

Eulio's arm went around his neck. "Oh Triani, this is awful!" he whispered.

"It's a new role, sweetie, but you'll learn it. You've got to dance with me again. I came back to this company because of you."

"A new role! This is my *life* you're talking about. My whole life! Don't you understand?"

Triani didn't answer. What did he know about Eulio's life outside the theatre? His own world was very narrow. Even the time spent with his lover was centred around dancing.

Eulio was wiping his eyes on Triani's tunic. "My whole life," he murmured. Sharp images flashed through his mind: he and Orosin making love in the pool in their bedroom,; the floating gardens outside their Merculian home; playing in concert with his parents and siblings and their friends during the long, pale twilight of a summer evening; the glittering terror of opening nights at the theatre. Perhaps Triani was right. He should concentrate on the dance, the core, the centre of it all.

"Look, sweetie, I hate to bring this up, but if we don't get out of sight, neither one of us might have a life to worry about. There's a stream to the right. It looks deep enough to get cooled off in, at least. And there's a little cover among the rocks." He stood up. Eulio looked so lost, crouched on the ground alone. He couldn't see the hand Triani thoughtlessly held out to him. "Shit," muttered Triani under his breath. He slipped an arm around Eulio's waist. "Come on, sweetie. You have to sort of bend over. It's very steep."

They stumbled and half crawled to the water, sinking down thankfully beside the rushing stream.

"Oh God! Everything hurts," gasped Eulio. He undid the pouch at his waist and held it out to Triani. It was filled with an amazing assortment of unmarked cylinders of different colours. "The pain killers are the little round white ones in the yellow container."

Triani opened it, gave him one and took one himself. "Lucky thing you always travel with your own dispensary," he remarked as he closed the cylinder and replaced it carefully with the others.

In a few minutes, the pill seemed to take effect. The water was very cold and tasted marvellous. Eulio splashed some on his face and shoulders and chest. "I suppose I look just awful," he said, smoothing his hair with his hands. "I don't look much like a diplomat. What's that?"

"Nothing. I just slipped on a rock. What the hell is taking those guys so long?"

"Maybe we should try it, the touch-dancing, I mean," Eulio said thoughtfully. "Do you think Nevon would allow it?"

"For you, anything," said Triani, soothingly.

"Oh, no. With him, it's for you, anything, Triani, and you know it."

"Then how come you always get top billing?"

In spite of everything, Eulio had to smile. "Are we back to that again?" This had always been a bone of contention between them ever since Triani joined the company as a leading soloist.

"As soon as our guides find us, they can tell Orosin so he can get you some help—"

"No! Don't let them send for Orosin! Please!" Eulio's body tensed, and his shoulders hunched as if he were cold. "You expect me to give in at once, don't you? You think I'm spoiled and temperamental and weak."

"Shit, baby! Who gives a sweet damn what I think? You're an Adelantis and you're loaded with class."

"I can still talk. I can listen. I can do it, but you have to help me."

"You got it. I know I haven't been any help at all, so far. I've been a regular bitch."

"So have I." Eulio squeezed his hand. "And it won't look good if we keep bickering all the time, will it? And please try not to antagonize Marselind."

"He hates my guts. I think he resents the fact that I slept with his precious Luan before he did. But what do I know? Maybe he'd hate me anyway," Triani finished philosophically.

"Well, try not to make things any worse."

"I might get an ulcer from all this sweetness and light."

"I'm so scared!" Eulio's small fingers dug into Triani's shoulder.

"Look, the company doctor will know just what to do. He always does, sweetie. You'll get better. You have to. Shit! I'm not going through the rest of the season with the Mincing Bastard for a partner!"

"Ah, Triani, Alesio's damn good and you know it."

"I want the best, baby, and that's you. Don't argue. Listen, I think maybe we'd better get out of the water. There's a sheltered rock just behind you. If we climb up there, I can keep an eye peeled." He helped Eulio up and lay down beside him, close enough to touch. He was worried about the patrols Luan had mentioned. If they were picked up by the Chief's men, what would happen to Cham? He shivered and rubbed his arms.

"I can do it," Eulio said with sudden determination, almost as if he had read his mind. "I'll get Chamion back. I don't need eyes for that."

Triani grunted noncommittally. It seemed to him that Eulio had no idea of the precariousness of their situation. Perhaps it was better that way. "Are you still working on that dance you mentioned last week?" he asked. "The Magic Garden thing?"

"It's all in my head," said Eulio.

"Tell me about it." Triani knew the best way to keep his partner's mind occupied.

As Eulio launched into a technical description of the dance, Triani scanned the steep cliffs that surrounded them on three sides.

But for all his vigilance, it was Eulio who heard the falling stones first. "What's that?" He tilted his head alertly and reached for Triani.

It was Marselind. "I'm sorry it took so long to get back to you. The animal was bitten by a *hyla* insect, which is very painful, and it ran a long way. Are you all right?" He was looking at Eulio who sat very still, staring straight ahead.

Eulio swallowed. "I can't see. I don't know what happened."

"Other than that, everything's just peachy, darling," said Triani brightly.

Eulio pinched him, hard.

Marselind passed his open hand in front of Eulio's face. "Holy stars! But surely your healers will be able to help. Are you able to continue?"

Eulio swallowed. "I am."

"This unfortunate accident with the animals is going to delay us a while. In order to avoid the patrols, we'll have to camp overnight below the falls. There's just enough time to get there."

Triani groaned. "I hope there's something edible in those saddlebags," he muttered.

"At least we can get some sleep," said Eulio sensibly.

"Luan is waiting at the foot of the hill across the stream. If you don't mind, it would be a lot easier if I carried you on my back."

Marselind sat down on the rock, and Triani guided his partner's arms around the man's neck. Eulio looked very small and very scared.

Triani patted his arm. "Break a leg, sweetie. It can't be any worse than opening night."

"It is," whispered Eulio through clenched teeth. "It's so…undignified!" He closed his eyes and tried very hard not to cry.

18

*T*riani looked around at the sheer cliffs towering above them. Even in the brightness of the early morning sunshine, there was a desolation about the place that made him shiver. The great woolly animals lay in a sunny corner of the nearly enclosed canyon, their bulging eyes half closed.

Triani glanced at Marselind. He looked the picture of assurance, but Triani knew he was troubled by something. All morning, as they followed the deep gorge into this narrow valley, Triani had felt the man's growing apprehension and concern, a wariness that was not openly expressed. Triani had thought it better not to mention what he was picking up, suspecting the man would not want it known. He worried in silence.

"We walk from here," Marselind said, leading them to the base of the cliff.

"I know we're athletic, sweetie, but even Merculians can't climb up sheer rock."

Marselind didn't bother to answer. He pushed aside a scraggly bush and pressed his hand to the centre of a boulder. It rolled aside with a dull growl, revealing a hole in the ground.

"Holy shit," muttered Triani, staring at the darkness yawning at their feet.

Eulio tugged at his hand fearfully. "What is it?"

"We have to climb through a sort of passageway," he said. The frightening fact of the darkness wouldn't matter to Eulio.

"I will carry you, if you wish," Marselind said to Eulio. "The going is rough, but it's not far."

Triani helped Eulio put his arms around Marselind's neck. Then he climbed down into the dark hole. His heart was in his mouth. "Luan?" he whispered, feeling in front of him. His hand made contact with solid flesh and closed around the boy's arm.

Luan took his hand. "I'm right here," he whispered back. "Come on."

It seemed a long way to Triani, stumbling along beside Luan in the semi-darkness. Although they had camped for most of the night, his sleep had been fitful, his dreams troubled, and he did not feel rested or refreshed on being awakened. Finally they came out into the light. They followed a narrow ledge, always mounting steadily upwards towards the rocky battlements of the natural fortification where Yonan's hidden camp lay sprawled behind its barricades. There were no watchmen that they could see, but they felt eyes following their every move.

At last, they came up into a large courtyard. Marselind exchanged a few words with one of the heavily armed guards, and a massive door was opened in front of them.

Eulio slid to the ground and reached out for Triani's hand. He was terrified. He clamped his jaw shut in an effort to stop his teeth from chattering. Yonan was just a man, after all. But how many people had this man killed? How many desperate schemes had he planned and executed? It was painfully clear to Eulio, all of a sudden, that he had no official standing whatsoever. He was not even protected by I.P.A. law, since Abulon was not a member of the Alliance. He had walked right into a dangerous situation without giving it much thought. And he was totally blind.

Triani felt the anxiety and patted his partner's hand reassuringly. "Hey, baby, you've met the ruling heads of five planets. Why are you so nervous of this nonentity?"

"That was different. I met them as a dancer, not a diplomat. Besides, I could see them."

"Stop worrying. All we have to do is pretend it's 'Homage to the King', Act III, scene 2."

"Without your flying exit through the window, I trust," said Eulio dryly. "How do I look?"

"Gorgeous—all things considered." Triani took a deep breath and straightened his shoulders. He held Eulio's hand high and to the side as if making a curtain call. "Ready?" Eulio nodded. "One, two, three…."

They moved forward in unison, Eulio concentrating on sensing the large room in front of them and picking up the messages from Triani which guided his movements. He felt surprisingly calm. His earlier choking sense of panic was gone. He was always fine once the curtain went up.

Triani took in the scene at a glance and bent his head towards Eulio. "A lot of them look like the androids in the city only they have long, wavy brown hair and they're very animated. They're quite attractive, even sexy." He paused. "I don't see anyone who looks like the man in the hologram. Someone is coming towards us making gestures of welcome. Handsome devil. I wouldn't mind sleeping with this one." They stopped together, waiting for the man to reach them. Eulio's left hand felt cold and clammy.

The man walked with the purposeful stride of a soldier. He wore a long sheathed knife at his belt but no other weapon. His rough stained leather shirt was open at the neck. He nodded gravely at Marselind, who had stepped forward to meet him. They talked together for a moment; Luan was introduced. Then they stepped back, and the man came on alone to meet the Merculians.

Triani bowed with a flourish. "It is my privilege to introduce the Conte Eulio Chazin Adelantis, Member of the First Order of Merculian."

The man hesitated, then bowed briefly in return. "It is an honour. I am Norh, first officer of Yonan. He wanted to be here himself to welcome you, but due to the unfortunate accident that delayed your arrival, this was not possible. At the moment, he is on patrol. Welcome, in his name."

Eulio moistened his lips. "Thank you, *chai* Norh. I bring greetings from the Ambassador of the Inter-Planetary Alliance, the Conte Orosin At'hali Benvolini of Merculian."

"Your Excellency, we live very simply here in the mountains. Please forgive us if our lack of knowledge of protocol offends you, but we would prefer to get acquainted in an informal way."

"Certainly, *chai*. I will respect your wishes."

"If you would both follow me, then."

"Are you taking us to Cham?" asked Triani.

"All in good time." He led the way to a small door at one side of the great hall. "This is where the captains, myself, and Yonan discuss matters in private," Norh explained, ushering them into the already crowded room. "There's nothing here but mats to sit on and a few low tables. Do you mind sitting on the floor?"

"Not in the least," Eulio assured him. He sank gracefully to the floor on a mat beside Triani.

"Each of us has a series of questions to ask," Norh began.

"Wait." Triani held up his hand. "We're not answering any questions until we see Cham."

"You will answer the questions first. All of the questions. It will take some time."

Eulio laid his hand on Triani's arm. "We will do our part, *chai*. Then you will be expected to fulfil your part of the bargain."

"Exactly."

What followed was a barrage of questions and they all required specific answers. Triani was thankful that he didn't have to answer them. The study of politics had formed part of Eulio's education, but it was obvious he found it exhausting. What was the make-up of the I.P.A. Governing Council, they wanted to know. How many representatives were sent by each member? How was the voting done? What were the criteria when considering new members? What would their attitude be towards a group like theirs? Did they ever deal directly with opposition groups? What armed forces did the I.P.A. control? If turned down once, could a planet apply for membership later on? Where did they stand on slavery? And through it all, Triani felt the tension in the air, an echo of other questions that went unasked. What was really going on here?

After what seemed like hours, Norh called a noon break. "There are refreshments in the Great Hall," he said, getting to his feet. "Afterwards, we will reconvene here for a final summing up."

Triani led Eulio into the Great Hall, where long tables covered with platters of food were set up against one wall. He scooped up a handful of nuts and pressed them into his partner's hand. "Will you be all right if I leave you for a moment?" he whispered. "I've got to find out about Cham."

"Be careful. It feels…dangerous here."

"Tell me about it." Triani looked up at the heavily armed men surrounding them and shuddered. "I see Marselind and some others over by the door. I'll ask him."

"Am I beside anything edible?"

"Right beside the nuts and black bread. I won't be any longer than I can help."

Triani sauntered up to the group and smiled archly at Marselind. "Hi, sweetie," he said.

There was a low whistle from one of the other men. "Have you been holding out on us, Captain? You never mentioned a girlfriend!"

Triani raised an eyebrow. "I'm sure there's a lot he doesn't tell you," he remarked, brushing dust off his tunic. "So, how am I supposed to find Cham in this place?"

"You might try asking politely," suggested Marselind. He tucked his thumbs into his belt.

"Well, well. Still mad at me, I see."

"I find you very irritating."

Triani shrugged. "The sooner you show me where Cham is, the sooner you'll be rid of me. Okay?"

"That's logical," remarked Marselind. "Come on, then."

Triani followed his reluctant guide out the main doors and down a narrow, twisting corridor, which had been tunnelled through the rock. Suddenly Marselind picked up speed and disappeared around a corner. Afraid of being lost in the dim maze, Triani started to run in an effort to catch up and crashed into him with a thud as he rounded the corner.

Instantly a strong arm clamped around his shoulders and a hand covered his mouth hard. Triani tried to bite the hand but without success. Marselind only pressed tighter until he stopped struggling. Then Marselind released him.

"Shit!" muttered Triani into the man's sweaty chest. Even in his confusion, Triani could sense fear. "What's going on?" he whispered.

Marselind hunkered down on the ground, dragging Triani with him. "I don't know yet," he said softly. "But something's not right. Yonan wouldn't go out on patrol like this when we were expected, especially when we were so late. Besides, most of my men have disappeared as well as three of the more conservative captains of the Kolari legions. Most telling of all, it doesn't make sense that Yonan would put Norh in charge. He is considered one of the more extreme captains."

"What about Cham?"

"When I left, he was being looked after by the Kolari women. Now I find out he has been put in the isolation cells. I don't like it. Not any of it."

"Can we get him out?"

"I think we'd all better get out while we can."

"Holy shit," muttered Triani. "Wait a minute. If all this is true, why did you wait for me to contact you? And why were you so…. Well, you weren't exactly eager to talk to me back there."

"The others would have been suspicious if I'd sought you out after the Q&A. I knew you'd find me."

"Yeah. Great."

"We are going to have to trust each other," Marselind went on, his voice tight. "You will have to get Eulio down to this passageway on your own. Can you find your way back with him?"

"If I have to. But what about Cham?"

"This tunnel leads to an exit onto the mountain. We can get to him through the air vent. I know the way."

"And Luan?"

"Luan is my business."

"How much time do we have?"

"About half an hour. I can arrange for a diversion in the Great Hall that should give you a few minutes. During that time, you must get Eulio out and down into these tunnels." Marselind stood up again. "Can I count on you to follow instructions?"

"Look, sweetie, I know you don't like me but I'm not stupid. You can count on me." On the other hand, he thought, as he followed Marselind back along the maze of passageways, this might be more difficult than it looks.

19

The woman stood in the sunshine, her fingers sifting through the myriad of silver threads that drifted from a series of curved pieces of wood fitted into the wall. Dreamlike sounds wafted through the air, layering, overlapping, creating a mood rather than a melody.

Thar-von was entranced. He sat motionless, leaning forward in his chair. The combination of visual and aural beauty was almost painful in its intensity. When she stopped playing, he was speechless for a full minute.

"You did not enjoy it?" she asked at last, her face clouded with concern.

Thar-von snapped to attention. "It is the silence of wonder," he said. "It is almost too beautiful."

She relaxed into a smile that lit her entire person. Around her neck, the Serpian figurine glowed in the sunshine. "I asked you here a little earlier than the Merculian," she said, "for a very selfish reason. We have had so little time together and yet I feel that we have so much to say to each other."

"I feel the same way," he agreed, knowing he should not say such things to her, that she would misinterpret his words. But he craved the intimacy of this moment, even if it would be only a short time before Beny arrived.

Outside, beyond the roof garden, the crowds of merry-makers in the street below shouted and waved their wooden clappers as the first part of the procession came in sight.

Xunanda rose and came towards him, holding a small object wrapped in flame red material in her outstretched hands. "Today is our Festival of Dreams," she said. "At this time of the year, it is one of the customs to make a mask of the special ones in our dreams to show what has been revealed to us about them." She laid the object in his lap. "It is only a symbol," she went on quickly. "It is not meant to be a portrait."

Thar-von unwound the material and looked at the small wooden mask, carved skilfully from the soft green wood of the *kahadari* tree. It was the primitive face of a stoic, long and narrow, quite unlike his actual face. The only thing recognizable about it was the symbol of Serpianus carved on the forehead.

"The clip on top is so you can attach it to your belt," she said.

Thar-von rubbed his long pale blue fingers across the soft swirls of the wood. For one brief moment he wished he was not a man of honour. The words would be very difficult to say. "I am not allowed to dream about you. It is forbidden," he said at last, holding out the carving.

"You cannot return a dream-gift," she said. She put her hands behind her back. Then she turned and walked onto the terrace, leaving Thar-von alone.

The Serpian clenched his right hand into a fist, willing his mind to clear of the swirling emotion that threatened to cloud his judgement. In a moment, he took a deep breath and followed her. "I apologize if I have offended you. It is the thing farthest from my mind."

She was standing by the flowers that spilled a riot of colour out of the pottery urns lining the edge of the terrace. One brown hand touched the figurine resting between her breasts. "I did not want to follow the tradition of the third party presence with you," she said.

"Explain what that means, please."

"It means behaving as if a third person is present when we are together. It means never touching, never really being…intimate in any way."

"I, too, regret that very much. But it is necessary, Xunanda. To behave in any other way is not possible for me. I am a Serpian. I have taken the vow."

She turned towards him and smiled, her face full of sadness and understanding. "So be it," she said. She took the mask from his hands and fastened it to his belt. When she turned away, Thar-von let out his breath. "This does not change why I invited you and the Ambassador here. The 'disappearance' of the young Merculian brings back painful memories to me. Someone close to me also 'disappeared'. His body was found months later in the hills. People are afraid, Thar-von. That's why there has been no response to the dance company's pleas for information. It is not the amount offered. If it were, I would add to the sum myself. It is fear."

"Do you not agree that if the reward is high enough, there is always someone who will overcome his fear in order to claim it?"

"It is possible," she said. "Fear is something that can be overcome." She turned and smiled into his eyes. Thar-von felt his familiar careful world slip sideways.

While Thar-von talked with Xunanda, Beny was dealing with an unexpected visitor. He gazed at the First

Minister open-mouthed. The Abulonian was resplendent in a long cloak of multi-coloured feathers. His chest was bare and around his neck on a leather thong hung a great painted bird, its wings spread wide, its beak pointed to the sky. He wore a short leather kilt, and two small masks carved from the green wood of the native *kahadari* trees were attached to his belt.

"Oh my," said Beny at last, in genuine admiration. "You look wonderful!"

The First Minister threw back his head and laughed. Then he was all seriousness again. "I wanted to see you before I join the procession. It seems such a happy time out there but let me assure you, there is great danger. I cannot spare any hunters to guard you. They are all involved in the ceremonies in one way or another. The degenerates in the hills would like nothing better than to disrupt this special day, and you are the perfect target."

"I appreciate your concern," Beny replied unsteadily. "I have issued orders to all my staff, as you requested."

"Good thinking," Tquan said approvingly. He reached over and punched Beny's upper arm, but more gently than usual, Beny thought. "We will see you at the banquet tonight?"

"Certainly."

"Good." With a final grin of good will, the First Minister swept out of the Merculian's apartment.

Beny rushed back into his sleeping quarters and began to get ready to meet Thar-von. Tquan had caught him in his yellow robe, which was probably just as well, since he certainly didn't look ready to go anywhere. For once, Beny thought, luck was on his side. But would it last? As his trembling fingers did up the buttons on his tunic, he wished Thar-von had not gone on ahead. How much danger would there really be out there in the holiday crowds? All the men carried knives as a matter of routine, he knew that, but who would really want to kill him? Not Yonan, surely. They were in the midst of negotiations. But suppose there were other factions out there, people who didn't agree with Yonan? Or with the Chief either, for that matter. And how much could he trust the First Minister?

Beny felt close to tears as he fastened on his jewelled dagger. Much good that would do me, he thought. It was for ceremonial purposes only, its real use lost in the mists of Merculian history. It was centuries since they had had to fight for their lives, nothing left of this era of their history but the jewelled daggers and a series of dance steps performed on certain holidays. No matter. He would keep his appointment with this Xunanda person. Eulio and the others would soon be there. Please, just let us all get there in one piece, he prayed.

He started down the long corridor, thinking again of the words of warning. He did not want to go out there all by himself. It would be difficult to find his way in the crowded streets, with the tall Abulonians blocking his way at every turn. Still, he had a map of the back ways that would be less travelled on this special day.

He paused outside the open doors of the festival office. It occurred to him that he ought to unlock his private drawer and leave the channel to the I.P.A. accessible, in case he didn't make it back. Only Talassa-ran was there, diligently tending to the humming machines and power packs, no doubt doing things twice, three times, to keep himself busy. Beny slipped past him quietly and opened the door to his private office.

As he closed the door behind him, a dark shape loomed up from behind his desk. Beny stifled a scream, both hands clamped down hard over his mouth, his round Merculian eyes stretched wide in fright. An Abulonian male stepped into the light, both arms held high in the air to show he was unarmed. His long greying hair was matted and tangled, his clothes and dark craggy face streaked with dirt.

"Who are you?" Beny stammered, when he could talk again.

"I am Akan. I come from the hills."

"How did you get in here?"

"The tunnels. There is no time to explain. You must warn the Great Chief his life is in danger. I cannot do this. My face is too well known. Once I show myself out in the open, I will be arrested as a revolutionary."

"If you're a rebel, why do you want to warn the Chief?" Beny asked.

"I was always against assassination. When the topic came up, as it did many times, I voted against it. I thought that saner heads had prevailed. Then one time last week, I was out on patrol, and I intercepted one of Norh's messengers. That's how I learned about the plan to murder the Chief."

"Oh god! When?"

"Today. During the procession, when the Great Chief is on his way to the Hill of Dreams." Akan stopped talking and held his side. He was breathing with difficulty. "Excellency, my family has disowned me. You are the only one I could think of who has a chance to get close to the Chief. He will pay attention to you."

"Well, I— Are you hurt?"

"It is not important. Go, now. There is no time to lose!"

Beny reached out to the man as he stumbled. The urgency of the feelings he picked up at the contact, made the Merculian jump back in alarm. "All right, I'll try. Will you be okay?"

"Just go!"

"Wait here. I want to talk to you when I get back." Beny spun around at once and went into the outer office. His heart was pounding. It was bad enough having to go outside at all, but now he would have to cut right through the most crowded part of the city, right across the procession route, in order to intercept the Chief.

Talassa-ran stood at attention when he saw Beny. "Excellency, the others have left their jobs and have their noses pressed to the windows," he said, disapprovingly.

"I just wanted to tell you that I'm going out."

"But Excellency, you yourself gave the order to stay indoors."

"I know. Something very urgent has come up. I must get to the Chief. I thought someone should know, just in case."

"You are not going out alone, Excellency."

Beny was startled by the unexpected tone of the response. "I know this could be dangerous, but there is a possibility that someone will try and assassinate the Chief. I must warn him. But I can't endanger anyone else on my staff."

Zox drew himself up to his full imposing height. "I was trained as a Serpian Raider. I am used to danger. If you need a guard, which you do, I am the obvious choice."

Bemy stared at the man, remembering Triani's accusations against him. Could he trust Zox? Did he have a choice? "You're willing to do this? For me?"

"I am simply following the Raider Code to serve."

"Well, I don't deny I need all the help I can get."

"That is true," Zox agreed, a little too quickly, in Beny's opinion. "This might be a classic case of misdirection," he added, as he carefully sealed the doors of the office. "A standard battle tactic."

"You could be right," Beny murmured.

"In that case, you might still be the target, and this merely a ruse to lure you into the open." Zox scanned the area as they emerged into the sunlight.

Beny shivered, in spite of the heat. He hadn't thought of that possibility. "Nevertheless, I have to act on this information and warn the Chief. If we cut across here, we can intercept the procession near the house where I am to meet Thar-von and —the others."

They hurried through the Public Gardens, which were almost deserted, but the streets and walkways were choked with crowds gathered to watch the procession. Beny was thankful for Zox. The Serpian opened a path for Beny force-fully, undeterred by the press of bodies and the noise, which rose like a palpable wave all around them. The people were chanting: "Am Quarr! Am Quarr!"

Beny squeezed through under Zox's arm and saw the great procession swaying towards them, children dancing before it. After them came a confused throng of brightly kilted young men carrying cages of woven rush filled with red and purple and blue-green birds, all screeching and squawking, adding their strident voices to the din. Beny winced, resisting the urge to cover his ears.

"Can you see the Chief yet?" Beny shouted.

"Yes. He walks under a canopy held by Imperial Hunters."

Beny started pushing forward and immediately the crowd surged with him, all seeing the Chief at the same time. They waved their wooden clappers and shouted at the tops of their lungs. One of the cages dropped and a swarm of birds flew upwards, circling the procession before disap-pearing into the bright lavender sky. The noise was deafen-ing to his sensitive Merculian ears and the heat and the colours swirled around him, in noisy chaos. He gritted his teeth and pushed on, forcing his way through the dancing children and the boys carrying their cages, the mask-bearers and the first group of Elders and advisors who smiled at him indulgently.

Beny waved his arms and shouted, but his voice was lost in the noise around him and his frantic gestures were taken as some sort of alien ritual of enjoyment. The Elders laughed good-naturedly. The Chief turned and saw him and the dark face lightened in recognition. He paused.

"No!" screamed Beny. He had caught sight of a movement from a rooftop directly opposite. "Watch out! Be careful!" He saw a flash. Heard a scream. Felt a sudden burst of heat. A body slammed into him. Everything went black.

Thar-von became aware of the noise below them in the street and snapped his attention away from Xunanda. The jubilation had risen to such a pitch that they had to practically shout at each other to be heard. Suddenly as the Great Chief came in sight, walking under a feathered canopy on his way to the Hill of Dreams, the noise level became deafening as everyone waved wooden clappers in the air. The crowd seemed to swell, surging towards their leader as if wanting to touch him. Then there was a loud scream followed by a series of sharp explosions.

The procession wavered, the patterns changed. People screamed and tried to break away. The canopy fell. For an instant, Thar-von saw the great Chief of Abulon lying on the ground with blood on his chest. He also caught sight of Talassa-ran Zox. He saw him push Beny to the ground and then the crowd closed in and he lost them.

Thar-von turned and ran for the door.

"No!" Xunanda flung herself in front of him. "There's nothing you can do!"

"I must go. It is my duty." Thar-von removed her gently but firmly and tried to open the door. It was locked. He glanced out to the terrace but knew it was too far down for him to get out that way. Instinctively he backed up against the wall, feeling cornered. Xunanda was watching him closely. Her hands were clasped together in front of her but she seemed calm.

"Am I the next hostage?" asked Thar-von coolly.

She shook her head. "You do not understand," she said. She went to the table and pushed a buzzer carved among the oddly shaped fruits and flowers around the edge. After a moment, a section of the wall opened and a man entered. He had light brown shoulder-length curls and the stocky build and copper eyes of the androids.

"What happened?" she asked.

"The Chief has been assassinated."

"It is too soon," she said.

"I agree. It is unfortunate, from that aspect."

Thar-von felt for the reassuring hardness of the small hand weapon concealed in his belt. He slipped it into the palm of his hand. As far as he could tell, the newcomer was not armed.

"I am going to the aid of the Merculian Ambassador," he said, starting towards the door in the wall.

They both looked at him, startled by the cold authority in his voice.

"It is already taken care of," said the man. "We saw what happened. My people will bring them here safely."

"Your people," Thar-von repeated.

"Kahar is a Kolari," Xunanda said.

Thar-von waited in silence for an explanation. He kept his back to the wall, afraid that his heart might be clouding his judgement, making it difficult for him to assess the exact element of danger.

"We Kolaris are the second race on this planet," Kahar began after a moment. "Long ago we were a peaceful, agrarian people living beyond the mountains. For centuries this natural barrier protected us and gave us a false sense of security. When the warrior Abulonians found us, we welcomed the newcomers, took them into our homes, and showed them the secrets of the amazing technology we had developed."

"My ancestors repaid this courtesy with treachery," Xunanda broke in with feeling. "We killed their leaders and elders and enslaved their youth. Eventually my people set up a system of breeding farms to ensure a constant supply of slaves."

"But why was the term 'android' used?" asked Thar-von.

"Originally it referred to the little mechanical servants the Kolaris built to do the heavy work on their farms. At first it was used in derision to apply to the slaves and little by little the original meaning of the word was lost."

"I see."

"You do not seem surprised," observed Kahar. It was obvious that he was still suspicious of Thar-von.

"The Merculian Ambassador had already discovered that the so called 'androids' are sentient beings. The I.P.A. has been informed."

"And?"

"There is no question of Abulon joining the Alliance under these circumstances."

Thar-von tensed as the door in the wall flew open to admit two more Kolaris who carried a wounded Talassa-ran between them. Beny followed, clutching the Serpian's jacket. Talassa-ran's tunic was scorched and torn. His head was thrown back and a dark ooze of blood covered his shoulder.

Thar-von stepped forward and helped lay him down on the floor. Xunanda rushed to the corner of the room to bring water and hand towels.

Beny knelt beside Zox. His face was smudged and streaked with tears. "He saved my life," he whispered hoarsely. "I was right in the line of fire, and he threw himself on top of me. I was trying to warn the Chief."

Thar-von tore the Serpian's tunic away from the wound and examined it closely. "A knife," he said. One of the Kolaris handed him a long hunting knife. Thar-von undid the fastenings on his sleeve and rolled it back above his elbow. "I am ready," he said to Talassa-ran.

"No," said Zox faintly. "It is too late for the mingling." He closed his eyes, too weak to continue.

"It is not too late," said Thar-von gently.

"It is my choice. Let it happen."

"But Ran—"

"No," Zox repeated. "I have bought back my honour with this act. Let it be."

"What does he mean?" asked Beny, looking from Zox to Thar-von in confusion.

"Triani and that other Merculian dancer took my honour from me that night at the party before we left for this accursed mission. I was helpless and they took advantage of me." Talassa-ran paused to gather his forces. "For this humiliation I arranged for him and the little one to be guided to the bar. It was in payment of a gambling debt. I did not know the little one would be taken as a hostage."

"You betrayed them out of revenge," breathed Beny.

"You are alive because of me," Talassa-ran reminded him. "The knife, Del-k'sad."

"You are aware?" asked Thar-von.

"Aware, yes."

Thar-von laid the long-bladed knife in the Serpian's hands and backed away. He helped Beny to his feet and moved him away from the wounded man. As Beny turned to ask him a question, Talassa-ran shouted, a harsh, strong, foreign sound in the sun-filled room. He rolled onto the knife.

The others stared, uncomprehending, shock on their faces.

"You knew this would happen," said Beny, at last. "Why did you help him?"

"It was his right as a Serpian Raider. He always tried to live by their code."

"That code saved my life." Beny spread the jacket over the body and turned away. "I do not understand," he murmured, wiping tears from his eyes. "The Chief! What happened?"

"He is dead."

"I was trying to warn him!"

"Was it Yonan?" asked Thar-von.

"Possibly. Life is not simple here," said Xunanda. "But it has never been just Yonan and the Chief. There are many factions. I myself help the Kolaris get out to the hills where they can be free. Many have joined Yonan. Many are on their own. Those who are more militant have chosen to follow Norh."

"So Norh could be the one behind this?" asked Thar-von.

"It is possible." She shrugged her elegant shoulders. "He is known for being hot-headed. We do not know for certain."

"I do," said Beny. Every eye in the room looked at him. He suddenly remembered who he was, what he represented. He glanced at Thar-von. "But I can say nothing. There's someone I have to talk to, first."

20

The Great Hall echoed with the deep-voiced conversations of the soldiers as they laughed and talked, eating from wooden bowls they carried from table to table. Luan fingered his blue beads thoughtfully as he watched the scene. He glanced sideways at the stocky brown-haired man with the coppery eyes who stood beside him. He couldn't get used to the idea of these people being accepted as equals. All his life he had been taught to see the 'androids' as a subhuman, unintelligent species of servant, with a status slightly below that of a watch-dog. The idea had been constantly reinforced. He had never questioned it. In the last few hours of their early morning journey, Marselind had explained the truth about the Kolaris. Luan was stunned by the idea that his ancestors had dehumanized an entire race.

The man at his side was staring back at him boldly, quite unlike the androids Luan was used to in the city. There was anger in the copper eyes.

"You don't believe what you've been told about us, do you?" the man said.

"I don't want to believe it but I guess I have no choice." Luan looked away, uncomfortable.

"If you were chief tomorrow, what would you do about us?"

"Look, I haven't had much time to think about this. Of course it has to be stopped, but you just can't let loose thousands of people who have never been allowed to think for themselves."

"So, what would you do?"

"Well, first I'd find out how *you* did it. How did you make the adjustment?"

"Good," said the man, nodding approval. For an instant, Luan was stung that this object should condescend to him, but he bit back the rebuke.

"You still feel uncomfortable with me, don't you?"

Luan shifted uneasily. He made himself look the man right in the eye. "You're the first andr— I mean Kolari I've spoken to as an equal, and it takes a little getting used to."

"At least you're honest." He nodded and turned away.

Luan watched him for a moment, a strong, self-assured man striding towards the door, his long, wavy hair rising and falling as he moved. How had he made the switch from dehumanized, unquestioning machine to leader? Luan started after him.

"Wait! Stop! I mean, please. I don't know your name."

The man turned, not trying to hide the amusement at the initial note of command in Luan's voice, which had changed in mid sentence to one of apology. "I'm Xenobar. I used to be an 'android' servant in Yonan's household. About eight years ago, he had the obedience devices removed from my head so no one could trigger any response in me that I had not reasoned out myself. He taught me to think. He let me grow my hair, an important symbol for us. He saw to it that I learned to read and write. Naturally I followed him to the mountains when your father threatened to imprison him for civil disobedience. Now I am one of his captains.

The other Kolaris here have come either with their ex-masters or they've been liberated by raiding parties. Does that fill things in for you?"

"Thanks," said Luan humbly.

"Why did you come here?" asked the Kolari. "Don't you realize the personal danger you are in?"

"I came to try to save lives," Luan said, colouring. The grandiose words embarrassed him even as he said them.

"You are either very brave or very foolish," remarked Xenobar.

Luan opened his mouth, then closed it as he saw Marselind striding across the crowded hall to join them.

"I have been looking for you," Marselind said to Xenobar, ignoring Luan.

"I have been making the rounds." The Kolari glanced about him casually, as if the conversation didn't interest him much. "While you were gone, I heard the *cewa* singing."

"When?"

"Two nights ago."

"The flock has been gathering."

Luan looked from one to the other, perplexed. "It is not uncommon to hear *cewa* birds at this season," he said.

Marselind turned towards him for the first time, and his eyes softened. "Lu, you know my feelings for you. I'm asking you to trust me now as I trusted you that first night by the reservoir."

Luan flushed. He was shocked that Marselind would acknowledge their relationship so casually in front of Xenobar, but he nodded, struck into silence by something indefinable in the man's face.

Before he could say anything, a loud squawking broke out as several crates of animals awaiting slaughter for the evening meal, crashed to the floor. The flimsy doors sprang open, releasing the terrified creatures who dashed about looking for an escape amidst the legs of the amused soldiers.

"Don't ask any questions," Marselind went on, ignoring the confusion around him. "Just go with Xenobar. Now." He glanced at the Kolari, turned away, and was quickly lost in the crowd.

Without a word, Xenobar started towards a small door at the side of the room. After a moment's hesitation, Luan followed. He was acting on instinct alone, his mind confused by the odd exchange he had witnessed, his feelings in a turmoil from Marselind's unexpected words. His silent guide led him into a hall and through another, smaller door to a flight of stairs that wound down into darkness. Xenobar never hesitated, never glanced back to see that Luan was following.

At last they reached a small chamber hollowed out of the rock. One lone candle burned on the floor, barely illuminating the figures of Triani and Eulio huddled miserably in the shadows.

"Come," said Xenobar. "This tunnel will lead us outside. Bring the candle if you need it."

"I don't know you from a faceless Lanserian gidget," exclaimed Triani, hotly. "Who are you to give us orders? And where the hell is Cham?"

But Xenobar was already nearly out of sight.

"Marselind trusts him. I trust Marselind," said Luan simply. He held the candle out for Triani. "We won't leave without your little friend."

"'My little friend'," mimicked Triani. "You make it sound so trivial."

"Oh, do shut up," said Eulio wearily. "Let's get on with it."

They soon emerged into a cave, which led out to the daylight. Marselind was waiting with three men, one of them a Kolari. They sat down at the mouth of the cave while Marselind explained the situation.

"I was right," he said. "Norh has taken over. Yonan has been killed and Akan is missing. Most of my men are dead or in prison and many of the moderates have fled. Our best chance is with the river. Do you agree, Xenobar?"

"I do. There are a lot of my men at the river encampment, waiting for news. After the coup, communications were shut off or jammed."

"The dancer is being kept in the old isolation cells. The only way in is through the air vent."

"But that's impossible!" exclaimed one of the newcomers. "Only a child could squeeze through there!"

"Let me try," said Triani at once.

"It's dangerous."

"What do you call what I've been doing? A day at the beach? Show me the vent."

Marselind pointed up the sheer side of the rock. "Up there, on top of the first ledge," he said.

"How far down is it once I'm through the vent?"

"About four times my height," said Marselind. "You'll need this braided rope. If you tie the knot this way, it will be secure." His large soldier's hands demonstrated for the Merculian.

"Is it dark in there? My eyes adjust very slowly to a change in light."

"It's dim, not really dark."

Not really dark. There were no gradations in shadow to a Merculian, but Triani didn't give himself time to think about it. He hung the rope over one shoulder and looked at Luan. "If I stand on your shoulders, I might be able to make it."

But he couldn't quite reach. He jumped down and Marselind took Luan's place. This time, Triani made it, chinning himself up the last few inches and crawling onto the ledge. The vent grew up from the rock like some sort of ugly metallic flower, open to the sun. He stuck his head inside and edged cautiously forwards. The rope was around his waist, one end tied to the base of the vent. Without warning, the pipe bent downwards and he started to slide, headfirst, into the dimness below. He felt the scream rise in his throat and willed it back. In the end he couldn't tell if what he heard in his head was real or imagined as with a sickening lurch downwards, he fell into space. The rope tightened painfully around his waist and jerked him into consciousness. He was swinging back and forth, back and forth. With an effort, he righted himself, undid the knot, and jumped to the floor, only a few feet below.

He hadn't had time to know what to expect. As he blinked and waited for his eyes to adjust, the scene came into view. Huddled on a shelflike bed suspended from the wall by chains, was Cham. Around his neck was a collar with a short leather thong attached to the wall with a metal ring.

"Triani?" The husky voice nearly broke Triani's heart. "Is it really you?"

"What have they done to you?" Triani gathered him in his arms. Cham wore a shaby dress of some kind and no shoes. He clung around Triani's neck, rocked with silent sobs. "Come on, baby. We've got to get you out of here." With his ceremonial dagger, he cut the leather thong. "Can you climb up there?"

Cham nodded, but when he got up and reached for the rope, he stumbled and fell. Triani scooped him up in his arms and lifted him in the air. "Try again," he whispered.

"I can't," sobbed Cham. "Do something, Triani! Someone's going to come! I know it!"

"Oh, shit! Climb on my back. Put your arms around my neck. That's it." Triani eased the fingers that threatened to cut off his breathing and took hold of the rope.

He hadn't considered how he would get Cham out of here, assuming he could climb on his own. Now, Triani felt panic and fear, which he tried desperately to block so Cham wouldn't pick it up. He was very strong, his muscles honed by years of punishing dance exercises, but apart from lifting his partner, he was not accustomed to carrying another person's weight, certainly not this far, and, although Cham might be small, he was solid. And Triani was very tired.

Cham had a death grip on his neck. His body was convulsed with suppressed sobs. "Can't you do it?" he whispered.

"Of course I can do it!" hissed Triani. With a great spurt of energy, he hoisted himself and his passenger about half way up the rope and paused. His hands, slick with sweat, began to slip. Desperately he grasped the rope with his knees and ankles and regained the lost inches, only to slip again— further this time. He felt Cham's hot tears on his neck. The kid was barely breathing. Triani gritted his teeth. He felt his muscles burn and pull as he desperately struggled to get further up the swaying the rope. The constant motion made him dizzy, and he had to pause again. A fatal pause. His hands slipped.

"No!" Triani tensed his thigh muscles and pushed upwards.

The rope began to move!

At this point, Triani didn't care who was on the other end, just so long as he got Cham out of the darkness of this inferno! When his hands hit the metal of the vent, he pulled himself and Cham up and into it's curving tube and lay flat on his stomach, still clutching the rope with his knees. The line pulled them steadily into the light.

Luan's strong arms hauled them into the fresh air.

"You are all right?" he asked.

"I don't know. Ask me again when we get back."

Luan handed Cham into the waiting arms of Marselind, and Triani was lifted down after him.

"Now what, sweetie? How do we get the hell out of here? I don't see any beasts around."

"We will go by S.D.T." Marselind was rolling up the rope and fastening it neatly with a clip.

"Translation?"

"Short Distance Transit-car. They're illegal now, but I have pieced one together from scraps, with the help of the Kolaris who understand such things. Come. It is hidden nearby."

"Won't someone else think of this?" Triani asked. "I mean, they know about your creation, right? So they'd want to destroy it."

"They know about it's existence, yes. Few people know where it is. Come. It's on the other side of the gorge."

Several of the men rigged up a sort of litter for Cham and Eulio, leaving the exhausted Triani to stumble along on his own.

When they finally reached a rocky hollow, strewn with great boulders, and Marselind uncovered the car, Triani gasped. He had never seen such an rattletrap in his life. It looked as if it had been cobbled together from parts left over from something else entirely.

"And you expect that thing to get us all out of here?"

"It should work," said Marselind calmly.

"Why? It looks like an antique desert glider after a major collision."

"I don't want to hear this," said Eulio.

"Neither do I," agreed Marselind, "so unless anyone has any other ideas, I suggest you all climb in. Merculians first."

The dancers huddled together, secured in place by a wide harness, made out of the rope Triani had used. Cham clung to him, his eyes tightly shut. Eulio couldn't see anything anyway, so Triani was the only one who took in the frightening details of the ramshackle craft's peculiar construction. He wondered if it would stay together, once it got airborne, if indeed it could get airborne. And how did Marselind know how to pilot the thing, since private vehicles were prohibited? He decided not to ask any questions. Marselind seemed to be full of surprises. And Xenobar, his Kolari captain, seemed right at home in the thing.

"Don't worry," Xenobar said to Triani, just before take-off. "We Kolaris have this knowledge in our genes."

With that, the craft roared into the air and dipped sideways, clipping off a tree branch and narrowly missing the top of the cliff. Triani closed his eyes and tried to remember how to pray.

It was, without a doubt, the worst air trip he had ever experienced. He was relieved when the thing clanked back to a landing with an ominous rattle that sounded as if it had lost a few important bits of itself.

Their arrival was heralded with much back-slapping and growls of approval by the men and women who swarmed out to greet them. Triani bit back the acid comments and concentrated on getting Cham and Eulio out of the cursed thing.

They were escorted to a clearing in the forest, where more men and women milled around. They looked as if they were used to a rough life, but they were friendly and very curious about the Merculians. Several of the women brought some hard round biscuits and soup for them to eat.

"This stuff is inedible," muttered Eulio, dropping a biscuit discreetly behind the rock he was sitting on. "When will we get out of here?"

"We will take a short rest, then travel down the river to the city," one of the women informed him. She reached down, retrieved the discarded biscuit and put it back in her bag.

"That sounds more like it," Triani declared. After all, anyone can navigate a boat, he thought, dipping his biscuit in the warm liquid to soften it for Cham.

But the tension and anxiety was all too much for the young dancer. Cham fell forward in exhaustion, into Triani's arms. Eulio, too, was drained. His eyes were closing, even as he tried to get comfortable amongst the rocks and stumps where they sat. In a few moments, only Triani remained awake, one arm around Cham, as he watched the soldiers milling about Marselind and Luan. The scene was like some weird dream to him, the smoke from the cooking fires, the blackened earth, the giant trees reaching up towards the lavender sky, and the murmur of alien voices just outside the range of his sub-trans, so he couldn't hear any words. All that came to him was a deep murmur, as if the ocean were rolling in around him. His head nodded lower…lower…

Luan felt increasingly confused by the attitude of the soldiers around him. It was unsettling enough being questioned by people he had always regarded as things, without this further insult to his honour. The questions rattled around him like gunfire. "Why are you here?" "Will you do anything for us?" "What is your motivation?" "Is this just an adventure to you? A way to prove your manhood?"

"Stop!" Marselind raised his hand imperiously. "This is Luan, am Quarr, and he deserves the courtesy of a chance to answer your questions, in his own way. That I vouch for him should be enough."

"I stand with Marselind on this," Xenobar said, taking his place beside his leader.

"Well I want more proof! I don't know this Marselind well enough to take his word on a matter this important!"

"How dare you question one of your leaders!" cried another voice.

"This whole movement is about questioning authority!" shouted a third man. "That's the whole point!"

"Wait!" Luan jumped up on a boulder that thrust out into the crude clearing. "I do not need anyone to speak for me. Listen, and I will tell you why I am here and what I dream."

The group fell silent, shifting back so they could stand in a semi-circle around the rock where he stood.

Luan took a deep breath and raised his head to look into the distance where the sun slanted through the trees like spears of light.

"You have a right to question my being here," he began. "It is only recently that I have glimpsed the dream about the mountains. I do not have the right to claim this dream, but I can tell you what I feel. I am a youth, and I have the strength and vision of youth. I was born into power, and I have drunk deep of that heady water. I am the dream-son of Quetzelan, and he saw my vision of the mountains, although it was very unclear." At this, a murmur swept through the crowd. Luan pushed on, not wanting to lose the thread. "I am not a hunter, but I understand the code of honour. I am not a traitor, but I understand your position. I am here because I think my father is wrong not to try to talk to Yonan. There *is* a way to work things out between us!"

His words were drowned out by a growing rumble of approval. Luan felt a great wave of energy pulse through him. He touched the amulet at this throat and reached for the words he felt in his heart. Somehow they arranged themselves in order. He talked about an end to fighting, to innocent lives being lost for something which could be worked out. He talked about the shock he felt when he found out about the Kolaris. He talked about the long road ahead, because his father would not come around easily. He admitted he had no easy answers to the questions he sensed hanging in the air around him. The only thing he could promise, when and if he had the power, was an amnesty for the rebel soldiers. This, too, would take long and careful planning. "But it can be done! In my dream, I see a land where Kolaris and Abulonians live together as equals! I see a land where there is no fear! I see a land where technology is again valued, where we are memebrs of the Inter-Planetary Alliance. This is my dream! Is this the dream of a traitor?"

A chorus of no's thundered into the air, followed by cheers and low ululating cries of victory.

Luan looked down at the sweaty, cheering faces and felt a power surge through him that he had never felt before. Perhaps Quetzelan was right. He looked around, and for a moment, he thought he saw the Dream Weaver standing far back in the crowd, leaning on his staff.

21

"What? What?" Triani blinked up at Marselind sleepily. It seemed only seconds since he had drifted off, though it was closer to an hour.

"The boat is ready," Marselind said.

"Boat?" Eulio sat up and felt around for his pouch. "If I am expected to get into a boat, I'm not doing it without help." He held out the pouch to Triani. "The pink capsules," he said. "Pass them around. Two each, considering the circumstances."

Triani did so, and without further comment, they all climbed into the waiting boat. Luan lashed them to the side and covered them with a waterproof blanket. In spite of this precaution, they were soon soaked to the skin.

Ever afterwards, the wild ride down the raging alien river was nothing but a nightmare of fear to Triani, interspersed with disjointed glimpses of lavender sky and frothing water, the sickening sensation of plunging into nothingness followed by the jarring splinter of wood against the rocks. The ramshackle air-car had been bad but this was far worse. It was so immediate!

Triani was more aware of the treacherous water than the other two, who were semiconscious from the pills. Triani had taken only one. He wanted to know. Even if he was going to die, he wanted to know. Rigid with strain, he clung to the side of the boat and watched unblinking as the alien countryside swept by in a kaleidoscope of swirling shapes and colours. The deep-voiced shouts of the Kolari oarsmen beat an uneven rhythm in his head.

Luan's long, black hair was plastered to his skull as a wall of water broke over them. He was laughing. At the camp, something seemed to have happened to the boy. Triani dimly remembered some speech, but he had dozed off without taking in anything else. Now he realized that while he had slept, Luan had become a leader.

Triani couldn't hold out against the synthetic languor of the single pill he had swallowed, in spite of his firm intentions, and at last he slipped sideways against Eulio, one arm flung out protectively across Cham's limp body.

When he came to, the stillness hummed against his ears. After the maelstrom of the recent river, the quiet of the sluggish backwater was unnerving. The light was fading, casting green shadows on the water and the high walls on either side. As he sat up, Luan put a finger to his lips.

"They are taking us to a safe house," Luan whispered, as the boat bumped softly against the wall of a stone building, covered with moss. A door opened in the wall and strong arms lifted the groggy Merculians inside.

"Not more dark passageways," moaned Triani.

"The last one," said Xenobar. "Let one of the men carry the little one." An Abulonian soldier reached down to lift Cham in his arms, but the young Merculian pounded him with his fists and fastened his teeth into one hand. Hastily the man set him down again.

Cham backed up against the wall. "Don't touch me!" he cried hoarsely.

"It's okay, lover," Triani soothed. "You can walk if you want to."

They went up a dim flight of stairs and along a narrow hall. Then Xenobar, who seemed completely at home here, opened a door into light. Thankfully they stumbled through.

"Xunanda," said Xenobar in greeting. "I bring strange news from the mountains."

"We have news, too," she said.

"Eulio!" Beny flew across the room and flung his arms around the exhausted Eulio. Numbly, Eulio returned the embrace. Triani leaned against the wall, holding Cham's hand tightly. He nodded wordlessly at Beny.

"Your news, Xenobar?" asked Zunanda.

"Yonan, our leader, is dead," Xenobar said at once. "Norh has taken command."

"Ah," she replied. "That would explain what happened here today when—

Suddenly everyone was talking at once. Even the lone Serpian, Thar-von, felt compelled to put in a few words.

"Enough!" Luan's voice cut through the babble. "First we must look after our honoured guests. Then we talk."

"We need sleep," said Triani at once.

"Of course." Zunanda and a Kolari girl led the Merculians to their sleeping quarters. When she returned, she found the others settled at the long table, Luan at the head. She joined them and at once told them what had happened during the Festival of Dreams.

"Who is responsible for this outrage?" demanded Luan at once, springing to his feet. "Who killed my father?"

"We don't know yet," she said. "Obviously it couldn't have been Yonan. And surely Norh couldn't have had time to set it up."

"Norh blew up the reservoir, though," announced a Kolari woman who was making some sort of a list. "We just found that out yesterday."

"I must go to the palace," said Luan. "I must leave my token with my father's body!"

"Listen," Xunanda said earnestly. "The First Minister has been broadcasting messages all afternoon announcing that you are a traitor, that you left the city with your rebel lover to join Yonan's camp."

"Tquan can't be saying this! Someone who is against me is doing this and using his name!"

"No. It is Tquan. His voice, his image."

"But that is only a half-truth!" exclaimed the boy.

"Welcome to the world of politics."

"But that's nonsense! I must talk to the man. I have to explain how it really was. Then he'll understand."

"Luan, it isn't safe," objected Marselind. "You are a threat to him now, don't you see? He has everything to gain by your disappearance."

"How dare you! If it wasn't for you, I would have been here for the festival, beside my father! Did you engineer things somehow to get me out of the way?"

Thar-von smoothed back his silver hair and looked around the table. "It seems to me that the First Minister has a lot to gain by the death of your father, Luan."

"What you're saying is impossible!" exclaimed the boy hotly. "He was my father's trusted friend."

"Really? Then why was the Dream Weaver appointed as regent in case you came to office while you were still under age?"

"How do you know this?"

"He told the Ambassador."

"Where is Quetzelan?" asked Marselind.

"We don't know," answered Xunanda. "He disappeared right after it happened and hasn't been heard from since."

"Your father was an astute man," Thar-von said to Luan. "Perhaps he didn't trust the First Minister as much as you think he did."

Luan didn't answer. The conversation was absurd. He couldn't believe that his father was dead. The words held no reality. He looked at Marselind, and felt the anger churn again in his stomach. Why had this man taken him outside the city and kept him from being with his father at the Festival of Dreams?

Luan got up and walked out onto the terrace. Down in the street there were few people for this time of day. Otherwise, everything looked very normal. There were no signs of the desolation he was feeling. He kept saying over and over to himself: I'll never see my father again. I'll never be able to tell him that I love him. Just a few short hours ago he had felt sure and proud of his own power. Now he felt like a child. His grand gesture was looking more and more like betrayal.

"Luan." Marselind's soft, intimate voice broke in on his thoughts. "I am very sorry."

"You hated my father."

"I hated what he stood for, not the man."

Luan swallowed hard. "I did not betray him," he said, his voice breaking.

"I know that."

"Everyone must know!"

"Tell them. Use the equipment from the Merculian office. It can be adapted quite easily for long range broadcasting. The Kolaris can guide you there through the tunnels under the city."

"What tunnels? They're only stories told to frighten children."

"No. There are miles of tunnels down there. They're used to get to the secret workshops where hundreds of Kolari slaves repair the machinery that runs practically everything in the city that still works. There are people down there who have never seen the sun."

"My father knew about this?"

"He would have told you on your Coming of Age day."

Luan shook his head, overwhelmed.

"Talk to the people," Marselind said. "Let them hear your dream."

"Why would they believe me?" Luan asked. "Why would they pay any attention to someone who is not a hunter?"

"You won over the people at the river camp."

"That was different!"

"You are your father's son, the rightful heir. Tell them plainly why you went to the mountains. You saved the young Merculian's life. Tell them about it." He paused. "If you feel my role in this might compromise you in any way, I will withdraw."

Luan turned on him angrily. "You have already compromised me! This is all part of some plot, isn't it? Someone sent you to seduce me, to get me out of the city? To discredit me!"

"What are you saying?"

"You used me! I am nothing to you but a pawn in a game of sexual politics! And I thought you were different."

"If you truly feel that way, I will get out of your life, give you a chance to think things over."

Luan didn't answer. He stared ahead of him, unseeing and wondered if he would ever feel anything again.

Marselind turned away and walked back into the house.

For a few moments, Luan stood alone, gazing over the city. It seemed to be washed of colour, sepia-tinted in the fast-gathering dusk. As he thought of his father's face, he saw the First Minister, always at his side, that streak of white hair gleaming against the black. It had been that way as long as he could remember, his father and Tquan. Marselind, this rebel soldier, had used him, was trying still to use him. Marselind did not know the inner circle of the Great Chief. The First Minister was trying to hold the country together during this time of upheaval. That was his job. All that Luan needed to do was explain the situation.

Inside, the others were now gathered around, studying some plans spread out on the table. Luan walked past them and through the door in the wall. Nobody noticed. He followed the narrow corridor to a small door leading to the river. He opened it, waded though the shallow water to dry land, climbed out, and stamped his boots on the wooden walk way.

He stood for a few moments in the dimness, getting his bearings, then started off in the general direction of the palace. He would talk to the First Minister, and then he would stand the midnight watch beside his father's body, as he should. His sisters could not perform that task. That duty done, he would find Quetzelan.

He turned a corner and stopped. Someone was right behind him. Quickly he flattened himself into a doorway. Holding his breath, he waited. Nothing happened. "Who's there?" he called, his hand on the knife he had never used.

"Someone has to look after you," said a voice. It was Xenobar. The Kolari leaned nonchalantly against the corner of the building, a faint smile on his lips.

Anger and relief flooded through Luan, fighting for control. "I didn't ask for your protection." he said.

"You didn't have the sense. Where are you going and why?"

"It's none of your business."

"If you really are the 'leader of the future', as you told us back at the camp, then it is my business. If, on the other hand, that was mere rhetoric…."

"I meant it. That's one reason I'm going to talk to the First Minister now."

"Just like that."

"Why not?" Luan started off briskly down the narrow street.

As he rounded the next corner, his head exploded in stars, and a searing pain sliced through his side. The breath was knocked out of him. His knees buckled. Eyes stretched wide in astonishment, he clutched at his stomach. Blackness caught him.

22

*B*eny gazed at the sleeping face of his jewelled love. Silent tears slid down his cheeks. After a rambling explanation of what had happened, Eulio had tumbled into bed, too exhausted to think of getting out of his ragged dirty clothes. He was asleep almost instantly. Hours passed, and still Beny knelt beside him, holding his hand, almost as if doing penance for what had happened.

"I shouldn't have sent you," Beny murmured, his voice hoarse from the litany. "I should have gone myself. I've already made so many diplomatic mistakes, what difference would one more make? I'm a musician! I should have stayed home with my music. Then you would still have your sight!"

Eulio moaned softly in his sleep and pulled his hand away from Beny's touch.

"I don't blame you." Beny got to his feet and paced around the small room, not even seeing the carvings that hung on the walls, or the feathery flowers nodding at the window in the gathering dusk.

This mission had been a disaster almost from the start. Even though he realized that much of what had happened was the fault of the original contact team, he still felt the crushing weight of his responsibility in the matter. A man whom he disliked had given up his life so that he might live. The Merculian whom he adored had been blinded trying to do what he should have done himself. Anyone else would have made the right decisions! It was too late to bring back Zox, but it was not too late to try to do something that would help right at least one of the wrongs.

With a last look at Eulio's pale face, he opened the door and slipped down the corridor. Back in the main room, voices were raised in argument. Thar-von came over to him at once.

"More bad news?" asked Beny, watching his face.

"Luan has disappeared," Thar-von said quietly. "He may have been killed. We must get back to our quarters at once. It is too dangerous to wait any longer."

"This is preposterous!" Beny exclaimed, shocked beyond belief. "Something must be done!"

"Not by us. Not now."

"But we have to help our friends."

"First we must be sure who they are," Thar-von pointed out softly. "Come. The Kolaris will lead us through the tunnels."

Xunanda joined them. "In the abandoned tunnels is a small rail car system. We can use that to transport you quickly and safely to the Central Complex."

"But Eulio is so tired—" Beny began. He shook his head. At least he was still alive.

Thar-von cleared his throat. "If you wish, I will carry Eulio. If he would not object to such close contact," he added quickly.

Beny smiled. "He's a Merculian, Von. Of course he won't mind. Besides, I don't think he could make it on his own, and I couldn't carry him far."

"It is my pleasure." Thar-von bowed formally and followed Beny to their room.

Eulio didn't even wake up as Thar-von lifted him from the bed and carried him down the long winding stairs hidden between the thick walls of the building. Someone had lighted scores of torches in deference to the Merculians, and it was easy to see the way. Triani and Cham walked hand in hand, Cham stumbling now and then but refusing any help from those around him. No one said a word.

Thanks to the boxes on wheels that served as a primitive transportation system, they arrived at the Merculian Festival office with surprising ease. The dusty winding tunnel came up outside the back door to Beny's office. So this is how Akan got in without being seen, Beny thought to himself, looking around. And then he felt it. There was no sign of his visitor, but Beny knew he was still there. Waiting. Hastily Beny stumbled after the others, carefully closing his office door behind him.

When Eulio was once again asleep in his own bed, watched over by Dhakan and the giant dog, Beny went back to his office and looked around. For a few moments, he just stood there, listening, every fiber of his being intent. "I know you're here," he said at last. He went over to his desk. As he sat down, his foot touched flesh. Fear coursed through him.

"How could you tell? I just this minute arrived!" The First Minister swept in without ceremony and threw himself down opposite him.

Beny froze. He felt a hand on his ankle and shuddered.

"Are you all right?"

Beny nodded, afraid to trust his voice.

Tquan looked exhausted. A wide piece of cloth bound his left forearm and there were scrapes and bruises on his face. "What a day! I find it hard to believe everything that has happened!"

"I am very sorry for your loss," Beny said carefully, unsure what the proper formula would be here.

"It is a bad time to switch leaders," Tquan agreed. "But at least we have the man who did it in custody. A rogue android. Not surprising, I suppose. I came to make sure you were all right, Ambassador. We can't have our honoured guests put through any more."

"As you can see, I am fine. But you— You're wounded?

Tquan glanced at his bandaged arm and shrugged."A flesh wound only. I regret that I was too far back in the procession to be in the direct line of fire. I tried—but the crush was too great."

"I thought I saw you pushing forward."

Tquan shrugged again. "But you, you are amazing," he remarked. "The last time I saw you, you were being abducted by rogue androids. What happened?"

"Well, I did so want to see the procession," Beny began, his voice shaking. "I should have paid more attention to your warning, I realize that now." The First Minister merely grunted. "Anyway, I saw the Chief and then— Honestly, I don't know what exactly happened. The Serpian who was with me kept me from harm. He was...killed."

"I'm sorry to hear that, but you were warned. You should have listened!"

"Well, yes, I know. But it seemed so safe—"

"Your Serpian companion found out just how safe it was!"

Beny swallowed painfully and blinked back tears. He clutched the arms of his chair tightly.

The First Minister sprang to his feet. "I must go. There are a million things to attend to before the reins of power are once more in firm hands."

"Luan will succeed his father?"

The First Minister look down at him and shook his head. "It saddens me to see the end of a great line of leaders, but it happens. I warned you about him, Excellency. Much as I loved him, he has always been a dark horse. Now he has shown his true colours, first running off with his rebel lover, then managing to get himself killed. In a way, that makes things much simpler."

Beny swallowed. "Then it will be Quetzelan?"

The First Minister swung around and impaled Beny with a black stare that alarmed the Merculian. "And why would you think that?"

"Well, ah, I don't know, exactly. I just thought...someone said—"

"Obviously you were mislead, Excellency." He smiled, all easy charm again. "Rest assured that I will continue the Great Chief's work with the Inter-Planetary Alliance. It will take some time for things to calm down again. Please be careful. Take my advice this time."

"Thank you. I will." Beny stood as his guest left the room. Then he collapsed back into the chair and activated the locks. For the first time, he looked under the desk. "You can come out now. It's safe."

Akan crawled out from his cramped hiding place and straightened up slowly. His face was ashen with strain.

"Tquan is a teller of half-truths and outright lies," he said. "He is the one who set up the assassination with Norh, and he planned to blame it on the Kolaris, as you just heard. He paid two Kolari marksmen to do it. But then Luan played right into his hands by going off with Marselind. It was a perfect set-up. Treason for love." He winced and lowered his tall frame into a chair. Beny noticed the top joint of his fourth finger was missing.

"You are a hunter?"

"Yes. Then I met Yonan and was won over by his ideas, his wonderful vision. But the more I stayed in the hills, the farther away it all seemed. Then dissension set in. Splinter groups formed. There was more and more killing that accomplished nothing. When I found out about the plot to kill the Chief, I suspected the First Minister was behind it, working with Norh. He must have promised him the moon and the stars. All he will get, is execution. So much for daring to dream without the gift." Akan lapsed into silence.

Beny got up and poured drinks for them both. "I haven't been much help so far," he remarked, handing Akan a glass.

"You made the effort. And you lost one of your men in the process."

Beny nodded and took a long drink of the Merculian sherry. He was exhausted, and it took all his concentration to keep the glass from shaking. "Is there any way to prove what you have told me?"

"If there were, I wouldn't be here," snapped his guest.

"You said there were two Kolaris involved. Tquan only mentioned one. Perhaps we can find the other one."

"Just how do you propose to do that?"

"Marselind, perhaps, or Xunanda. There's a network, if we can let them know about this."

"Xunanda? I've heard about her." The colour had come back into his face at the thought of action. "Where can I find her?"

Beny tried to describe what he could remember of his journey through the crowds and tumult. Then he remembered the map. "I can give you a map," he said, reaching into a drawer, "and a com device so we can communicate."

"Why are you doing all this?"

"I owe it to Luan," Beny said simply. "It's the least I can do to honour his memory."

23

The flames crackled and leapt against the brilliant hardness of the noon sky as thick ribbons of smoke spiralled lazily upwards. From the huge crowd surrounding the funeral pyre came a steady, low keening as the mourners swayed gently shoulder to shoulder, causing a ripple of motion. The tremendous heat from the flames had forced them back, leaving a wide, uneven circle around the towering pyre and the peculiar twisting metal stairway-like construction that snaked around and over it.

Beny stood with Thar-von in the front ranks of the crowd. The alien scene shimmered in front of him, made even more unreal by the heat, the roar of the fire, and the strange, sharp smell of the spices and incense burned as part of the ceremony

The very idea of a state funeral was alien to him. Back home on Merculian, saying goodbye to a loved one was a very private affair. Celebration on a grand scale was for life, not death, and a party would be held the following year on the date of a loved one's birth. Beny realized that this would probably seem barbarous to these people. He looked around at the mourning crowd and wondered at this public out-pouring of emotion. How much was mere ritual and how much genuine? Who, outside of the family, had really cared for the Chief? And yet everyone looked as if he had lost his best friend, even the hundreds of armed Imperial Hunters who mingled with the crowd.

Beny was the only Merculian there. He had insisted that the others stay inside for their own safety, in spite of reassurances from the First Minister that all was now under control. He would have liked to have Eulio beside him, but Eulio had flatly refused to get out of bed for any reason whatsoever, announcing firmly that his job was finished. His life was over. He wasn't needed any more.

"But I need you!" cried Beny pleadingly. "Besides, the diagnosis is temporary trauma blindness, Eulio. This will pass." But his lover turned away and buried his face in the pillow.

Beny stared at the empty throne-like chair just visible through the smoke at one side of the circle. Luan should be sitting in that chair, Beny thought bitterly. Tears spilled down his cheeks. The boy had made a tremendous effort to help. He had kept his promise to bring Eulio back again, not quite sound but at least safe. And now there was no way Beny could repay his debt, except to try to get behind the lies and rumors spread by the First Minister's broadcasts, the hypocritical sorrow behind the words that branded Luan a traitor. It wasn't true! And with any luck, they would soon prove it! The marksman who had been taken into custody was dead, supposedly killed by another enraged prisoner before he could be properly interrogated. Now Beny had to count on Akan. The man had been in touch, but so far all he could report was that the other Kolari marksman was in hiding.

A high-pitched shriek jerked him back to the scene in front of him. Three Imperial Hunters rushed forward, holding short lances with decorated streamers of paper attached to the end. With a blood-curdling yell, they leapt into the lower part of the fire and buried the points of their lances in the coals. At once, the paper caught fire as blue flames raced to devour it. Thin spirals of coloured smoke curled upwards.

"They are sending good wishes to guide their Chief on his last journey," explained the hunter who stood beside Beny.

The Merculian nodded, incapable of speech. No sooner had he recovered, then the scene was repeated by another threesome, then another, and another, until the thin membranes of Beny's ears were vibrating painfully from the noise and the stress of watching the young men endanger their lives so recklessly. He was beginning to see why the women were nowhere in sight. He had been told they remained wrapped in their red veils of mourning after participating in the preparation ceremonies. He wished he were with them.

Thar-von's navy blue eyes were following the ritual, but he was thinking about Talassa-ran Zox. He had ordered the flag of the Inter-Planetary Alliance to be lowered to half mast for his Serpian colleague, but even this recognition had been taken away. Everyone would assume the flag honoured the Great Chief. Talassa-ran's entire life was the history of a man whose search for recognition always just missed the mark, a pattern which eventually lead to bitterness and vengeance. But he was not an evil man. At the end, he had made the grand gesture of atonement and Thar-von was determined that he would go home to Serpianus with his honour intact. Beny had agreed to keep part of the story a secret, realizing that if Talassa-ran had not led Triani and Cham into the trap, there would have been another Merculian hostage. There was nothing to be gained by discrediting Thar-von's countryman.

In front of him, Beny was swaying with fatigue. The gray and mauve uniform of the Merculian Diplomatic Corps had not been designed for such heat. Thar-von steadied him unobtrusively with a hand under one elbow.

Beny turned towards him and whispered wearily; "Will it ever end?"

"'Even though the sun may shine on your neighbour's cornfield, the grain will also grow on your side of the fence'," replied Thar-von, quoting an old Serpian proverb that he had always found comforting.

Beny smiled. "Somehow, I think that one lost a lot in the translation," he said.

An eruption of drumming made Beny snap his head back to the fire in time to see the First Minister step into the circle and draw the knife he always wore strapped against his left bicep. Another man appeared, holding what looked like a large white satin square, the corners embroidered with symbols. The drums stopped, just as suddenly as they had started. Tquan raised the knife above his head. The sun glanced off the glittering blade in bright shards of light that made Beny blink. Slowly, the knife was lowered again and with a long smooth gesture the man touched the razor-sharp tip to his bare chest, drawing it down from left to right, leaving a scarlet ribbon of blood in his flesh. As he repeated the gesture, he threw back his head and began the ululating cry of mourning that had been heard off and on throughout the ceremony.

Beny felt his stomach heave unpleasantly. Once again he was thankful for the reassuring touch of Thar-von behind him. At his side, he sensed a sudden tenseness in his own personal hunter guard. Was this an unexpected development? He looked back at the First Minister in time to see him grab a lock of his long black hair and shear it off with the knife. He laid the hair on the white cloth, now sprinkled with his blood, and added a paring from his thumbnail. The hunter beside him moved his hand to his long knife, just as a cry rang out in the smoke-laden air from the back of the crowd.

"No! You have no right to the mourner ritual! That is for his son to perform! I—"

The voice was cut off suddenly. A murmur went through the crowd, people craning their heads trying to see who had dared to voice a challenge.

As Tquan hesitated, a young man rushed out of the crowd, holding what looked like Luan's flowered vest in his hands, along with a lock of black hair. Without a pause, he rushed across the open space and leapt onto the winding metal steps that led up and around and over the funeral pyre. The crowd burst into a loud keening as the figure made his way swiftly up the steps, until he was obscured by the thick smoke.

Beny leapt forward, hands stretched out to the rapidly disappearing figure. At once, strong arms caught him and he was dragged back by the hunter.

"Stop him!" Beny cried. "He's committing suicide! Can't you see?"

"Perhaps this is supposed to happen," Thar-von pointed out. "We were not prepared for a state funeral."

Beny twisted his hands together, wincing with the pain in his aural membranes.

"The young man means to take the honour of principal mourner from the First Minister," the hunter explained, still holding him in his steely grip. "Only the Chief's son has that right, and since Luan is dead, someone should be sent in his place."

Suddenly, the young man tumbled from the high scaffold into the fire, his smoke-streaked body writhing in the flames, a knife plainly visible in his chest.

Beny screamed.

"You ought not to be here," said the hunter quietly. "They should have insisted you stay with the women, where it is safe."

Beny cleared his throat. "I am all right now. Please let me go. It was a shock, that's all."

Reluctantly, the hunter released him and stepped back, but only one pace.

When Beny forced himself to look at the pyre, he saw no trace of the young man's body.

Then the drums started up again, and, from somewhere out of sight, the low tremulous call of Abulonian horns shivered through the crowd, silencing all but the most ardent keening. The First Minister took the white cloth from the priest like figure and walked to the steps. As the drums beat louder, he started up into the shimmering heat. The crowd began to shout encouragement to him as he moved slowly, surely, up into the swirling smoke. Everyone craned their necks, pushing forward to watch his progress with rising excitement.

Beny felt as if his breath was coming in short gasps. He imagined the heat Tquan must be enduring, the difficulty in breathing.

Tquan dropped the white cloth bearing his blood and hair and nail clippings into the fire and then disappeared from view.

"Oh god! Now what?" asked Beny, looking up at his mentor, but the hunter hushed him, his eyes never leaving the top of the twisting steps.

A cheer went up, and suddenly, there was Tquan on the ground again, holding the Great Chief's staff of office in his soot-streaked hand.

"He did it," breathed the hunter. "He retrieved the staff from the pyre! He now holds the power."

"Why?" Beny asked.

"It is ordained, even though I see he has not brought back the cat's-eye pendant, as is the custom."

Beny looked at Thar-von, his round eyes wide with the shock he was trying to control.

"It is said in my country, that the ruler of the beasts is not always the largest or most powerful in the timberland," Thar-von remarked.

The hunter gave him a strange look, then deftly caught Beny just before he passed out.

24

On the fourth day after the funeral, people began to emerge cautiously from their homes, going about their business again with one eye on the armed guards, who were everywhere. The Imperial Hunters, on the other hand, were no longer a strong presence in the city.

Beny opened the theatre for rehearsals, mostly to keep the company busy, but he urged the Merculians not to wander around in the city and even appointed a guard to accompany them. He was waiting for final word on the arrival of the I.P.A. ship that would take them all home, but there were unexpected delays.

"Just my luck to get us passage on a ship belonging to the fleet of His Supreme Highness, the Veershtag of Ultraat," he muttered as he glowered at the monitor. Several times a day he checked for the latest reports and they were always unclear, very friendly, but vague to the point of being almost meaningless. This one said: "We look forward with joy to the voyage with us of our esteemed Merculian friends, but our engines continue not to respond. More anon." What did that mean?

"Any news about the ship?" asked Thar-von, closing the door behind him.

"Same old song of joyful anticipation, plus 'more anon'." Beny sighed and turned away from the console. "Between the Veershtag's casual approach to engineering, Eulio's withdrawal, and Triani harassing me about doing a final performance, I'm at my wits end."

"A final performance?"

"Triani's determined Cham's going to get his chance to dance with the company, no matter what cataclysm is unfolding around us."

"Are you considering it?"

"It's out of the question, Von, although it would be a nice gesture of farewell from us to Luan's memory. Since he is apparently viewed as a 'traitor', there will be no state funeral, did I tell you? I got that from the F.M. himself. And now I hear Quetzelan has disappeared. He may be dead, too." Beny sniffed and wiped his eyes.

"Ben, I must tell you something of the utmost importance." Thar-von sprung the privacy lock on the door and came over to stand in front of the Merculian. He handed a thick envelope across the desk. "My resignation," he said. "I have overstepped my authority. I should have contacted you at once before issuing—"

"What— What are you talking about?" Beny collapsed into his chair. "I'm not accepting your resignation! I don't care what you've done!"

"You're very loyal, but if I don't resign, then you will be held responsible for my actions."

"Stop this talk about resigning, sit down, and tell me what you did."

"First of all, Luan is not dead." Thar-von hesitated, then sat down opposite Beny. "Right after the funeral, Xunanda's brother dropped in to see me. It turns out he's one of the Imperial Hunters, the Chief's elite bodyguard. They're practically a law unto themselves, apparently. He told me most of them have watched Luan grow up and they are fiercely loyal. Because of his connections with Xunanda, he found out that Luan had been saved from his attackers by Xenobar and is being cared for in the tunnels. But he needed medical attention beyond their skills. So I sent the company doctor."

"You sent a Merculian underground."

"With a good supply of day-glow torches. Now will you accept my resignation?"

"Certainly not. How is Luan?"

"Apparently, he is progressing well."

"That's wonderful news! Any more surprises?"

Thar-von studied his hands. "Other than okaying the technical equipment for Luan's broadcast, nothing."

"I'd agreed to that one earlier, so it doesn't count." Beny picked up the envelope by a corner as if it were contaminated and held it out to Thar-von. "Put this thing in the disintegrator. When is the broadcast?"

"Frankly, I didn't want to know."

"Well, I do. And it better be soon. I'm sick to death of dealing with the First Minister. He doesn't take me seriously, Von. He doesn't even believe me when I tell him the I.P.A. will not consider a state as a member that condones slavery. He just laughs and says I don't understand them yet. It's insulting. You know, I sometimes wish he was the one who'd been assassinated."

Thar-von looked at him askance. "Ben, please do not say those things. It does not become you."

"Maybe not, but it's true. And he's always teasing me about fainting during the funeral. As if that's something to laugh about." He shook his head. "He's changed, Von. A lot."

Thar-von looked at the wall thoughtfully. "Sometimes the truth is like a shy woman who can be more forthcoming in the dark."

Beny stared at him. Then he started to laugh. "It's not like that with Merculians," he said and laughed harder.

Thar-von shrugged. "Serpian proverbs do not always translate well, cross-culturally speaking."

Beny jumped to his feet. "All right. Enough of this chit-chat. Something must be done! Von, take me to Luan!"

For days, Luan floated in a sea of pain and confusion. He felt as if he were packed in layers of gauze, and he had no clear idea of the exact confines of his own body. At times he could smell dampness and decay and the medicinal sharp-ness of ointment, and he thought of his mother, with her cool hands and lulling voice, and the sweet spiced drinks of his childhood. When he surfaced, he had the impression of being in a cave, deep underground, of one lone flaring torch and leaping shadows.

Then came a time when he opened his eyes and looked into a Merculian face that was unknown to him, with long pale hair and round green eyes. His conscious mind told him he ought to be concerned, but there was something in the touch of the alien hands that calmed and reassured him, in spite of the strange cavelike surroundings. Once more he drifted off.

Now he had the feeling of weightlessness, a happy care-free feeling that made him smile in his sleep. When he woke up and looked around, his damp cave was infused with every colour of the rainbow. It was beautiful! He reached out and touched the glittering rock wall beside him and studied his fingers in wonder.

Finally, he woke up as if from a natural sleep. He turned his head and looked into copper eyes that were examining him at close range. There was something familiar about them but his fogged brain would not supply any answers. He tried to sit, to take inventory of his surroundings, but his own weakness overwhelmed him, and he sank back against the pillows. Above his head, on the rough wall, a slick of dampness gleamed in the light of a single torch.

"Where am I?" he asked at last. His own voice sounded old and rusty from disuse.

At once a young man appeared beside him. One half of his face was horribly scarred. "You are safe with me, lord." The voice was low and musical, the eyes a glowing copper.

In spite of the scars, the face was strangely familiar. "What place is this?" Luan asked.

"We are in the tunnels. Xenobar brought you here to recover after the attack. Please rest. It will help the healing."

Luan closed his eyes for a moment, remembering at last the sickening blows and the confusion of pain and the panic of not being able to breath. Someone had tried to kill him! Even now, suffering from the results of this attack, it was difficult to grasp the concept. Perhaps Marselind was right about the First Minister. Or perhaps it had been one of Norh's men, or a member of one of the fanatic splinter groups, or....

Luan focussed again on his companion. "Something about you is familiar," he said slowly. "Do I know you?"

"You have forgotten, lord. I am Sinxin. I served you for three years."

"I remember now. But I thought you— " He stopped himself. He was about to say 'I thought you broke down'. "I thought you were reassigned."

"I was liberated soon after one of the elders threw a pail of chemicals at me for being too slow."

Luan winced. The young man began sponging his face and chest with gentle, sure strokes. The skin on his hands was a dull red, tight and shiny like plastic.

Luan forced his mind away from the ugly picture of casual savagery. "How long have I been here?"

"Six days. You lost a great deal of blood, lord. But you will be well, soon. The Merculians sent their healer to you. You are doing much better now."

Luan was shocked to discover the length of time he could not remember. The alien drug…. That explained a lot: how he felt like a different person, even though his head ached, and his ribs still reminded him of his ordeal if he made a sudden movement. It explained why he was having such a problem with time. The strong alien medication that had been injected into his body had compressed days into what seemed like minutes.

"How old are you?" asked Luan suddenly.

"I don't know. I suppose there must be records some-where. Not that it matters."

Luan shook his head at the immensity of the task he had set himself. "I need writing materials. I must prepare my speech to the people. There is still time?"

"Yes, lord. The Day of Awakening in still three days off." Sinxin handed him paper and pens.

"So soon? Oh ye gods! What am I going to say?"

"I am told you were very good at the river camp."

"That was preaching to the converted. They were pre-pared to accept me. These people have been hearing noth-ing but lies about me for days. People will believe anything if they hear it often enough."

"Not everyone."

Luan dropped the book he had just scribbled a few notes in. His heart thumped painfully against his sore ribs. Marselind stood in the doorway. His long hair was tied back, and his clothing was covered with dust as if he had been travelling for a long time.

"Where have you been?" asked Luan. The light from the torch showed up Marselind's chiselled high cheek bones and the strong line of his jaw.

"I have been to the mountains. Norh's men are deserting him in great numbers. Some have joined our ranks. I assured all our supporters you would speak out on the Festival of Awakening, if you are well enough. They are moving into position in the tunnels, in safe houses in the city, and just outside in the caves. They have orders to take over key points around the city during your speech. They are counting heavily on that amnesty you promised them."

"If I get elected. That's a big 'if'."

"Not so big. The Imperial Hunters are with you, remember. After your speech, others will be, too." Marselind paused. "There are some personal things I wish to discuss." He looked pointedly at Sinxin, who got up and left the room with a bow. "The days have been very long," he said, with his slow, gentle smile. "Have you sorted things out?"

"There's so much to think about," Luan faltered.

"I mean, about us."

Luan looked up at the fine sculptured face, the steady dark eyes, the elegant arched eyebrows. All the words he had rehearsed for this meeting, all the politics he had been immersed in, everything evaporated on the air. He swallowed, groping for words. "Marse, I just—" He felt a sudden storm gathering inside, the tears he hadn't shed yet breaking through.

Marselind crossed the room and carefully pulled him into his arms. Luan clung to him, his muscles taut with strain, gasping in his grief and pain, not trying to stop the tears that finally came. Marselind said nothing, his cheek resting against the glossy black hair, as he waited for the storm to end. Gradually the boy's body began to relax against him. He loosened his arms.

"Are you all right now, Lu?"

He nodded.

"That was the first time, wasn't it? The first time you cried?"

Luan nodded again. "I'm sorry, Marse. Your shirt's all wet."

"I don't care about the shirt. I care about you."

"Even after what I said back at Xunanda's?"

"You were upset. It doesn't matter now." He cupped Luan's chin gently in his big soldier's hand and kissed him. "I've missed you," he said softly. "And I've been so worried. Are you really all right?"

"I'm fine, now. Just don't go away again."

"Not without telling you."

"Marse, even if this speech doesn't work...I mean, if I don't become Chief, will you stay with me?"

"Of course."

There had been no hesitation.

"Then you accept me as your Life's Companion?"

"I do."

Luan didn't know what to say next. He tugged at his hair and laughed to cover his embarrassment. "I guess we can't do anything official yet."

"That can wait." Marselind reached up with one hand and took off the thong holding back his hair. He cut the leather strip in two with his hunter's knife and handed half to Luan. "Tie the knot, Lu. That's official enough for me." He held out his left hand.

Luan smiled and tied the thong securely around the man's wrist. Then he kissed the warm open palm, looked into Marselind's eyes, and held out his own wrist.

For a few moments they sat in silence, fingers entwined on the rough blanket.

"I guess you were right about the First Minister," Luan said after a while. "It's scary, isn't it? I thought I knew him."

"Power is a sickness in some people. The executions have begun, you know. He is trying to eliminate everyone who speaks against him."

"Why doesn't Quetzelan do something?"

"He's biding his time, waiting for us to find evidence, waiting for you to speak out."

Luan picked up the notebook. "I guess I could start my speech by saying I will not do things the way my father or the First Minister did."

Marselind shook his head. "Too negative. No one wants to hear what you won't do. They want to know what you *will* do."

"I'll put a Kolari on the Council."

"My dear Lu, there's going to be tremendous opposition to Kolaris in any position of responsibility, let alone on the Council. Slow down. Don't try to do everything at once."

Luan pushed at his hair in exasperation. "Then help me! Tell me what to say!"

"You don't need anyone to tell you what to say. You are a leader, by birth and by training."

"But I'm not a hunter!"

"You've got to remember who you're talking to here."

"The people."

"Yes, but even more important, you're talking to the elders, the members of the council. You must get their support, so they will vote for you at the leadership meeting the day after your Coming of Age. They will want to see your dream."

"Marse, I don't know if I can—"

"Listen, the Council agrees that we need the Inter-Planetary Alliance. Who did the I.P.A. send as their representative? The Merculians, a race as different from us as night and day. Was it a hunter who reached out to these people, who understood their ways, who communicated so well with them? No! It was you, Luan am Quarr. You are the leader we need!"

"Gods, Marse! You've almost convinced me!"

"And that's only the beginning!"

"And let us hope that beginning will start soon!" Beny appeared in the doorway, smiling. He held a day-glow torch clutched in his hand and a bunch of red and yellow flowers in the crook of his left arm. "They're beginning to wilt a bit, I'm afraid, but I know you love flowers."

Luan stared at him, seeing again his vision of the Merculian with his arms full of flowers. "Thanks!" he stammered, trying to recover. "Thanks for everything. Sending your healer and the flowers…and coming yourself, of course."

"Don't try to get up. Please. And it was Thar-von who sent the healer." Beny sat down on a stool and laid the flowers on the bed. "Is there anything else I can do for you?"

"You have done enough, Excellency."

"There is something," Marselind said, speaking for the first time. "Luan will speak to the people, thanks to your equipment, and that is a wonderful gift. But he must appear in person, to speak of his dream. We need a public venue in a contained space, something we can control and yet that is open to the public."

Beny ran the tip of his tongue over dry lips. "Like our theatre, is that what you mean?"

"Exactly. If your company could give a final performance…."

"Dancers on a stage are very vulnerable," Beny said slowly.

"I understand your concerns about safety," Marselind interjected, "but we have a great deal of support, now, and we can fill the place with hunters."

"Luan, we Merculians owe you a great deal. At one point I *was* considering a final performance, I thought as a memorial to you but thankfully that's not necessary." He smiled, one small hand smoothing the material of his tunic. "If you would like to make your first public appearance in our theatre, perhaps that could be arranged."

"Thank you," Luan said. "That would be a perfect place." He took one of the flowers and handed it to the Merculian. "Now I am beginning to see the truth behind my dream. You are indeed the sun but in a way I was not expecting."

That night, Luan woke up from a deep sleep and knew something incredible was about to happen. The cave was full of a soft blue light, glinting against the damp streaks on the walls, making the ordinary bits and pieces of furniture, the sconces on the walls, glow. Beside him, Marselind slept peacefully, his face buried in his arm. Something told Luan not to wake him. Whatever was about to happen, was for his eyes alone.

The light shimmered and then grew stronger. The low sound of a horn reverberated on the air and he was there. Quetzelan. Standing tall, almost filling the cavelike room with his commanding presence. Luan had never seen the Dream Weaver like this. The old man seemed to be young again, his eyes bright with an inner light, his long hair stirring as if it, too, were alive. Luan leaned against the cold wall for support and lifted his hand in greeting.

There was a tinkling sound, as if a breeze stirred a number of tiny bells tied to the branches of a tree. When Quetzelan spoke, it was like hearing the words inside his head. He knew the old man could hear his thoughts clearly. There was no need for words.

"Luan, you are my dream-son. I am proud of you, of who you are, who you have become, and what you will do for your people."

"Tell me what to do."

"You know what to do, my son. You had already started along that road when last I saw you. And you have made great progress. You will open your heart to the people, show them your dreams, and they will follow you."

"Do you really believe that? I don't mean to question you, but—"

"I know it is yourself you question, just as all leaders do from time to time. But your feet are set upon the path now, my son. You cannot lose. Speak the words that are in your heart on the Day of Awakening. On the day of your birth, go to the dance festival for the Merculian's final performance. Everyone will be there, including the Merculian Ambassador. His presence will give the seal of I.P.A. approval to your leadership."

"I know, but I have been thinking about that. The clan leaders will be there! The sub-chiefs! Will they follow me? And what about the First Minister? He will never allow this!"

"Luan, my strength is weakening. Listen to me. Tell Xenobar he will find the man he seeks hiding in the Cave of Dreams. When that man tells what he knows about how the First Minister plotted with the rebel Norh against your father, others will come forward to speak against him, too. You are the Great Chief of Abulon, my son. My dream is yours."

The light in the cave was dimming. A dull echo filled the space, a rising and falling as of laboured breathing.

"Wait! Quetzelan, don't leave me!" For the first time, Luan was afraid.

"You are my dream-son, Luan. I leave you my strength, my vision, and my love. You will never be alone."

There was a flash of blue light and then darkness. Luan began to shake. He realized his face was wet with tears. But his heart was singing. On the floor lay his father's cat's-eye pendant, one of the symbols of his power.

25

*C*ham was running…running…trying to get away. If only he could go faster, leap higher, he would be able to escape. Rough hands caught him, throwing him down. Strong fingers tore at his clothes and grasped his arms and legs, pinning him to the ground.

Cham screamed.

He tried to fight free of the encircling arms. Eyes wide open now, he stared right at Triani and screamed again.

The door burst open. A young Kolari strode in, his long knife raised above his head in the throwing position.

"Get out!" shouted Triani. "It's just another damn nightmare!"

"It's okay, Jaxor." Cham pushed the damp hair away from his flushed face.

"I know Xenobar assigned him to you as a bodyguard, but I wish to hell he wouldn't take his job so damn seriously! Doesn't he ever sleep? No wonder everyone believed they were androids." Triani got out of bed and pushed one of the chairs in front of the door. "Maybe that'll slow him down a little."

Triani poured himself a glass of wine. He was worried. If anything, Cham's nightmares were getting worse. Every night he woke up in a cold sweat, shaking with fear. If Triani touched him, he cringed away as if expecting to be hurt. It was very difficult to cope with.

Triani was consumed with guilt. He still felt it was his fault he had not been able to protect Cham. He also felt guilty that he couldn't control his own physical longing. His desire for Cham seemed to grow more fierce the more Cham drew away from him. In an effort to satisfy his cravings, he had gone to Serrin, but the result was to make him want Cham even more. He knew Cham could feel this and was frightened by the sheer force of Triani's lust. This, too, made him feel guilty.

Triani picked up the bottle of Crushed Emeralds and went back to bed. "Maybe you should see the doctor again," he said.

"What for? He said I'm okay physically. I'm just a little out of shape because I haven't danced for a while, but I'm working on that."

"Chami, let's cut the crap. You know that's not what I'm talking about."

"He said I'm okay," Cham repeated stubbornly.

"Than why are you screaming in my ear in the middle of the night?"

"Maybe I should sleep in the other room."

"Oh for god's sake—"

"Stop it! Please don't shout at me."

"I'm not shouting!" Triani poured another glass of wine. "Chami, tell me what the doctor really said. I tried to talk to him but he wouldn't say anything to me."

"Of course not. It's private."

"Look, sweetie, I'm your lover."

"Maybe."

"What? Maybe?"

"You don't love me. You never said you loved me. Never. And you sleep around all the time." Cham covered his face with his hands. "I'm sorry. I didn't mean to say that."

"Why not? It's true, isn't it?" Triani lay back against the pillows and studied the wine in his glass. "Do you remember how all this started? You followed me around for weeks. You were there when we were rehearsing. You even slept in my doorway so I'd fall over you when I came home late at night. And I always sent you home. Then you hid in my dressing room and danced for me naked late one night when everyone had gone."

"I don't know what I would have done if you hadn't taken me home that night. I was in a real bad state over you. How come you gave in?"

Triani grinned. "It was the kind of stunt I might have pulled myself at your age. Besides, when I finally got a good look at you how could I resist? But all I wanted was a pretty kid to sleep with. I didn't know it would be…anything more than that."

"Everyone warned me about you."

"You should have paid attention."

There was silence in the room for a moment, each one enclosed in his own thoughts.

"When we get back home, maybe you should stay with your parents for awhile," Triani said. It was hard for him to say. He had no respect for parents who had given up their only child so easily to a person with his reputation. But they were parents nonetheless. Maybe they could do for Cham what he couldn't do.

"Are you trying to get rid of me?" Cham asked, raising his tear-streaked face.

"Look, sweetie, if that's what I wanted, I'd have left you with the rebels. I know what you're thinking, but as you so astutely remarked, I can get sex anywhere. There are a lot of star-fuckers around. What I get from you is different." He stopped to think about what he had just said. It was the first time he had formulated the thought, and it surprised him. "Let's put it this way," he went on. "If I didn't think you were something special, I wouldn't be sitting here in the middle of the bloody night, racking my brains to try to explain something I don't understand myself to a pretty kid I laid my life on the line for just recently."

"I think you're something special, too." Triani waved the comment aside. "Tell me," Cham went on. "When it happened to you, the rape you mentioned before, it wasn't a Merculian, was it?"

"No, sweetie. It was a Serpian male. He was drunk out of his skull, and he was like an animal. I suppose that's why I have a thing against Serpians. It's not a conscious thing. It just comes out now and then."

"Like with Zox."

Triani nodded. "I suppose so."

"I feel that way about Abulonians. Except Marselind. While he was there, everything was more or less okay. They even tried to find things I could eat. It wasn't until after he left...."

"When Norh and his bunch took over."

"I knew there was fighting going on. Then some men came and threw me in that cell and took my clothes and turned off the lights. It wasn't so bad in the day but at night—. They thought it was funny, seeing how terrified I was."

"It's okay, sweetie. You're with me, now."

"It's not okay! It keeps going around and around in my head. It was torture for me, and they laughed. Then those two men came in with the dress I was wearing when you rescued me. They said if I did what they wanted, they'd leave the lights on. But they didn't. They came back later and threw me on the floor and raped me anyway. Both of them. It was after that they tied me up to the wall. I didn't see anyone again until you came. I thought everyone had forgotten about me, and I was going to die."

"Not a chance, sweetie." Triani leaned on one elbow and studied the haunted face. "Look, we have to get some sleep. There's a rehearsal called for tomorrow. Do you feel up to it?"

"I can handle it."

"Good. There's a rumour going round there might be one final performance before we go home."

"You mean I might get to dance with the company after all?"

"Don't get too excited yet. If they decide to do it, I'm asking Nevon to do 'Twilight Kingdom'. There's a solo in it for you. What do you say?"

"You mean the Moonbeam Child? You taught me that months ago. I won the National Competition with it."

"I know. It was that performance that really got you this trip. Are you up to dancing after what you've been through?"

"How long have we got?"

"That's more like it! Probably about four or five days."

"Do *you* think I can do it?"

"Yes. If, that is, we get some sleep. Now, will you take one of those damn sleeping pills of Eulio's?"

Cham smiled. He was looking more relaxed than he had for some time. "Will you hold me after I take the pill?"

"That's what I'm here for, sweetie."

"Just hold me, though. Promise?"

Triani sighed. "And he thinks I don't give a damn," he muttered, taking Cham in his arms carefully.

The next morning, Triani insisted on seeing his partner.

"But the Conte Chazin Adelantis is in bed," said Dhakan worriedly, as he followed Triani across the room. "Let me find out if he wishes to see you."

"Shit, man! He's always in bed! That's the problem!"

Dhakan stepped nimbly in front of Triani and blocked the door to the bedroom with his stocky frame. "Please. I am supposed to look after the Conte for the Ambassador."

"Look, sweetie, you're doing a fabulous job. So fabulous he doesn't need to get out of bed at all, don't you see?"

"Those are my orders. That is what the Ambassador wants me to do." He didn't move from the door.

Triani tapped his foot impatiently. "Hell, I haven't got all day for this. Wouldn't you like to do something really terrific for the Ambassador?"

Dhakan's copper eyes glittered as he stared down unblinkingly at Triani. "I would do anything in my power for him," he said, with such intensity that Triani stepped back involuntarily. "Explain what you mean."

"I can get Eulio out of bed, if you let me in there." Triani looked up at Dhakan, one eyebrow raised questioningly. "What do you say?"

The man was silent a moment, his expression uncertain. "You will not harm him?"

"I don't make a habit out of beating people up. Besides, he's as strong as I am; he just doesn't look it."

Dhakan continued to stare at the Merculian, obviously trying to make up his mind. He was not used to having to make decisions.

Triani sighed in exasperation. "Shit, man! He really will get sick if he goes on lying there feeling sorry for himself!"

Slowly, Dhakan nodded his head. He opened the door. "You have a visitor, Conte." He stood aside to let Triani past. The copper eyes, full of pity, looked at the slight figure on the bed and glanced back at Triani. He closed the door quietly behind him.

Eulio lay back against the pillows, his eyes closed, a lacy white shawl over his bare shoulders. The fine bones seemed very prominent in his pale face. His hair had been carefully brushed.

"Who is it?" he said listlessly. "I don't want any visitors."

"Just me, sweetie. I came to dish a little dirt and see why you aren't up yet."

"Why should I get up?"

"Why the hell not? You're a dancer, baby, not a vegetable!"

Eulio turned his head away and didn't answer. Triani wandered around the large, sunny room examining the ornaments on the shelves; the bottles of perfume and cream; the brushes, combs, and lotions set out on the dressing table and along the edge of the pool. He ran his hand over the narrow engraved case that held Eulio's Merculian pipes. At last, he stood by the bed, staring down at his partner, a calculating expression in his black eyes.

"Don't stare at me!" snapped Eulio irritably. "I can feel it."

Triani sat down on the edge of the bed. "Just what the hell are you trying to prove?" he asked conversationally.

"I don't have to prove anything. Not to you. Not to anyone."

"I wouldn't have believed that you'd just give in—abdicate like this. You're turning everything over to the Mincing Bastard on a silver platter."

"You don't know what you're talking about," said Eulio wearily. "You can't even begin to imagine what it's like morning, noon, and night. Darkness and fear and helplessness. So just go away and leave me alone!"

"Oh, baby, you're a bundle of laughs today! No wonder poor old Orosin looks like death warmed over these days. You probably won't even make love to him any more."

"Shut up!" Eulio's hand, aimed at the sound of Triani's voice, was very accurate. He hit the side of his face a glancing blow. "Get out of here, damn you!"

Triani laughed and caught his wrist. "That's more like it! Did I get too close that time? Can't get it up any more, sweetie? Not feeling sexy in the dark?"

With a cry of rage, Eulio kicked free of the bedclothes and leapt at Triani, feet first, lashing out at him with all the power of his well-developed muscles. Triani was not prepared for this. With a grunt of pain, he dropped Eulio's wrist and bent over his groin protectively.

Eulio scrambled back to the other side of the bed, waiting, tense, crouched ready to spring if attacked. His deep blue eyes were wide open and bright, his cheeks flushed with colour. The sun turned his hair a dark, gleaming gold.

"Holy shit, Eulio! What are you trying to do to me?" Triani massaged the inside of his thigh. "If you'd been a bit more to the left...." He turned his head to look at Eulio and suddenly grinned. "Hey, you're gorgeous when you're mad. Especially naked and mad."

Eulio pulled the covers around himself hastily. "I'm not naked," he said stiffly.

Triani shrugged. "That little piece of lace doesn't count." He straightened up cautiously. "It would be a pity to let all those lovely muscles deteriorate, wouldn't it, baby?"

"You've got a colossal nerve, Triani."

"I know, sweetie, and I agree. Your sex life is no damn business of mine. Besides, it's probably one hell of a lot more interesting than mine is these days."

"That's not what I hear from Serrin."

"So, you have had some visitors." He flexed first one leg and then the other. Satisfied, he sat down again. "Want to hear the latest? We're going to give a final performance. Apparently Luan is alive after all, and we're going to dance for his Coming of Age day, or whatever the hell it is."

Eulio stopped rubbing his wrist and raised his head alertly. "Go on."

"We're doing 'Twilight'." Triani was watching Eulio's face closely.

"I don't believe it!" The colour drained from Eulio's cheeks. "Tales of the Twilight Kingdom" was one of his most famous roles. It had been created for him to dance with Triani six years ago. No one else had ever performed it. More than any other work, it was a celebration of their peculiar, intense partnership. "It's not true. Is it?"

"Nevon announced it this morning."

"The bastard!" Eulio pounded the bed with his fist. "That's mine! He can't do this to me!"

"You're doing it to yourself. What do you expect? He's got a company to run. It was on the closing night program in the first place, and this will be our farewell performance."

"But it's my part!"

"Baby, you've done nothing but sit around on your gorgeous ass for days. Nevon did try to see you. Remember? You wouldn't let him in."

"But he promised! It's mine! I always …I—" Eulio was incoherent with emotion. "Oh, Triani, you're not really going to do that show with…with Alesio?"

"The Mincing Bastard in person, sweetie. It wasn't my idea, but what can I do? It's in my contract. If you're not available, I have to dance with your understudy." He moved nearer to Eulio, watching his face intently. "Are you available?"

Eulio didn't answer right away. His small fingers were twisting in the sheets. "Damn," he said softly. "He's not going to get away with this. He didn't even have the courtesy to tell me."

Triani began to smile, a look of satisfaction spreading across his face. "You didn't answer me. Are you available?"

Eulio drew his knees up to his chin under the blankets, a worried frown on his face. The sudden anger was beginning to fade now, and he was starting to feel fear. Triani could sense it. He moved closer and took Eulio's hand. He didn't say anything.

"You're serious about this touch-dancing thing, aren't you?" said Eulio

"I'm serious."

Eulio moistened his lips. "It could work. There aren't many solos." He was running over the choreography in his mind. "We'd have to make a few changes. The section with all those pivots in a circle would have to go, for instance."

"We can work all that out."

"Triani, this is asking an awful lot from you. I mean, you'd be going way out on a limb trying a crazy stunt like this. What if I fall flat on my face?"

"You get up again. What else?"

"It could be dangerous."

"We're on Abulon, sweetie. Of course it could be dangerous. You probably haven't noticed, cooped up in here all the time, but the whole place is an armed camp."

"I don't know. There's not much time to rehearse."

"Shit, baby! You know the damn part inside out, and the stage is exactly the same dimensions as the one at home."

"I'm scared." Eulio was trembling.

"Baby, I'd rather dance with you deaf, dumb, and blind than with anyone else in the universe."

There was a short silence. Triani dropped Eulio's

hand and moved back to the edge of the bed.

"I feel that way about you, too," said Eulio, smoothing the blankets over his knees.

"Oh, shit! Let's cut the sentimental crap and get down to work, okay?"

"Thanks, Triani," said Eulio.

26

The First Minister sprawled half naked on the pile of furs on his couch, picking his teeth with the point of his hunting knife. He had just dismissed the young girl who had been warming his nights lately. Even she was no longer able to distract him. Thanks to the meddling of the wretched Merculians, things had moved much too fast. Tquan was beginning to sense he was no longer a favourite at the gaming tables.

He strapped his knife back on his arm and got to his feet. Outside, an uneasy stillness hung in the late morning air like a fog. Tquan shrugged into his soft leather shirt and pulled on his boots. It was almost time for the head of his secret security force to check in.

For years these top secret meetings had been held every morning at the same hour. This was how Tquan kept in touch with the complex web of intrigue spun from his fertile, devious mind. For Tquan, there was no such thing as loyalty. It was always possible to find someone to betray a friend, a master, anyone in a position of power over them, for a price. No one could be trusted, and it was important to keep reminding those who served him how much they owed to him, how easily he could ruin their lives, should they decide to betray him. Everyone would soon know that Tquan was a name to be reckoned with, despite his humble origins. Why should ties of blood be stronger than natural ability? Of what use was a well-known clan against native intelligence? It was *his* understanding of the role of technology, *his* vision that had led a reluctant Chief to seek membership with the I.P.A. It was *his* voice that had counselled against leniency for the rebels. And he had been proven right! He, Tquan, should be the leader of his country, the country he had worked so hard to bring out of the dark ages, not an inexperienced, lovesick youth like Luan. Abulon was well rid of the boy.

He smiled to himself, knowing that even now his men were on their way to Norh, to cut the last link between himself and murder. Of course there was still that damned elusive android marksman, but he couldn't hold out much longer. He was merely an android, incapable of acting on his own for any sustained period of time. Tquan rolled the word around his mouth thoughtfully. It was ridiculous how the Merculians had reacted to that simple word, the nonsense they talked about machines Slavery. It was only a word! He shrugged. When the time came, he could explain it all to everyone's satisfaction. What mattered was that at the final performance of the Merculian National Dance Company, he, Tquan, would be in the place of honour, the chair of office that up till now he had forced himself to appear too humble to occupy. It was lucky for him that the Merculians were insisting on holding one last performance. They were so soft and easy to fool. The very thought of their Ambassador was enough to make his lip curl in derision.

Suddenly, the sound of drums reverberated from the square outside his windows, the din echoing up and down corridors, resounding from balcony to balcony, as if the noise itself were a live thing. Outside, the clamour was augmented by voices, as crowds began to gather, looking about for the source of the noise, asking each other what was happening. It was the Day of Awakening. Was this some new ceremony? Tquan rushed outside, too, peering over the stone balustrade at the swirl of humanity that grew as he watched.

And then, Luan's hated image appeared on the wall. Tquan stared in horror as more and more hologram images hung in the air, reflected off buildings, projected anywhere people could gather to see and hear the son of the Great Chief of Abulon. Luan wore a leather kilt and a plain vest. An angry jagged scar was visible on his bare chest and his face was drawn and haggard. His large dark eyes were unafraid. "Am Quarr!" someone shouted, and then Tquan saw it; the cat's-eye amulet of power hung around the boy's neck. In the streets all over the city people began to cheer.

The First Minister swore and turned on his Chief of Security in fury. "You told me he was dead!" he shouted. Without hesitation, he pulled his knife and plunged it into the man's heart. Too late it occurred to him he may have killed one of his few trustworthy followers.

Tquan rushed to the speaker tube on the wall and bellowed into it. The frightened man in the control room beneath the palace was almost incoherent, but it was obvious that all efforts to jam Luan's transmission were of no avail.

"Whatever they're using to power their equipment, it's much stronger than ours," he babbled.

"Keep trying!" shouted Tquan. "Shut down the air-circulation system and reroute the extra power! Pour everything you've got into it! Now!"

Outside, the crowd had fallen silent as Luan began to speak. His young voice echoed eerily in the still air, fading in and out as the makeshift equipment worked overtime, surmounting all efforts to interfere. He spoke simply, standing unblinking in the bright lights with the rough walls of the tunnels behind him, and opened his heart to his people.

"Those two-faced little alien hermie fuckers!" raged Tquan. "He couldn't have done any of this without them!"

Tquan had realized from the beginning that the rebels knew about the tunnels. Like rats, they had now gone underground. He was glad he had taken the precaution of sealing off all entrances that gave access to the palace. Now, he saw his mistake. He should have sealed them all in with the miserable androids, and left them to die! He thumped his fist on the balustrade.

Then, the android marksman who had eluded capture, appeared beside Luan, and Tquan knew he had lost. There was nothing left for him now but escape. Like everything else in his careful plan, this too he had prepared for. The route was charted, the place prepared and waiting.

He turned away and hurried into his apartment. He was totally surprised by the sudden entrance of the Merculian Ambassador.

"Good afternoon, Tquan." Beny stopped and stared at the body on the floor.

"As you can see, it is not a good day for everyone," remarked Tquan. He wiped the blade of his knife on the dead man's long hair, relishing the shock in the alien's delicate face.

"I don't want any more bloodshed." The Merculian's voice shook slightly, and Tquan smiled.

"Then why are you here? Are you people fond of sacrificial gestures?"

Beny cleared his throat. "Far from it." His face was pale, and one small hand was clenched around the hilt of the ridiculous jewel-encrusted toy dagger. "I have come to appeal to you, one more time."

"I warned you when you first came here that you should never beg. Have you learned nothing from your stay?"

"I have learned that the Great Chief spoke the truth when he told me there are people who cannot resist the lure of power. It is like a fatal disease, insidious and eventually deadly."

"If you came to moralize, little one, you chose the wrong moment. Out of my way."

"No." The Merculian stood his ground.

Tquan began to laugh. "It's a little late to make a grand show of bravery. There's no one here to appreciate it but me, and I'm leaving."

"No, you are not going anywhere."

"Watch me." Tquan drew his knife and advanced on the trembling alien. "Don't even try to fight me," he said softly. "I don't want to harm an ambassador, but I will. It makes little difference to me, now."

"It does to me!" The Merculian leapt at him, taking him totally by surprise, and fastened his teeth in the man's upper arm.

Tquan howled, more with rage than pain, and tried to shake the creature off. But the small body clung to him tenaciously. As Tquan drew back his free arm to plunge the knife in his assailant, his wrist was seized in a grip of steel.

"It is over." The man was an Imperial Hunter. His sister had been under suspicion for dealing with the rebel androids. Apparently, the rumor about the beautiful Xunanda was true.

"It took you long enough," stuttered the Merculian, adjusting his silk tunic. His face was ashen. "I thought you said you'd be right behind me. I was just supposed to stall him."

"My apologies, Ambassador, but we ran into a few delays."

His two companions tied Tquan's hands behind his back.

"The game is not over yet," Tquan said, with an unpleasant smile. "There are still the elders and the sub-chiefs to persuade. You can't arrest them all."

"They are not criminals," said the Merculian. "You are."

"Can you prove it?"

"Oh, yes. There will be no difficulty with that."

Tquan shrugged. "So you say, but I have been around far longer than you, your *Excellency*. Take it from me, your boy doesn't stand a chance of making it to chief."

As he was marched off to a cell, his mind was busy with the odds. They had swung heavily against him, for the moment. But there was always another day. Another game to play.

27

"*B*envolini has no right to order us to perform under these conditions!" cried Alesio, tossing back his red curls.

"He has every right," Nevon reminded the soloist. "It's his job to run the festival."

"Festival? There *is* no festival any more!"

"Alesio's got a point," another principal pointed out. "He's stopped the other performers from coming here because it's too dangerous."

"That's because the I.P.A. has withdrawn its sponsorship of the event, thanks to what's been discovered about the Kolaris," Nevon pointed out.

"Be that as it may," said Lari, the lighting designer, "but giving a performance on that day as a gesture of support to Luan is a political act. Is this not going too far?"

"From what I hear, Luan might not even appear at this great Name Day event or whatever they call it," said Alesio. "Then where would our great gesture of support be? We'd look like fools!"

"That wouldn't be hard for you, sweetie!" Triani shouted. "For god's sake, we've been dancing here every day anyway. What's the difference?"

"Oh, we all know why you're behind this mad scheme!" Alesio shouted back. "Anything to get Cham on stage!"

"You seem to forget that this 'mad scheme' will also get you on stage, Alesio, dancing Eulio's solos for the first time ever!"

"Of course I'll be on stage! I'm a principal! And I should be dancing the entire role!"

"So that's it!" Triani snapped his fingers. "And you accuse me of having an agenda!"

Serrin stepped forward and laid a hand on Triani's arm. "There's another difference you seem to have forgotten between a practice session and a performance. There'll be an audience here. A possibly hostile audience, armed, dangerous, and unpredictable."

There was silence for a moment. The dancers were standing on the stage in the glare of the working lights. Most of them were in dance clothes, having come ready for a company workout. The young members of the chorus lingered in the shadows, watching the principals tensely, murmuring amongst themselves.

Cham hovered off to the side in an agony of anxiety. He wanted his chance to dance so badly it was making him physically ill, but the fear on the part of the others was valid. They were not allowed out in the city. An armed guard escorted them to and from the theatre. From their windows, they could clearly see the ravages of the civil war that seemed to be still smouldering, in spite of the First Minister's arrest, the Elders' frequent calming bulletins, and the sudden appearance of Quetzelan in the public square. There were growing rumours of the First Minister's secret execution, which only added to the confusion. Even now, there were guards posted around the theatre, outside and in.

A noise behind him made him spin around, his heart in his mouth. "Oh, Ambassador, you scared me! You were so quiet!"

"I was concentrating." Beny smiled. "Next time I'll make a noise, although with all the commotion in here, I don't think any more noise is what's needed."

Beside him, Eulio held tightly to his hand, staring straight ahead. Sweat gleamed on his pale forehead. "Did we interrupt something?" he said. His voice was calm, clear, and pitched to carry across the stage.

The others clustered around him, welcoming him back, but although their pleasure at seeing him was genuine, there was no real joy.

Beny walked to stand beside Nevon, leaving Eulio with the others. He clapped his hands for silence. When he had their attention, he began to speak.

"Whoever said this was a political event was right. This whole festival, our presence here, everything that has happened is political, and we're fooling ourselves to think otherwise. This is Abulon's first experience of Merculians. People call us 'the entertainers to the galaxy', and in this role, we have made quite a splash here." There was a low murmur of assent at this understatement. "However, I want to give them something more; something they will understand in the context of their lives; something that will show them how we think, how we live, how we support our friends."

"Like Luan," Eulio said.

"We came here to represent our culture, to show them what belonging to the I.P.A. means. To me, it means supporting other members. Luan needs our support to get him this last step of the way, so he can take over from his father and complete the work his father started. This young male went out on a limb to help us. Surely we Merculians can go out on a stage and do what we do best—entertain!"

"What about the danger?" called a voice from the chorus.

Triani spun around. "Who said that?"

"He's right," Beny said. "There will be danger. But we knew that when we agreed to come here, implicitly, at any rate. Precautions will be taken. We will have experienced Abulonians and Kolaris to guard us, people who know about such things. Merculians have not had to fight for over two centuries. The symbol of warfare, our daggers, has become nothing but an ornament to us. The soldiers will do their job. Let us do ours!"

It was Eulio who started the clapping, Cham noticed, but the others soon joined in, growing more and more enthusiastic. Cham wiped the tears from his face with the back of his hand.

"Holy shit," muttered Triani. "I didn't know you had this in you, Orosin."

"Neither did I," Beny returned under his breath.

An hour later, the company went into rehearsal.

Cham was happy. In spite of the armed guards at the stage door. In spite of the tension that crackled like static in the air. A few days ago he wouldn't have thought it possible that he could feel like this, light and high, full of hope and plans for the future. Triani had brought him back to life, back to the world of the dance that they both loved with such passion. He thought of Triani, as he had seen him so often, backstage in the glare of the rehearsal lights, his body an instrument of fluid beauty under his total control, practising alone by the hour, searching for perfection. He thought of him arguing for the final performance, not because he cared about Abulon, but because he cared about Cham. "That's the person I love," Cham thought. "And that's what I want to be."

Cham sat in the narrow hallway leading to the stage, with his back against the wall, waiting for his call to go on.

His stomach was doing odd flip-flops, but other than that, he felt reasonably calm. Beside him, his Kolari bodyguard, Jaxor, played idly with his long hunting knife.

"I wish you'd put that away," Cham said. "It makes me nervous."

Jaxor slipped the knife into its sheath at once. "Forgive me, master."

"You're not supposed to say that any more."

"Oh, yes. I keep forgetting." He smiled shyly and touched the soft fuzz of brown hair that covered his head. The feel of it was still unfamiliar to him.

Cham had grown quite fond of his Kolari companion. While he was in the mountains, the Kolaris had been unfailingly kind to him, and Cham now thought of them as protectors. Jaxor made him feel safe, especially now, when the tensions in the city threatened to explode into violence even in the theatre.

"I'm going to miss you when I go home," Cham said.

"Maybe I go with you," Jaxor suggested, hesitantly.

"You don't have any papers. I explained about that."

"Dhakan is going with his ma— I mean, with the Ambassador."

"I know, but that's a special case. I'm sorry. You have to stay here. Things will be different, now. Better. You'll see."

"The man on the wall said we all have to go to school," said Jaxor glumly.

"That was Luan. And he meant just until you learn about things. Other Kolaris, like Xenobar, will teach you."

But although Cham cared about Jaxor and sensed his confusion clearly, he was too excited to concentrate on the young man's problems. He was finally going to dance a solo! Alone in the spotlight! Part of the famous Merculian National Dance Company, if only for one night. This role was always danced by someone very young, the 'up-and-coming youngster destined for great things', as the critics would say. It was a tradition. If only nothing went wrong....If only he didn't make any mistakes.

A buzzer sounded on stage. Cham jumped to his feet. "It's time, Jaxor! Wish me luck."

The young Kolari looked at Cham solemnly. "May you dance always in the sun," he said.

The Merculian paused, realizing the significance of the words for a man who had been born into slavery, perhaps destined never to see the daylight.

"Thank you." He bowed and raced back to the stage area. Jaxor hesitated, then followed at a distance.

Cham had never danced on stage with Triani before. Now he was thankful for the long hours of practice they had done together. Without this, he would never have been able to cope with the utter impersonality. This was no longer his tender, teasing, demanding lover. This was a stranger. Triani, the great dancer, who lived only for his art. Cham was shaken. Before, when they had practised together, Triani had played the part of the teacher. Now they were fellow artists. There was no personal link. He gave perfection and demanded it from others. After an hour and a half, Cham was exhausted, his bright pink top soaked in sweat. Adding to the tension, he couldn't help being aware of the watchful alien presence of the guards.

Dancing with Eulio, he soon discovered, wasn't much better. He was equally demanding, although not so verbal about it. Even though he couldn't see, he seemed to be able to tell exactly the height of Cham's extension or the curve of his back simply by the light touch they always maintained. It was uncanny. Both dancers had quick tempers and lost patience with him often.

"You're not this mean with Alesio," muttered Cham to Triani, trying not to cry.

"Alesio is a pro, for god's sake!" exclaimed Triani.

Finally, by forgetting who these people were and thinking only of the roles they were dancing, he was able to win their acceptance. Nevon even praised his work.

At last, shaking with exhaustion, Cham dropped down into the fifth row to watch them work on the duets. The glare of the lights didn't reach here and there were no armed guards in his line of vision. Nevon had finally banished them to the back regions of the theatre, claiming they were too distracting.

On stage, Triani and Eulio were discussing with Nevon what changes ought to be made, what sections cut in order to keep as much contact as possible between the dancers. There would be no physical set. The entire effect would be achieved by lighting, so Eulio would have one less thing to worry about. Lari was experimenting with the projectors and already the magic was beginning to happen.

Hearing someone coming down the aisle, Cham turned. He got to his feet as the Ambassador stopped beside him.

"I can't believe it," murmured Beny. "I was afraid for awhile I'd never see this again." He watched the two elegant, remote, serenely smiling figures weaving gracefully between the blue shadows. "It must take one hell of a lot of concentration for both of them."

Cham nodded, but the Ambassador was already moving down the aisle. He vaulted on stage as the last chords of the music died away. Triani winked at him and moved away from his partner. Left momentarily alone, Eulio's face lost its serene smile and a look of fear flashed into the staring blue eyes. This changed to surprise and then joy as Beny threw his arms around him and burst into tears.

"Oh *chaleen*!" cried Beny. "It's so good to smell your sweat again!"

Suddenly, Cham sensed a presence behind him. He gasped, just as a large hand was clamped over his mouth. He felt sweat and fear and hatred. Although it was general, not focused on him, Cham went cold with terror.

A rough voice whispered in his ear: "Tell the boy traitor that if he appears here on his Name Day, he will be killed." Then the man was gone.

It took Cham a moment to find his voice. He screamed.

28

*C*losing night! In spite of the threat of danger, there was a magic about the words. Cham had been through so much here, but being part of the final performance on Abulon would make it all worth while.

He had come to the theatre early with Triani and had gone through a variation of the same long, rigorous warm-up. Now he enjoyed having the junior dressing room to himself for a short while. His table was piled high with cards and flowers, welcoming him back. Like getting a prize for surviving, thought Cham bleakly. Suddenly everyone was so friendly, so concerned, but always underneath was that cold, prying edge of curiosity that had nothing to do with friend-ship or caring.

Except for Quana. She had visited the theatre with her parents during rehearsal earlier that afternoon. She had given him what she called 'a friendship token', odd violet-coloured things shaped like disks. He was unsure whether he was supposed to wear them or eat them, but he appreciated the gesture, especially since she would not be in the audi-ence tonight. Although nothing was said, he suspected her parents thought it would be too dangerous.

Now Cham stood in the wings, made up and in costume, listening to the wash of sound well up from the theatre. The stage manager showed him where to stand to get a glimpse of the house, rising in long, gentle crescents of deep blue, lit with low-hanging, glittering, star-shaped globes. The balcony seemed to float suspended in the centre, sweeping off to both sides in a gilded curve. Dark, animated faces turned to talk and laugh to each other in the golden light. But even from his vantage point, Cham could sense more than just the usual eager anticipation. Everyone had come expecting something extraordinary to happen. Luan's dramatic broadcast had been seen throughout the city. Now there were heavy wagers being made as to whether he would show up for this celebration of his Coming of Age, or whether the opposition of some of the major sub-chiefs would succeed in keeping him underground. The tension was electric. Cham could feel it in his stomach. He heard again that dark gravel voice threatening to kill Luan, and he closed his eyes, fighting nausea.

There wasn't even standing room tonight, the stage manager informed him with satisfaction. Competition for tickets had been so fierce, fights had broken out earlier in the day, and the Officers of Concord had had to bring out the riot squad. Imperial Hunters were everywhere, especially around the glittering balcony where the Great Chief always sat, after making his grand entrance through the theatre.

Cham turned as Beny came up to him. "Chamion, I don't think I can stand this!" He was clasping and unclasping his hands, his sherry-brown eyes anxious with worry. "Eulio fell this afternoon. It left a mark." He rubbed one hand abstractedly over his right buttock.

"It's supposed to be a good sign when the final run-through of a show is a little rough," Cham said in an effort to reassure him. He had never seen the Ambassador like this, and it made him even more nervous. He was relieved when Thar-von appeared and laid a large, steadying hand on Benvolini's arm.

"Ben, you cannot stay backstage. You're the Ambassador. Your place is out front."

"But Von! I can't leave Eulio at a time like this!"

"This is a difficult night for all of us."

"I never should have agreed to this performance," muttered Beny distractedly. "I thought things would be all right with the First Minister out of the way, but this place is a powder keg. I've never seen so many weapons in my life. The whole bloody damn audience is armed to the teeth!"

"Nevertheless, you promised Luan your support. You told him you would be at his side."

"He might not even show up!"

"That is beside the point."

"I'm resigning from the Diplomatic Corps, Von!"

"That's fine, but you'll have to do it tomorrow, on the way home."

"If anyone's still alive by tomorrow."

"Ben, you are being overly dramatic. No one is threatened here but Luan."

"And you want me to be beside him!"

"Metaphorically speaking."

"Oh, wonderful," muttered Beny, but he went with Thar-von, back to the auditorium.

They had just reached their seats when a long wail of Abulonian trumpets sounded from the entrance. A hush fell on the theatre as a slow, deep-throated drum started up, soon joined by others, weaving rhythmic patterns around the heavy beat. Finally, with a jangle of bells, Quetzelan appeared carrying a bowl of incense in his outstretched hands. Behind him was Luan, resplendent in a long multihued cloak of feathers and a wide band around his head, encrusted with large blue stones. He carried his father's staff of office in one hand and wore the famous cat's eye pendant around his neck. Behind him walked Marselind, his hunter's knife sheathed in an intricately carved scabbard, and behind him, walked Xenobar, his long wavy brown hair a defiant symbol of his freedom. Slowly, the small procession made its way through the hisses and growls of the audience, to the balcony.

Once there, Luan turned and faced the rumbling, uncertain crowd. This was the first time he had appeared in public since his father's death. How did this crowd really feel about him? he asked himself. Where did they stand? Would the presence of a Kolari in his party jeopardize his possible election? He was so nervous his hands were shaking, and he lowered the staff out of sight to hide the fact. Marselind reached out and took his hand and together they faced the throng.

Luan sought out the sub-chiefs gathered in a row below him. This was where the official opposition would come from. As he expected, quite a few had their standards raised defiantly to show they did not recognize his authority, and more were joining these, an obvious reaction to Xenobar's presence. He could feel their hostility coming at him in waves across the crowded space. But a few seemed uncertain, and these were the ones Luan singled out. Deliberately, he held the eye of first one, then the other, trying to force them to his will. He had seen his father use this tactic often. He wondered now if he, too, had ever felt the sick stab of fear in his gut. He could hear the whisper of knives being loosened in their sheaths. Behind him, he heard the word 'traitor', breathed on the air.

Marselind heard it too, and his hand sprang to his knife.

"No!" hissed Luan. He blinked as a tendril of blue smoke from the incense stung his eyes. And suddenly he knew what to do.

He held out his right hand over Quetzelan's brazier. There was a gasp from below, but he did not hesitate as he plunged his hand into the burning coals, grasped one, and withdrew it. He held it over the railing in front of him, letting the heat pulse through his skin, hot, burning, yet with a pain that served only to focus his thoughts. He felt the power and began to speak, hearing the beat of each word a split second after he had uttered it.

And then he saw the images slowly form in the air. Total silence fell over the audience as he went on speaking, telling of his love for his father, his love for his country, and the battle between these two. The figures swayed like smoke over the heads of the spellbound listeners, as he told of the power of his dream to carry them forward to a new peace. When he stopped speaking, there was not a standard raised in the house to oppose him. He dropped the coal back into the bowl, bowed to his people, and sat down. Only then did he feel the pain, slicing like knives through his arm with such force that he almost fainted.

At that moment, the house lights dimmed. Nevon's light voice came over the speaker system. "Ladies, gentlemen, and Merculians: For tonight's special performance in honor of Luan of Abulon, the role of the Moon God will be danced in all the duet scenes by Eulio Chazin Adelantis." There was applause and even cheering from the audience, most of whom had heard the story of Eulio's accident. The voice went on: "The Moon God solos will be performed by Alesio Fadra Consadrine. The role of the King of the Night will be danced by Triani and the Moonbeam Child will be performed by Chamion Adino Eseris, who is making his debut with the company." The applause grew tumultuous as the audience remembered the name and made the connection with the kidnap stories they had heard.

This is really it, thought Cham on hearing his name and his hands turned cold in sudden fright. This is it. I'm not dreaming. He watched Alesio, dramatic in silver and gold costume with sequins on his eyelids, take his place centre stage for the opening number, surrounded by the shimmering chorus. He watched the curtain go up, the lights play over the dancers, creating the illusion of leaves, shadows, mists, and water. Time seemed to telescope for him, and suddenly he was the one center stage, aware of the tier upon tier of upturned faces yet strangely and completely alone, the only alive thing there besides himself being the music, moving through his body like a current. He spun downstage, sinuous and lithe, smooth and glittering. He seemed so small on the bare stage, yet vivid and pulsing, the very essence of light and life. He felt, rather than saw, the stage lighting shift as the music changed, quickened, taking his heartbeat along with it. He was no longer alone. As he turned and touched the slender outstretched hand of the King of the Night, the audience could feel the contact, the spark tossed back and forth between them.

Time took another leap, and he was with Eulio, aware now of the need to send directional signals to his serenely smiling partner, to think of the whole rather than only the part. The music lifted him forward, an almost physical thing. The lights broke over his glittering body in bars of colour. He leapt for the King of the Night and Triani's arms as the curtain fell with a triumphant crash of trumpets.

It took Cham a few seconds to realize that it was over, and he advanced to the footlights holding Triani's hand tightly. He could see Eulio on Triani's other side, holding Alesio, while waves of applause broke over them. Cham felt stunned, clinging to Triani as if to a lifeline, his smile on automatic. As Triani urged him forward alone for a solo bow, he came to life. He ran to the front of the stage, scooped up an armful of flowers and searched the dimness beyond the footlights for Luan. When he found him, he smiled and blew kisses and held out the flowers to him. People craned around in their seats, trying to see who was being singled out. Several stood up, their eyes fixed on Luan, creating a wavelike ripple of movement as others followed their example. Soon the whole theatre was standing, applauding their young chief enthusiastically. In a final gesture of thanks, Cham threw the flowers to one of the Merculians close to the front, who ran off to deliver them to Luan. Cham slipped back beside Triani.

Finally the curtain came down for good, and Beny, tears streaming down his face, hurried Eulio off to his dressing room.

"Thank god that's over!" exclaimed Triani. "And not a drop of blood shed!" He dropped an arm around Cham's shoulder.

Cham looked up at him anxiously. "How was I?" he asked, his voice husky.

Triani raised an eyebrow consideringly. "You'll do, Chamion Adino Eseris," he said and gave him a sudden hug.

For the first time in days, Cham's response was instant and heartfelt. He returned the hug.

"Let's go home."

"You don't want to go to the party and say goodbye to Luan?"

"I've said my goodbyes," said Cham. "You go, and you can tell me all about it tomorrow."

Triani paused outside his dressing room door. "No," he said after a moment. "If you don't go, I don't go."

Cham stared at him in amazement.

Triani grinned suddenly and disappeared into his dressing room.

For a full minute, Cham stared at the gold star pulsing on the door above Triani's name. Then he knocked and went in.

"Did you mean that?" he asked.

"I don't say things I don't mean. Which reminds me, don't ever upstage me again, okay?"

Cham closed the door behind him. He ran across the room and put his arms around Triani's neck. "I love you," he whispered.

"I know, sweetie. I love you, too."

Coming in 2002 ~

> *The Danger Dance*
> by Caro Soles

The second book in the Merculian Series is a prequel which takes place before the events in *The Abulon Dance*. Beny and Eulio, enjoying their newly 'jewelled' status as a couple, are suddenly torn from their safe, calm world and sent on a dangerous mission aboard an I.P.A. ship by the menacing Praetan of Merculian. Using the scheduled tour of the Merculian National Dance Company as cover, Eulio and Beny start off well but are soon hopelessly over their heads. Triani's shadowy sadistic Terran boyfriend, Lucius, complicates things dangerously. Even Thar-Von Del despairs when his Merculian friends are reported killed by Serpian pirates and the Captain of the *Wellington* refuses to investigate.

Available now from Baskerville Books:

> *Bloodlover*
> by Nancy Kilpatrick

> The long awaited fourth novel set in the popular
> Power of the Blood Vampire world.

Julien has been around for almost 500 years, and most of that time he's been alone. Relationships are a power struggle for him, extremely violent, and he intends to hold the reins. Jeanette has her own problems with relationships. To her, Julien is just another man to be manipulated. When these two strong, determined personalities clash, power changes hands again and again and again. Who will win, who will lose? And who, ultimately, will survive?

The Danger Dance
Opening

Beny raised his head and listened, his hands poised motionless over the silver keyboards of his instrument. It wasn't a sound that had disturbed him, exactly. It was more like a whisper in the air, a feeling as if a cool breath had passed underneath his skin. All traces of the music he had been working on were gone, pushed out of his mind by this alien something, this subtle change in the atmosphere.

The slight Merculian got to his feet and looked around the familiar room, confused. But everything was the same: the glowing blossoms of the flowering root plants made phosphorescent patterns against the glass of the underground window; the blue of the morning sky flooded in through the transparent bubble of the roof; the instruments and recording equipment were ranged around the walls of the workroom as always.

Uneasy now, Beny ran one small hand through his thick reddish gold curls and decided to check with Eulio. Had he, too, felt that strange disturbance? Eulio was more finely attuned to atmosphere than most Merculians. Beny opened the door and hurried along the quiet passage. He knew Eulio would be rehearsing at this hour, stretching and toning those beautiful muscles, making them perform the impossible feats of the dance that looked so effortless on stage. He passed the courtyard with its floating garden, the brilliant, changing colours swaying in the bright water, and came to the door of the rehearsal area. He could hear the music, but through the glass wall he saw that Eulio was just standing there, wiping the sweat off the back of his neck with a towel, a puzzled expression on his face.

"You felt it too," said Beny, opening the door. He went over to Eulio, took the towel from him and wiped his back and chest tenderly. The love jewel resting in the hollow of Eulio's throat pulsed a deep violet.